VERLAND

THE TRANSFORMATION

B.E. SCULLY

ISBN: 1460907000
ISBN-13: 9781460907009

To Traci Scully and Jane Scully,
who helped give this book both its life and its meaning;
and to Bob Scully, who went in search of that which comes next.

To Montserrat Fontes; and to Verland,
for telling his tale and entrusting it to this writer's care. Believe!

CHAPTER 1

It was a good day for talking with the dead. The din from Wilshire Boulevard had ebbed into an early evening hum, and the clusters of tourists looking for Marilyn Monroe were more sparse than usual. Even the weather was cooperating—mean-looking threads of black streaking the gray skies, wind rattling the leaves around like the very bones beneath her feet. In other words, a thoroughly untypical Los Angeles afternoon.

Elle headed toward the northeast corner, passed Frank Zappa, #100 and unmarked, then Dorothy Stratten, #118. One more beautiful woman cut down by violence. And there it was, #127:

Helen Bramasol
March 1949–June 1989
Loving wife, mother, daughter

Those four words never seemed like enough. Elle sat down at the foot of the grave to wait.

"Twenty years," she told the small plaque, which as usual offered no response.

Every time it was the same—she got restless so quickly, even though patience was the most important part. If she ever expected to receive a message from her mother, she should at least be willing to wait. Elle thought twenty years was a pretty good wait, though.

She looked up past the buildings and billboards and scanned the skies. Her mother had loved to watch birds from their deck.

"Helen, come out here and look at all of this bird shit," her father would say.

"Bird shit everywhere, on the chairs, the steps—look at these piles wherever they sit!"

"Perch."

"What?"

"Birds don't sit. They perch."

"Well, whatever they do, they must shit the whole time they're doing it!" her father would roar. But her mother would just smile, and the bird feeders would stay.

Twenty years ago, she had come home from school, flopped on the couch, and turned on the TV just like she did every other day. The after-school special had just started, and she felt the hazy drift of sleep coming on when something crossed the deck, flicking the room into shadow. She sat up to investigate and saw a golden-brown hawk settle on the porch railing less than four feet away. She went to the screen door expecting it to fly, but it stayed put even after she was right in front of it.

"You're kind of far from home, fellow."

There were plenty of hawks in the San Gabriel mountains where she and her friends went hiking sometimes, but she had never seen one this far in. It stared at her, fierce and secret and knowing. She took a step back.

"And what can I do for you?"

Its *caw-caw-caw* of an answer caused the cat to flee under the couch in terror and Elle to retreat from the screen door. But it kept up the racket, and she edged forward to see what was wrong with it. The hawk went silent, locking her in its gaze. She should probably shoo it away—what if it had rabies or something? But she couldn't break the fairy tale spell of its golden eyes. It stayed still a moment longer before shrieking one last time, and then in one great flap of wings, it was gone.

Wait till she told her mom—talk about bird shit! And then the phone rang and just like that, a perfectly ordinary Friday afternoon became the day when everything collapsed, when nothing would ever go back together in quite the same way. It was someone from her mom's job, and at first Elle couldn't put the words together, couldn't figure out how they related to her. Everything slowed, as if she had been plunged into freezing water, and for some reason, it was impossible to put down the phone, to place one foot in front of the other and answer the front door, to form words and make them come out of her mouth.

Only years later did Elle realize how brave her neighbor had been to tell her the truth.

"Honey, your mom has been shot. I'm sorry, but your mom is dead."

Until that moment, Elle had only known death in passing—someone's grandparent or a car wreck, the occasional premature heart attack or fatal disease. But on June 17, 1989, death stepped forward and fully introduced itself, shook her hand and whispered its secret, terrible name into her ear: *Never Again.*

She had not really believed in death. She knew that her parents would die someday, and she would, too—everyone did. But knowing a thing and believing it are two entirely different things, and who believes in his or her own death? Afterward, in the streets, at restaurants and shopping malls, Elle would look at people drinking coffee or going about their business, and she would know that each and every one of them would die— *must* die. And yet the amazing thing was that none of them seemed to understand this to be so.

She forgot about the hawk in the bewildering chaos of funeral, police, trial, the steady forward-march of routine. But months later when she came upon her mother's death certificate, she reconstructed the timeline: shot at 3:52 p.m., fatal hemorrhaging within minutes. Time of death approximately four o'clock on a Friday afternoon, when a backyard bird enthusiast or daydreaming kid might have spotted an unlikely golden-brown hawk cruising low in an otherwise perfectly ordinary suburban sky.

Ever since then, Elle watched for hawks everywhere. She still saw them while hiking the canyons or driving through the hills, and sometimes they turned up in unexpected places: a freeway sign on the 101; the ledge of a seedy motel on Ivar Avenue, of all places. But she'd never again felt the kind of connection that she'd had on that Friday afternoon, and with each passing year, she saw fewer and fewer hawks no matter how hard she searched for them.

She shifted position and resisted the urge to check the time. Just out of college, Elle had dated a science teacher named Rick who at two and a half years still qualified as her longest relationship, not counting Gary. Rick had considered Elle's graveyard ritual unhealthy. He used to tell her about the stages of grief as if they were one of the scientific theories he taught to bored teenagers every day. They had argued about it, one of those "relationship will never last" warning signs that she'd chosen to ignore. But that had been over ten years ago, and Elle was beginning to wonder if old Rick had been right. Maybe a part of her had stopped believing in the hawks, and that's why she couldn't find them anymore. Or maybe they had stopped finding her.

She closed her eyes and pressed her hands against the ground.

"Where are you, Mom? Are you out there somewhere?" Elle whispered to the silent earth. "Can you hear me? *Can you give me some kind of a sign?*"

A vibration shot through her and she cried out, jumped to her feet—and then cursed her foolishness. She had forgotten to turn off her phone again.

It was Sam Forsythe, her agent. When Elle had started looking for an agent, she had found in Sam a kindred spirit: smart, ambitious enough, but with a reflectiveness, a distractibility that meant he was never going to cross the corporate finish line first. And maybe that's why he had taken her on, as well— they had sized each other up and found a perfect fit. Sam had helped Elle get her first contract at Greene Line Publishing after her articles about the Crazy Girl Killer, a psycho who had stalked strippers at the infamous club on La Brea. The media had gone wild for the case: strippers, grisly murders, and a perpetrator who turned out to be a former child actor who had once played a character with the nickname "Chop-Chop."

The book offers started coming in before Chop-Chop had even broken in his prison uniform, and Elle's career as a "true-crime writer" had begun. Her last book, about a physician in Pennsylvania who killed his terminally ill patients and buried them in the garden of his country home, was her fifth. Crime, it seemed, was steady business.

She waited until she'd cleared the gates before calling back; taking a call in a cemetery felt creepy even by L.A. standards.

"This is it, Elle. The big one."

"You always say that, Sam. How about 'This is it, Elle. The medium one.' Or even 'the downright small but it pays the bills' one."

"Oh, no. Not this time. Greene Line has got a big one for you, and I mean a *really* big one. Really big." Sam was practically panting.

"OK, Sam, I'll play. Which homicidal maniac do I get to spend the next six months with this time?" Elle waited, knowing Sam wouldn't be able to resist a dramatic pause.

"Eliot Kingman." She took the phone from her ear and gaped at it in cartoon character astonishment.

"Elle, are you there? I knew it! I knew you wouldn't believe it. This one is going to mean movie deals, TV specials, who knows what all—we have to work the contract really well on this one, and—"

"Sam, wait a minute, slow down. Why is Greene Line giving me such a big story? What's the catch?"

"There you go. The doubter. Because you're good, how about that's why? And because—and this is how I know we're going to negotiate the hell out of that contract—because Kingman himself contacted Greene Line about the book and *specifically asked for you.*"

"Why would Kingman ask for me?"

"Why did Kingman stab some poor schlep through the heart for no apparent reason when he's a gazillionaire movie producer? You can't ask why about something like that—just thank the gods of Hollywood, whatever publicity-starved has-beens they may be."

It was true that this was huge; Eliot Kingman had been one of the biggest names in Hollywood. Rumors had circulated for years about his erratic behavior and penchant for dark hobbies, so when one of his assistants turned up dead at his mansion one day, no one in the industry had been all that surprised. What *had* been a surprise was that Kingman had been charged and eventually convicted for the crime. After a typical L.A. circus trial that had included everything from a necromancer on the stand to Kingman's newly minted wife being removed from the courtroom for drug possession, Kingman had gone from a multimillion-dollar estate in Malibu to the California Department of Corrections for nineteen years to life.

Back in her apartment, Elle closed the blinds against the city. In the days when she had been living paycheck to paycheck, she had taken a one-bedroom apartment in a building at the wrong end of Sunset called The Bradbury, a gone to seed relic from the 1940s Golden Era still holding ground against

Hollywood's perpetual attempts to reinvent itself. The rent had risen ridiculously ever since the Boulevard had replaced its rundown T-shirt and sex shops with an upscale mall and movie theater, and for a while Elle had gone to look at slick modern apartments with doors that didn't weigh a hundred pounds. But she had finally admitted to herself that she didn't really want to move: The Bradbury, with its down-at-the-heels charm and hints of faded glamour, was like a place out of time, and that suited her just fine. Whenever she stepped into the ancient elevator with its scrollwork gate and tattered velvet wallpaper, she felt like a character in a noir film, maybe the femme fatale with a dangerous secret and a heart of gold.

But instead of a dashing, hard-boiled dick in a fedora, all that awaited her were two hungry cats.

"Hey, greedy little great-beings, can you at least wait until I'm in the door?"

They indicated that they could not, and after taking care of the most important members of the household, Elle rummaged for her own dinner. All that turned up was a container of stale-looking rice and shriveled edamame beans.

"I've got to start getting out more," she told the cats, who couldn't have cared less. She ate standing at the kitchen counter before grabbing a Dogfish Head Pale Ale and settling down in front of the computer. She started with Kingman's much-publicized arrest.

Tuesday, February 4, 2007

Malibu, Calif.—Legendary movie producer Eliot Kingman was arrested Monday for investigation of homicide after the body of a man was found at his home, authorities said.

Kingman, 52, was arrested at his estate around 3 a.m. in this wealthy oceanside community about 40 miles northwest of downtown Los Angeles.

The police responded to an anonymous call and discovered the body of a white, adult male, a police spokesman reported. The man had been stabbed and was pronounced dead at the scene. An antique dagger was taken into evidence as the possible murder weapon.

Authorities have identified the man as 28-year-old David Klee, employed by Kingman as a research assistant. Police stated that Kingman is the only current suspect in the murder. Bail was set at $1 million.

Kingman wrote and directed hit movies such as *Break of Day* and *Running on Empty,* and has received academy award nominations for his work as both a producer and director. He has two children with his ex-wife, the movie actress Niki Cole. His last movie, the 2005 release *By Night,* was about a vampire searching for acceptance in modern society. Friends and associates say that Kingman's behavior grew increasingly erratic throughout the making of the film.

The film's lead actor Nathan Owen reported that Kingman "would always talk about things like death and the afterlife, and hang around all these freaky people. But I guess that's what really great artists do, you know, get into the work like that."

Elle got another Dogfish and retrieved a notebook from the pile on her desk. Even though she couldn't imagine how writers had managed before Microsoft, when it came to research nothing could replace the tactile pleasure of an old-school black-and-white Mead.

She searched the daily updates from the courtroom, remembering what a zoo it had been. Kingman's lawyers had pinned their case on reasonable doubt, starting with Kingman's lack of motive. Then they floated every alternative theory for the murder, from a mysterious third party to the possibility that Klee had killed himself. Despite having the best defense team his considerable amount of money could buy, Kingman himself had proved the most damaging piece of evidence. During initial questioning, he had changed his story several times, which looked even worse once he admitted that after he found Klee's body, he had taken the time not only to remove the dagger but also to wipe it clean before police arrived.

One entry caught her eye for its ludicrous title alone:

Necromancer Takes the Stand

A self-described "necromancer" named Zor Pithador (aka Brian Williams) took the stand today as a witness for the prosecution. Mr. Pithador, who calls himself "a practitioner who summons spirits of divination in order to communicate with the dead," testified that he and Kingman made several visits to the city morgue in an attempt to receive messages from the recently deceased. A spokesperson for the L.A. County Morgue declined to comment about how Kingman and Pithador gained access to the facilities, but said that they are investigating any possible employee misconduct.

In light of the long-standing rules of Los Angeles, where reprieve from any vice can be bought for a high-enough price, no one had ever expected a conviction. But the prosecution had taken every chance to portray Kingman as an unstable man whose growing obsession with death had ended in murder, and Kingman's bizarre behavior had done most of their work for them.

Elle took off her glasses and rubbed her eyes. She wanted to spend some quiet time in her favorite spot, an old recliner that had been in her family for as long as she could remember. It had been reupholstered three times already and the gears were going bad, but she couldn't give it up just yet. Flipped back with the lights off, a Dogfish in hand, and cats in lap—that was Elle's version of meditation, and right now she needed to think. Why would Eliot Kingman want her to write his story? Greene Line had several authors who made the kind of money that someone like Kingman was used to. Elle had a solid enough fan base, but she wasn't even close to being one of Greene Line's top sellers. So Sam's endorsement aside, why would Kingman specifically ask for her?

She had decided to let these questions wait until tomorrow when her phone rang. It was Sam again, who didn't hesitate to call at any hour of the night when either inspiration or anxiety struck, the latter being the much more frequent motivation.

"Get ready to not sleep tonight."

"Sam, I'm already not sleeping because I'm on the phone with you. Is this a sign of things to come until the Kingman contract comes through?"

"Probably, but that's not why I called. It's actually bigger than that."

"Bigger than a contract? What, is Kingman going to give us the scoop on who shot JFK or the whereabouts of the Roswell alien?"

"OK, joke. Laugh all the way to Delano State Prison, in fact."

"What?"

"It turns out Kingman's lawyer has been in touch with Greene Line for over a month now. He wants an interview, and you've already been cleared."

"Seems like Kingman is calling the shots from inside the same way he did on the outside."

"Ain't money grand?"

"We wouldn't know. When's it going to be?" Interviews often produced some great material, but they could be difficult to arrange. So many things could go wrong, from obstinate prison officials and cautious lawyers to interfering family members. The subjects themselves often turned skittish or manipulative from one visit to the next.

"Tomorrow." Sam must have known what was coming.

"You've got to be kidding! I just found out I was even *doing* the Kingman story—I've had *zero* time to prepare!"

"It's a two-hour drive to Delano. Prepare on the way."

"Sam, there's no way I can go in cold like that. Tell Greene Line to reschedule."

"Elle, this is Eliot Kingman. You can't reschedule Eliot Kingman, even in prison. Listen, this is the biggest story of your career. Ace this story and you're set. Seriously."

"You mean *we're* set."

"Well, of course, *we're* set! And since we're in it together, I'll go with you tomorrow and do all the driving so you can prepare. Come on, Elle. We're going to have to do this one a bit differently."

"Which means Kingman's way, right?" When Sam didn't answer, Elle gave in. "OK, you win. But you're driving *and* buying lunch."

She sat watching the deepening shadows of evening before heading back to the computer. Sam hadn't been kidding about that sleepless night.

CHAPTER 2

North Delano State Prison went from Level I, for low level offenders, to Level IV, the maximum security section. Kingman was in the Protective Housing Unit, designed for prisoners requiring "extraordinary protection from other prisoners." Anyone rich, famous, or notorious enough ended up in the PHU, and since Delano was the nearest prison to L.A., it never had a shortage of special cases. In Elle's experience, the PHU was the most tranquil part of the prison; the inmates had sincere reasons for wanting to stay there.

Elle had been to Delano before, but she was always taken aback by the way it materialized like some barbed-wire oasis out of the barren landscape. The only other thing around was the town of Delano itself: population, 14,458; points of interest, zero. Like most of California's prisons, Delano was a self-contained city, with 942 acres and an inmate population of 5,544. At night, you could see the lights from miles away.

Visitors had to go through two security gates to get onto the grounds and then pass through a metal detector so sensitive that showing up in a bathrobe was the only real guarantee. Elle had once had some trouble with an underwire bra, and another Greene Line writer had been denied a visit after the copper attachments in her hair extensions had gone off. If you cleared the first phase, the next obstacle, the oracle whereby all must prove worthy in order to pass, sat waiting behind the Visitor Control desk.

Sam dropped her off at the front entrance without getting out of the car.

"Meet you in two hours. Have fun, but most important, remember where you are—Sociopath Inn, despite the ambiance and snack machines."

"You can wait in reception, Sam." Elle knew that certain types of institutions gave Sam the creeps—prisons, hospitals, mental wards—anywhere, he'd once told her, where people could go in and not come back out.

"No thanks. I'll take my chances with the locals."

"Half of them work here anyway."

"That's fine, as long as I'm not in there with them."

Whenever she did interviews, Elle never forgot that the guard at the door was the only thing standing between her and a convicted killer. Unlike some crime writers, over-identification with the subject was not a hazard of the job for her.

Kingman was escorted in, and then they were alone. Most law-abiding citizens carry themselves with a sense of legitimacy, sending out a set of signals that convey their rightful place in the world. But if that legitimacy is stripped away, a furtiveness creeps in, the wounded survival instinct of a once-beloved pet turned out of doors to fend for itself. If nothing else, the lousy food and interrupted sleep and endless drag of days in prison usually wear down even the hardiest of constitutions.

But Kingman looked exactly the same as he had strolling down the red carpet with a starlet on his arm: tall, thickly built, shock of sandy-brown hair engaged in curly battle with his forehead—broad shoulders not the least bit beaten down. He was starting to go soft in the middle, like a former college quarterback who had settled into an accounting job and a two-kid marriage in Anytown, U.S.A. There wasn't a dark or gothic edge on him, and Elle had a hard time imaging him spending time in morgues with someone called Zor the Necromancer.

Kingman's background was as ordinary as his appearance. His mother had been a librarian; his father, a police officer. He had studied philosophy in college before dropping out and working part-time as a truck driver in order to finance his first project, a ten-minute science fiction film called *Galaxy Genesis*. After that, he had worked in everything from special effects to script consultation before getting his break directing the blockbuster sci-fi film *Break of Day*, and the hits kept coming after that. An all-American success story all the way down the line—until ending up a convicted murderer, that is.

Kingman sat down, clasped his hands, and leaned across the table. Elle marveled at how tenaciously the privileges of power clung to those who had once possessed it. Kingman carried himself as though he'd just entered a high-powered production meeting that couldn't start without him instead of a prison visitation room where he couldn't even use the toilet without permission. Accordingly, he didn't wait for Elle to get things started.

"Elle Bramasol, thirty-five years old. BA in English literature from UCLA, author of five books. All of them about killers. Single, no children."

"If you don't count the cats." One of the first things Elle had learned about working with sociopaths is that manipulation and control are as essential to them as eating or sleeping. In order to get a good interview, she often had to play the game by their rules.

Kingman continued his rundown, reciting from memory like a news report.

"Mother, Helen, shot to death at age forty by John Danoff, age thirty-seven, at Omni Group Advertising Agency on June seventeenth, ninety eighty-nine. Danoff, a former employee disturbed by his recent termination, shot three other people during the rampage, including Ally Hill, age twenty-nine, who died three days later. Convicted on two counts attempted murder and two counts first-degree. Currently on death row in San Quentin."

Kingman paused and leaned even farther across the table, uncomfortably close.

"Do you plan to attend the execution?"

Elle hesitated. This was not territory that she liked to play games with, book of a lifetime or not.

"I'm not sure. Do you believe in the death penalty, Mr. Kingman?"

"I believe that some people die for a purpose more important than their own lives. Do you, Ms. Bramasol? Do you believe that death can serve a higher purpose?"

Before she could answer, Kingman leaned back and closed his eyes.

"You're wondering why I chose you. For one reason, Ms. Bramasol, and one reason alone—because you understand death."

"Actually, I don't understand a thing about death. If anything, writing about it for the past seven years has taught me that death is the most perplexing subject of all."

"Exactly. And that's why you're here. The Highway Five case."

Elle's third book, about a killer who had driven up and down a rural highway in Kentucky, looking for women with car trouble and then strangling them. Afterward, he would pose them sitting upright, hands on the wheel as if still alive. Once he had even placed an open cell phone in one of his victim's hands.

"You understood what even the killer himself couldn't explain," Kingman continued. "That one of the reasons he killed those women was because it was so easy."

"That's right. He said that when he killed his first victim, he had expected to feel this debilitating sense of guilt and remorse. But it hadn't happened; his life went on exactly as it had before. Not one thing had changed."

"So how much did a life matter, if any ordinary fool like him could end one so easily? Even the grieving families would eventually go on with their lives. Because that's what we do, don't we?"

"Yes, but not without a permanent loss."

Kingman's voice rose in irritation. "But that's not what we tell ourselves. We don't say, 'I *can* go on, but with a permanent loss.' No, we say, 'I can't live without her,' or 'I don't know what

I'd do without him.' *That's* what we say about our husbands or our wives or our children. And yet we know *exactly* what we'd do—the same thing that billions of people have done billions of times over since life began—go on with our lives. Doesn't the very ordinariness, the very commonality of 'moving on' strike you as extraordinary?"

Elle's father had married a woman fifteen years younger than him four years and seven months after her mother's murder; their son had been born less than two years later.

"Yes," she said. "Yes, it does."

Kingman nodded. "If our loved ones meant as much to us as we believe they do, as we *say* they do, their deaths would mean only one thing: suicide. That's what it *really* means to not be able to live without someone. Do you mean it enough to make it literal? If not, then you don't mean it at all. There's no in-between."

"Romeo and Juliet?"

Kingman smiled for the first time, a strange, secret smile. "Shakespeare got a lot of things right."

"Is that why you killed David Klee? Because his death wouldn't make a difference?" Since Kingman had never admitted to the crime, Elle knew that bringing up Klee's death was a gamble. Kingman's lawyers had started working on the appeals before the verdict had even come in, but if the legal thin-ice of his situation concerned him, he didn't let it show.

"David Klee's death was going to make all of the difference. But that's not what I brought you here to talk about."

"Well, much as I enjoy philosophizing about death, I'm not sure my publisher is going to go for it."

"You'll get your story. That's how I make my living, you know—telling stories."

Elle noticed his use of the present tense. "And now you're interested in stories about immortality? Is that why your last film was about vampires?"

"Do you know what did it for me, Ms. Bramasol? My father's death. I had just been nominated for an Academy Award. I had two great kids, a beautiful wife. I had never, not even *once* in my life, considered that I couldn't get what I wanted as long as I was smart enough and worked hard enough. Then I get a phone call at nine o'clock on a Wednesday night, and just like that, he's gone. Massive heart attack while taking a bath. This was a man who wore a uniform almost every day of his life for twenty-five years and then put on a pair of pressed pants and a suit jacket every day after that. And he was as naked as a newborn when the ambulance came for him. He wanted cremated right away, so I think he stayed that way—naked, I mean—right up to the end. Went out of this world literally stripped of everything."

Kingman paused, remembering. "When I started to clear his things away, I found the shoes he had set out for the next day. They were perfectly polished, those shoes."

He framed his hands in the air around an imaginary movie scene; the classic director's gesture. "It's been almost five years now, but that image has never left me: my father sitting there in his room, polishing a pair of shoes that he'd never wear again. He could polish a pair of shoes so that you could see your reflection in them! My father was sixty-nine years old when he died. He'd had a great life. That's what everyone kept saying: 'He had a great life.' But that didn't make it any easier at all."

"No, it doesn't."

"You know, your parents form a sort of barrier against death. Did you ever think about it that way? And once they're gone, nothing separates you from death except time. It made me realize that it didn't add up to anything, this stumbling around in the dark. I've spent my entire life creating the kinds of movies that only one in a million people can make. Yet it won't stop me from going out just as naked and alone as my father did."

Elle let the silence alone until he was ready to continue.

"Do you ever think about it? What happened to my father? Not to his body, but to his essence, his soul—whatever you want to call what made him who he was. What happened to his love of jazz music and his cop stories and his goddamn shoe-polishing secrets? Are you telling me that's just nothing? Just gone? Where is your mother now, Ms. Bramasol? Just went to work one day like a million other people and never came back."

Kingman was clenching and unclenching his fists. Elle imagined him on some movie set, terrorizing his crew into seeing the same visions he saw.

"I think about it a lot," Elle told him. "What about religion? You don't believe in an afterlife?"

"It doesn't matter what I believe, or what anyone believes. I can *believe* whatever I want. But that doesn't change the fact that I don't *know* even the most basic thing about what happens after we die. And neither does anyone else—not the mystics or the prophets or the scientists or the philosophers. And that's why we're all so obsessed with it."

Kingman didn't wait for Elle to agree. "Have you ever seen the cave drawing of the dead figures rising toward 'heaven'? Created twenty thousand years before Christianity. Every culture on earth has some version of an afterlife. It's what I call *totem*—the kind of universal, primal instincts that cross time and place. The power of motherhood, the urge to procreate. The belief in a higher power. That's all totem."

"If belief in an afterlife is totem, then it follows that there must be something to it."

"Look at it more carefully. A *belief* in the afterlife is totem. We obviously have this need to believe in something bigger than ourselves, in something that extends beyond our deaths. But that doesn't mean it exists; only that our *belief* in it does. And that's not good enough for me."

"Is that where people like Zor come in?"

"I know most of the 'black arts' are as much of a rip-off as any other New Age crap. Or any organized religion, as far as that goes. But that doesn't mean all of it is crap. Have you ever tried to talk to the dead?"

"I have."

"And has it worked?"

"Sometimes I think there have been signs. Other times I think the mind can convince itself of whatever it wants. As you say, there's no way to know for sure."

"And why is that? Why have we been given the power to create art of breathtaking genius, to break down the very workings of the universe, to map the essence of life itself to the last chromosome—and yet we still know absolutely nothing about death. *Nothing!*"

Kingman was almost shouting now. "Why have we been denied this? Shouldn't we be given the answer to the most important question of all, the only one that really matters? The one that if left unanswered makes all of the other answers useless, nothing but wasted time before the abyss? *What the hell kind of a deal is that?*"

"I don't know. I don't know any more than you do."

In an instant, he had regained his composure. "You're right, I don't know. But I didn't get where I am in life by accepting raw deals or lousy contracts. Over thirty years in the movie business has taught me that there's *always* a way around a problem if you find the right tools for the job. And I've found the right tools, Ms. Bramasol. I know the way around."

"The way around what?"

As he leaned towards her, Kingman's entire body—entire *being*—seemed concentrated into this one point. "*The way around death.*"

Elle had a sense of sliding reality, like finding herself cast in the supporting role of a madman's puppet show. And Kingman had gotten very rich on the power of his puppet shows.

"My wife Vita will call you within the next few days. She's going to give you something that will change your entire life. I'm trusting you with this item, but you cannot tell anyone else about it. Not your agent, not your boyfriend. Not even your damn cats."

"Will you tell me what it is?" Elle felt her stomach knot with the possibility of a previously undiscovered suicide note or some hidden piece of evidence that would break the case wide open.

"It's a book."

A book. Not exactly the smoking gun Elle had been hoping for, but then again when it came to Kingman, anything was possible.

He motioned for the guard and stood up to leave. "This is no ordinary book. It tells a very strange and interesting story. That's totem, too, you know. Our need to create and tell stories."

And our need to believe them. Elle had a feeling that where Kingman was concerned, she would do well to keep that in mind.

CHAPTER 3

The next day started with a phone call to Gary Holland. Gary was a homicide detective with the Los Angeles Police Department, one of those contacts every crime writer needs to access otherwise off-limits information. He was also a friend, and sometimes more. They had met when Elle was working the Crazy Girl story and had connected despite the differences. Gary was exactly what tourists expected to see when they came to California: tall and square-jawed, with tousled blond hair as if he'd just stepped off a surfboard ad. And he had in fact grown up on the beaches of La Jolla, excelling not only at surfing but also at football, track, and water polo, of all things. Gary's family had money, and he'd gone to one of San Diego's most exclusive private schools.

Elle's middle-class high school hadn't even had a pool, let alone a water polo club. She had never played a sport in her life, and her fair skin was genetically incapable of getting a tan. She was probably one of the few women in Los Angeles who didn't belong to a gym. Had they been classmates, Gary wouldn't have known Elle existed, and she would have written him off as a superficial jock without an interesting thought in his head.

The differences didn't stop at the surface. Gary was as gregarious and easygoing as Elle was introverted and cautious. She didn't consider herself a pessimist or a cynic, but no one would describe her as particularly sunny or light of spirit, either. Already solitary by nature, Elle had turned even further inward after her mother's death, which was one of the reasons she was so well suited for writing: it allowed her to connect with humanity while remaining separate from it—fellowship without friendship, involvement without intimacy.

Elle's father had waited until she'd finished college before relocating to Arizona and starting a new life, complete with new wife and new kid. For a while, she had considered moving there to be closer to him, but the more years that had passed, the easier it had become to maintain an affectionate but limited distance—too many memories for him, too many adjustments for her. Now Elle had her life narrowed down to a short list of essentials: research, write, feed cats, feed self, sleep. Wake up, repeat. Throw in a couple of Dogfish Head, and life was good. Gary, who liked people and who was therefore liked in return, balanced her solitude.

After finishing college, Gary had pursued whatever new adventure caught his attention, from trekking through South America to playing drums in a rock band that had actually had a hit before calling it quits; it still surprised her to run searches and turn up pictures of five brooding young men, the spikey-haired blond one looking familiar. But eventually Gary had run out of adventures. During a late-night TV-and-beer session on the heels of his thirtieth birthday, an LAPD recruitment ad had come on. His friends had joked about going downtown and trying out, and the idea had stayed with Gary long after both the beer and the friends had disappeared. His family hadn't objected to this sudden and unlikely career choice, but they hadn't exactly been supportive, either. He had once told Elle that the police academy had been the first thing in his life that he'd really had to work for.

She'd asked Gary to dig around on Kingman's case, and he was stopping by with his customary dinner of take-out pizza. As soon as he walked in, Elle could tell that he'd been working too many long hours again. Gary was more cagey than most men about his age, but Elle knew from piecing together his timeline that he was somewhere just north of forty, and when he was tired or overworked, his leanness edged into gauntness, which wasn't helped by his lousy eating habits. Elle had once looked in his refrigerator and found nothing but a half-empty can of tomato soup, a carton of milk, and a box of Saltines. When Gary's eyes were sunken with fatigue and the angles of his face too tautly drawn, Elle could glimpse the old man that he would become, still far away but no longer out of range. But Elle also knew that bone structure like that never failed. With most good-looking people, beauty emerges in youth and then peaks somewhere in the twenties, maybe sticks around a little longer before heading out of town like a retiree on a pension. But Gary's was the permanent resident kind, settled in for life.

"Here, have a Dogfish." Elle slid a bottle across the kitchen counter and held her own up to the light to catch the swirling amber. She had discovered the Dogfish Head microbrewery while working a story in Delaware, and had become addicted to the stuff enough to pay a small fortune to have a crate load shipped to L.A. twice a year. A costly but worthy indulgence.

"Palo Santo Marron—brewed in handmade vessels made from Paraguayan Palo Santo wood. Hints of caramel and vanilla in a malty brown ale."

"You sound like a menu," Gary said, taking the bottle. "According to the German Beer Purity Law, true beer can only have three ingredients."

"Well, so much for German purity laws."

Gary took a long drink and flipped open the pizza box.

"Do you ever stop to think how lucky we are to be in a time and place where we can have pizza and beer pretty much any time we want it?"

"You mean *you* can have pizza and beer pretty much any time you want it." At five feet nine with size 10 jeans and what was commonly referred to as a "full figure," Elle had never been slender. But after turning thirty, her metabolism had apparently taken out a restraining order forbidding her from coming within a hundred miles.

"I like a woman with a little pizza on her." Gary came around the counter and slid his arms around her hips. "In all of the right places."

Elle leaned into his muscular build and inhaled his musky smell. At one time, they had drifted toward a serious relationship, but life kept intervening with plans of its own—Gary's long hours, Elle working on a story halfway across the country. The state of affairs in China. Now they had settled into a comfortable place where friendship intersected with sex only when it worked out for both of them. They had an unspoken agreement that if one or the other ever found a partner, the sex would end without affecting the friendship. But so far, neither of them had tested that theory.

"What happened to Cynthia?"

Gary never had difficulty attracting women, many of whom had high-paying jobs or huge divorce settlements to go along with their looks. His upbringing allowed him to mix easily in their world, but none ever lasted. Whether that was because of his job or his persistent inability to stay focused on a relationship, Elle didn't know. Probably both. "Cynthia decided to give it another try with her ex-husband, and even as we speak is probably lying poolside on an estate in Bel Air, sipping a cocktail delivered by a twenty-year-old servant boy with swarthy good looks and a mysterious past."

"Lucky Cynthia."

"No, lucky us. With that pesky Cynthia out of the way, we're free to copulate all night like the unfettered animals we are." He leaned over and buried his face in her hair. "Mmmm, girl hair. One of nature's finest aromas."

Other than her fair skin, Elle's hair was one of the few features she had inherited from her mother, who came from a long line of Irish beauties with the same delicate bone structure and peculiar shade of cherry-Coke colored hair. Her father's Italian side, on the other hand, was all strong contours and bold lines, and Elle was the kind of woman people referred to as "attractive" or "handsome" rather than "pretty." Which suited her just fine—she wasn't a pretty kind of person, and tended to agree with Proust that pretty women should be left to men devoid of imagination. She slid out of Gary's arms and gave him a kiss before delivering the ultimatum.

"First, tell me what you found out."

Gary sighed and headed for the couch. "This can't go on, you know. I won't allow myself to be used like this, a manservant of information for your insatiable fact-finding desires."

"You know you love it, so don't hold out. Give a girl what she wants."

He retrieved a dog-eared notebook from his back pocket. Like Elle, Gary was one of the last vanguards of the dwindling pen and paper kingdom.

"OK, first up, Vita Mae Lee. Kingman's latest wife, twenty-seven years old."

"Did you ever notice that when men over fifty remarry, it's never to someone, say, their own age?"

"That's because most men sincerely believe that their biological age is permanently fixed somewhere around thirty—which makes it perfectly reasonable to marry a seventeen-year-old and have a baby at eighty."

"Does that mean you have a seventeen-year-old stashed away somewhere?"

"A sixteen-year-old, actually. But his name's Connor, and I think we might be related."

During his musician years, Gary had gotten married to a girl he'd met on tour. It had fallen apart quickly, and only after she'd moved back to her hometown in upstate New York did he find out that she was pregnant. Gary loved his son, but nothing could change the fact that there had been thousands of miles between them from the very first day of Connor's life, and apart from a summer vacation or a long weekend now and then, it had remained that way ever since. For Elle, remembering that Gary had a kid out there, a living remnant from some long ago life of rock-'n- roll excess, was always difficult.

"What else?"

"Turns out that Vita Mae only sounds like she's a stripper. She actually has a BA in art history. Drifted around after graduation, ended up in L.A. a few years ago. Worked as a bartender at a club called Stigmata before signing on with Kingman about three years ago. Married him right before the trial started."

"They were dating before that though, right?"

"She was a part of the crew working on that vampire film, and they probably got something started then, but it doesn't look like there was much to it. The marriage happened because he needed a pretty young wife by his side during the trial, and she needed the money. So there you go. Just one of a million young girls drifting through L.A. who gets lucky and hooks up with one of the big fish."

"The only thing she's lucky about is that she wasn't the one on the end of that dagger. What about Klee?"

"David Klee, twenty-eight at time of death. Died from a single stab wound to the upper left chest. Ivy League master's degree in Religious Studies, concentration in contemplative religions, whatever the hell that means. Aren't all religions contemplative?"

"In theory. In practice, pretty much the opposite, at least for most people. Seems like Kingman liked to surround himself with well-educated people."

"Yep, and well educated in things like art history and religion, which leads to the second criteria for playing on Kingman's team—having little to no employment prospects. Klee was even more of a drifter than Vita. By the time he was twenty-six, he'd lived in four states and tried everything from teaching at a private school to working in a home for mentally handicapped teenagers. He landed a gig with Kingman as a research assistant and was with him right up until the end. His own, that is."

Elle had gotten used to Gary's gallows humor over the years. It went with the territory for people whose jobs brought them into face-to-face contact with the kind of gruesome tragedies that for most people never come any closer than a TV screen.

"What about Klee's suicidal behavior?"

"First off, there was no suicide note. Just a few e-mails to friends and family saying how excited he was about something 'big' that Kingman was working on. Lots of stuff about death and immortality. But that was all related to the vampire film. Kingman's assistants had been doing the research nonstop for months, and it seems like all of them got a little obsessed. The defense produced tons of emails and memos about the undead and black magic and that sort of thing. They argued that working on the film caused Klee to become morbidly obsessed with death, and eventually it got the better of him. Without a note, though, it wasn't enough. Klee had prescriptions for Paxil and Zoloft, but list me ten people in the movie biz who aren't on some kind of antidepressant."

"List me ten people in L.A. who aren't." Elle checked her notes from the trial. "One of their experts testified that it would take someone with a deep personality disorder to commit suicide that way, and Klee didn't have any history of mental illness, Zoloft aside. So the suicide theory was pretty weak right from the start, even without the note."

"True. Then again, almost nothing is too bizarre to consider suicide. There are cases where people have cut off limbs or slashed their own necks trying to do themselves in. A cop I know worked a case where a guy bled to death after slashing off his own penis. It was eventually ruled an accident, but since the guy had made previous attempts to kill himself they couldn't really be sure. It's a weird world out there, Elle. Weirder than most people could ever imagine."

"I'm convinced enough of that."

When Elle was researching a case, she and Gary often played devil's advocate over the evidence. Elle had never once believed that any of the killers she'd written about were innocent, and Kingman so far was no exception. But coming at a case objectively uncovered shades of gray that the black-and-white perspectives of prosecution and defense often missed.

Elle reviewed her notes again. "Typically a suicidal stabbing is to bare skin, with the clothing removed or pulled aside, because the clothing actually offers the greatest resistance to penetration. And Klee's shirt was wide open when they found him, with his own fingerprints all over the buttons and no evidence of tampering. Why would he remove his own shirt in order to be stabbed by Kingman?"

"Maybe he had it open before the stabbing. I myself have been known to walk around bare-chested, you know. You should try it." To help her along, Gary began undoing the top buttons of her shirt.

"But how easy is it to stab someone in the heart? Wouldn't Klee have put up some resistance? I mean, they didn't find any defensive wounds."

"People overestimate the amount of force it takes to produce a deep stab wound. The main factor is how sharp the point of the weapon is, and that dagger was *sharp*. With no clothing involved, the point would have penetrated the skin surface fairly easily, and then the blade slips right into the deeper tissue like a ripe melon. Speaking of which…"

He slid his hands inside her shirt. Elle flushed with arousal like she always did at his touch, but she removed his hands and got him another Dogfish to keep him occupied. There were a few more points she needed to clear up, and once Gary left a topic, it could be hard to get him back onto it.

"The prosecution also brought up the lack of hesitation wounds." Elle had discovered that many suicide victims have shallow cuts caused by attempts to test the effectiveness of the weapon or to build up courage before the final cut. Klee hadn't had even one.

"Well, not all suicides practice first. Some have the nerve to just go for it right away, I guess. But yeah, the lack of hesitation wounds was just one more factor to support homicide."

"But what about the lack of blood splatter on Kingman's clothes? He only had blood on his hands, which he claimed came from touching the body when he found Klee."

"There wasn't much blood, period, let alone splatter. A penetration wound can look like practically nothing depending on where it is on the body. The damage is often really deep, which means very little external bleeding. I've seen corpses with wounds so small and clean you have to shake them to make sure they're really dead. Now, can we consider penetration of an entirely different kind? Here, let me demonstrate…"

"Just one more thing, I promise. What about the so-called third party defense? And the nine-one-one call?"

"That's two things. First, no evidence turned up to indicate a third party was involved in the murder. No forensics, no witnesses, nothing."

"But the defense claimed the nine-one-one call proved that someone else had to have been on the grounds. Kingman's mansion is on three acres of property with a secured perimeter and a gated entrance, and none of the servants were on the grounds that night."

"Which was suspicious in of itself given the fleet of them that usually hung around. A few even lived on the grounds, but Kingman just happened to give every one of them the night off right when a murder takes places? Not to mention that all of the security cameras covering the grounds *and* inside the house also just happened to have been turned off that night."

"And they never determined who made the nine-one-one call?"

"No. There wasn't much to it. Male, probably somewhere in his thirties. The recording was hard to make out. Real quiet and muffled, like the speaker didn't want identified. Plus it was right out by the ocean, so that interfered with the sound quality as well."

"But couldn't they just trace the call?"

"Normally, but it was a prepay."

"So?" Elle had a hard time believing that anything was truly untraceable these days.

"Look, I could walk into any major chain store right now and get a pre-paid phone. I pay cash; they turn the phone on. I buy a phone card, put the minutes on the phone, and off I go. No record of my name is ever attached to that phone. We can use cell towers to pinpoint the general location of where the call was made, but that's it."

"OK, but most people just have regular phones. It seems like a pretty big coincidence that whoever witnessed the crime just happened to have an untraceable phone handy. What do the cops have to say about it?"

"The general opinion is that it's pretty unlikely it was just some random witness. But if the call did come from someone involved, then whoever it was didn't want to do Kingman any favors. With his kind of money and power, there's no doubt he could have cleaned up the crime scene and gotten a hold of some people in pretty high places if he would have had more time. He might have even gotten the body out of his house and disposed of it altogether; it's happened before. But the police had the scene secured in less than twenty minutes, and the press got a hold of the story almost as fast, which didn't help. The body was still warm, and Kingman was the only one there to answer for it. But without that nine-one-one call, Kingman would probably still be walking around free today, visiting necromancers to his heart's content."

"This is turning out to be a strange case so far, Gary."

"And I'm going to turn into a strange case if we don't stop talking and start something far more pleasurable."

Gary slid his hand back into her shirt, and this time she didn't stop him.

"Quite a high opinion of your abilities, isn't it?"

"Well, why have a false sense of humility?"

And he devoted the rest of the night and well into the next morning making good on his claims.

CHAPTER 4

By the time Elle straggled out of bed the next day, Gary was already gone. She was always amazed at how little sleep the man needed, though one of these days he would have to slow down. Elle knew that someday Gary would get married again and settle down into his own peculiar version of domesticity. When that happened, things would change between them, and not just the sex. She knew that it was selfish, but she couldn't help but be relieved whenever the latest girlfriend came and went. But sooner or later, one would stay. Elle decided to save that thought for another time.

She was halfway through her first cup of tea when her phone rang. Kingman's wife, just as he had promised. Her voice was so faint that Elle had to strain to make out what she was saying.

"My husband told me to contact you about the book. He's ready for you to read it now."

Vita made it sound as if Kingman was there waiting for her, and it struck Elle that no one seemed to believe that Kingman was scheduled to spend the rest of his life behind bars, including

Kingman. It was as if he were off on a movie shoot somewhere and everyone was just handling his affairs until he came back.

"Now as in *right* now?"

"Well, yes. It's very important that you read the book right away."

Elle sighed. It wasn't as if she was eager to start writing or anything.

"OK, today is fine. Where should I meet you?"

"Come to the mansion. But don't bring anybody else with you. Eliot said that if anybody else is with you, I absolutely can't let you in."

Elle was eager to the visit the site of the murder. After Kingman's conviction, the press had speculated that he'd sell the house, but he'd held onto it; his wife still lived there with half of the rooms shut up like some eerie mausoleum. During the trial, the jury had toured part of the house and grounds, and it had turned into a circus. One juror had lain down on the spot where Klee's body had been found, and another had sent the prosecution into a frenzy by ogling over a collection of Kingman's awards and movie memorabilia.

Elle hoped to get a look at the exact room where the murder had taken place. She liked to get a physical sense of a crime scene, to stand where the victims had stood, to see what they had seen, and to imagine what they had thought or felt. There was something powerful about being in a place where a violent death had occurred, and sometimes if Elle closed her eyes and let her mind go, she could feel the restless spirit of the dead requesting all those who stood there to bear witness and remember. This wasn't always the case; some murder scenes seemed so ordinary that Elle had to remind herself what had happened there. She wondered which type Kingman's mansion would be.

On the long drive out to Malibu, she couldn't resist calling Sam. "You'll never guess where I'm headed right now."

"Let me see. Where would you normally be headed on a Thursday afternoon—the liquor store on the corner of Sunset and Vine? Or maybe the taco cart with the bicycle horn that so charmingly honks up and down your street all day long? Okay, I give up."

"Laughs on you this time, Sam. I am, as we speak, on my way to the notorious Kingman estate, where the mysterious Vita Mae awaits to buzz me through the gates of doom and into the mansion of mayhem and murder."

"My God, Elle, that could be the opening for your book! How did you get an interview with her so fast?"

"How else? Kingman arranged it."

"It seems like Mr. Kingman has done all of the work so far. Why not just let him write the book?"

"He probably should; it would sell a hell of a lot better than my version. To be honest, I'm not sure what he's up to, Sam."

"Well, why worry about it? Just go along for the ride, because it's probably going to be the biggest and best one of your career."

"I don't know…something just seems off about this one."

"Off? What's 'off' is our lousy contract percentages, lousy royalty schedules, and lousy advances. What's 'on' is calling the shots from here on out. Don't be such a doubter!"

"I know, I know. Look, I'm almost there. I'll call you back if anything big turns up."

After miles of twisting canyon roads, the Pacific suddenly emerged along with the million-dollar mansions that dotted the coastline like jewels on a very costly necklace. Elle eased up to the gate of Kingman's estate, the modern equivalent of a medieval fortress designed to keep the serfs at bay. Elle was surprised when Vita herself opened the front door.

As they headed for the living room, Elle got a better look at her. She definitely didn't fit the stereotypical image of the Hollywood wife. She had on an inexpensive peasant skirt and black bodysuit; no jewelry; and very little makeup. No obvious signs of big money here. Vita was the type of small-boned, fragile-looking woman that always made Elle feel as if she should be holding a spear and wearing an animal skin, an Amazonian who had wandered too far from her tribe. Vita had dark hair that framed her face in tights waves; large, brown eyes; and a cupid-bow mouth. Add to this the air of vulnerability and the effect was of a silent-movie star thrust from her own era into a harsh modern world she was ill equipped to survive. All in all, not the usual type to swim in the piranha-infested waters of Hollywood wives.

"Would you like something to drink?" Vita offered. "I could make some tea or something."

"Tea would be great, thanks."

Elle was glad for the chance to get Vita out of the way. She got up and went into the hallway. She knew from studying maps of the house that the hall she was in now went in a circular pattern past a large dining hall, where once upon a lifetime Kingman had hosted lavish dinner parties attended by the rich and powerful. Klee's murder had taken place in an isolated room at the back of the house that Kingman used to display memorabilia from his filmmaking. Elle thought that she could find the room if she had enough time. She followed the hallway past the dining hall and several small rooms before coming face-to-face with a tall figure grimacing at her like an apparition out of an old haunted-house film.

"You startled me!"

"What are you doing back here?"

"First of all, my name is Elle Bramasol, and I'm here at Mr. Kingman and his wife's invitation." She extended her hand, hoping to divert the apparition from the fact that she hadn't actually answered his question.

"I know who you are and why you're here, and it doesn't include a tour." He gave a dismissive glance at her outstretched hand and made a dramatic sweep of his arm back toward the living room. "After you."

Vita hadn't returned with the tea, and they sat in silence for a while before Elle ventured a guess. "Are you one of Kingman's assistants?"

Kingman was notorious for his exhaustive attention to detail when he was researching a film. Nothing escaped his scrutiny, from the kind of tablecloth a middle-class family would own in 1940s' France to the scientific principles of concepts like time travel. Kingman employed a small army of assistants who pored over research manuals, antique books, hand-pressed memoirs—no source was too obscure and no fact too trivial for his team to track down. While making a film, Kingman often required his researchers to stay in a wing of the mansion set up especially for them, complete with their own set of servants. Elle had once read that the atmosphere was like a war strategy room in full-engagement mode.

"I'm Nyholm Quinn. Mr. Kingman's head research assistant, actually."

He said this without any enthusiasm, and Elle wondered what this job entailed now that Kingman's moviemaking days were over. Before she could respond, Vita returned with an antique Japanese tea pot and four small cups on a lacquered tray.

"This is Nyholm Quinn, Mr. Kingman's…"

"Head research assistant," Elle finished for her. "We've met."

As Vita poured the tea, Elle noticed that she left the fourth cup empty. The silence took uncomfortable root, and Elle realized that she was going to have to take the lead here. She didn't have all day to sit and watch steam rise from a cup of tea.

"Mr. Kingman said that you have a book for me?"

"Not just *a* book," Nyholm corrected.

Elle decided that so far she did not much care for this man.

"It's an irreplaceable artifact," he continued. "Maybe the most important document in all of written history." Vita nodded her assent.

What these two lacked in conversation skills, they certainly made up for in overdramatic flair. "Does it relate to Mr. Kingman's case?"

"It's of far greater importance than a mere criminal case."

From where Kingman was sitting, Elle couldn't imagine what would be more important than a "mere" criminal case. Vita's gaze had drifted out the window, and she seemed more interested in a large fountain gurgling in the inner courtyard than in a discussion of the most important document in all of written history taking place with a total stranger.

Nyholm sprang up and crossed the room with a speed and agility out of place in such a sickly looking frame. He went to a glass corner shelf, opened it almost reverently, and returned with an old leather-bound book held close to his chest.

"This book," he explained, "rarely leaves the most secure safekeeping that money can buy. I'm the only one who has ever handled it. Other than Mr. Kingman, of course."

His tone made it clear that he was not at all eager to add Elle to this elite list. She felt her irritation rise at the growing absurdity of the situation; between the book, the incorrigible Mr. Nyholm, and the mentally departed Vita, her patience was wearing out.

"May I see it?"

When she reached out, Nyholm actually recoiled, clutching the book tighter against his chest.

"That's why I'm here, after all. As Mr. Kingman requested." It hadn't been *her* idea to come to this creepy mausoleum and usurp some old book.

The reminder of who was still really in charge had the intended effect. Nyholm wilted onto the couch with a sigh, and handed her the book.

"You can look at it briefly, but please…be careful with it."

It was bound in dark green leather; the front and back were pockmarked with all variety of cracks and nicks and scrapes. It didn't have a title, but she could see a worn-down image of what looked like a tree...she squinted and held the book closer. Yes, it was a tree with branches in a circular pattern and what looked like images of animals or birds of some kind interwoven among the leaves. She ran her hand over the tree and looked closer...or were those *human* faces? She jumped when Nyholm spoke, breaking her concentration.

"It seems to change every time you look at it. After a while, alone in a darkened room, it can start to get to you, believe me."

"I can imagine." Elle opened the cover and carefully leafed through the pages. Nyholm leaned forward, his intensity between them like a force field. The first entries were dated around the late 1800s, and the script was florid and close-set.

"It's written in...German?"

"A German dialect, to be exact. And it's actually written in three different languages, only one of which is English. I translated it myself. I'm a double PhD in ancient and modern European languages."

"I see." Another one of Kingman's well-educated drifters. Elle turned some more pages. In places, the ink was blurred and almost indecipherable. Based on the dates, it seemed like some kind of a diary. Some entries were long and written so carefully that it looked like a manuscript, while others were little more than a few scribbled lines. Some of the pages were torn or marred by stains, and if Nyholm had been given the job of translating this thing, no wonder he was so high-strung. She noticed that in some places, the dates stopped for long periods and then picked up again. The language eventually changed to Spanish, and the ink and writing style became more modern. Toward the end, it was written in English.

"Is this some kind of a family history? A generational memoir or something like that?"

"Something like that."

"Well, it's a very interesting historical piece. But I'm not sure why Mr. Kingman wants me to read it. How does it relate to the book I'm writing about his case?"

"That's for you to discuss with Mr. Kingman. I'm only here to show you the book and to give you a copy of my translation. There are some very important rules that must be followed, though."

Rules? Elle had to bite back the urge to ask if there would be a test at the end. She got the impression that Nyholm's sense of humor wasn't one of his strong points.

"OK, I can do rules."

He retrieved a file folder from the bottom drawer of an imposing old sideboard. Elle had read that Kingman had a penchant for antiques, which is probably how he acquired this mysterious book that seemed to have everyone so entranced. Nyholm sat down and began separating the contents of the folder into several piles.

"Here's a translation of the first few chapters."

"So I'm not taking the book with me?"

Nyholm looked as if she'd just suggested capital murder. "Of course you're not taking the book. I told you, no one handles this book except for me. You can't take anything with you. Mr. Kingman was very insistent that nothing leaves this house.

No copies can be made, and you can't take any notes. In fact, you'll have to give me your phone and bag. Follow me and I'll show you to the library."

"Actually, I hadn't planned on staying that long."

He seemed relieved to hear it. "Suit yourself. I guess you can read it some other time."

She hesitated. As Kingman had known all along, curiosity won out. "OK, fine. Today is fine."

With this set of oddballs, Elle couldn't be sure she would even get another chance to read it, and she did want to know what it was all about. She couldn't imagine how, but the book had to be related to Klee's murder. Why else would Nyholm be willing to protect it like the Holy Grail? And why would Kingman be so eager for her to read it?

Nyholm led her to a large room with floor-to-ceiling windows framing the Pacific swelling less than a few hundred feet from the back of the mansion. The other walls were filled with shelf after shelf of books and manuscripts. The soft light of the late-afternoon sun bounced off the sea and filled the room. She had to admit, The Bradbury was no competition as far as reading rooms went. Nyholm handed her a sheaf of paper and suddenly turned solicitous.

"Make yourself comfortable. Vita can bring more tea if you'd like."

"No, I'm fine, thanks."

Elle could see where a person could get used to this. She sat for a while admiring the breath-taking view that people like Kingman paid millions of dollars to possess. Settling deep into her chair, she took out her reading glasses and picked up the first page.

CHAPTER 5

09 September, 1870; The Kingdom of Prussia under his Majesty Kaiser Wilhelm I

This is not written for the young or the light of heart, not for the tranquil species of men whose souls are content with the simple pleasures of family, church, or profession. Rather, I write to those beings like myself whose existence is compounded by a lurid intermingling of the dark and the light; who can judge rationally and think with reason, yet who feel too keenly and churn with too great a passion; who have an incessant longing for happiness and yet are shadowed by a deep and persistent melancholy—those who grasp gratification where they may, but find no lasting comfort for the soul.

This story begins on the first of September, 1870, at the great battle of Sedan. Though I no longer know who or what I have become, I was then an officer with the Second Army of the Rhine, under Prince Frederick Charles. The French had declared battle in July, and people erupted into cheers in the streets. Having from the age of seventeen sworn an oath of loyalty to the fatherland, I was prepared to die in service of that oath, though that sentiment seems meaningless to me now, a creature without a nation and worthy of no king.

My squadron was assigned to lead an advance attack of La Garenne hill. If we could take and hold that hill, the French would be forced into retreat, and Sedan would be ours. A warehouse outside the town had been set on fire by the shelling, and the area was engulfed in smoke. As we advanced on the hill amidst the roar of battle, the ground trembled beneath the tread of a thousand horses. All one could do was move forward and pray. Everywhere men and horses lay wounded and dying. My own horse's legs had been stained crimson by the carnage, and he soon joined the fallen when a musket ball passed through his neck at the crest of the hill. More men fell around me, their saddlebags blown straight off their backs and the contents scattered across the hill. Men too exhausted to move forward came together in confused heaps near the ammunition wagons.

As I crawled from beneath my horse, I learned that my right leg had been broken in the fall. I then knew that I would most certainly die, and I did not have long to wait. I saw the flash of a French Cuirassier's helmet and breastplate, then his sabre, which he thrust to the hilt into my chest. I fell to the ground to await my death, but it came for my vanquisher first—the Cuirassier had not advanced four feet before his head was smashed to atoms by a musket shot, leaving the headless trunk to sink beside me in a ghastly pantomime of my own fate only seconds before.

I know not how long I lay on that blood-soaked hill in a state of wavering consciousness, but the hospital assistants began arriving at the same time the skies opened up in torrents of rain. I watched as they searched for the living, sticking fast in the ankle deep mud and stumbling over corpses as thick and high as a city wall. Finally, an assistant knelt at my side and stripped me of my tunic. He placed his mouth against my wound; I felt a strange sensation and heard equally strange sounds issue forth. I had heard stories of men who could put the breath of life back into the mouths of the dead, and I felt hope revive—perhaps he was breathing life back into me through the gash in my chest! And yet I only seemed to grow weaker the longer he worked. Finally, he drew away from the wound. I felt his hand move gently across my face, and then I heard his voice close to my ear. I will try to record his words the best that my faltering awareness allowed me to comprehend:

"Soldier…you have delivered death to many men; now you in turn lie dying. The wheel has turned, and all are stained with blood. This, then, is the hell on earth that men create—look!"

He shook me with some force, but my eyes were long past sight.

"Look what men do to each other! This is your legacy. So tell me, solider—do you still wish to live?"

I struggled to speak but could not find the strength. He shook me again with more violence.

"Do you still wish to live?"

In that last moment of life, I went down into the deepest reserves of my soul, where enough will remained for just one word: "Yes."

He let go of my shoulders, and when he spoke again, the anguish had left his voice. "And so once again, it is yes. Always, they wish to live."

He drew a small dagger and made a deep gash along the length of his arm. The red stream mixed with the falling rain and splashed upon my face, so that the very sky above me seemed to be crying blood. He leaned over and placed his arm to my mouth. He spoke again, and despite the ghastliness of the situation, his voice filled me with the kind of unblemished peace one usually feels only in the innocent days of childhood.

"Drink, and you will live."

It did not occur to me to disobey. The liquid was thick and bitter, and I disgorged the first swallow. However, he kept his arm pressed against my mouth, and eventually I drank easily, even greedily, before he finally withdrew.

I heard voices, and the next thing I saw was the rough blue wool of my cloak being drawn over my head. I heard his comrades ask if he required a transport, and imagine my horror when he gave his reply: "No, this one is gone."

That was the last I heard of that strangely compelling voice, for suddenly I was alone among the dead—and yet *I* still breathed with life! My abandonment could only mean that despite the attendant's odd ministrations, I could not be saved, and I closed my eyes in acceptance of my fate. But instead of the comforting sleep of death, my living nightmare had now begun.

The groans of the dying blended with the wind to form a ghastly lamentation. I know not how much time passed as I awaited death, which stole upon me in slow, agonizing stages.

First, I lost what little movement remained in my body. My limbs stiffened into cruel, rigid postures, and I lost all bowel and bladder control; yet through this misery, I retained the ability to feel and, worse still, to think. I prayed for death, and my prayers seemed answered when a terrible burning sensation tore through my chest, as if a fire had been lit at the very center of my heart. The pain radiated out to every point of my body, and my jaw locked shut as if by an iron trap. I could feel blood vessels breaking, and my scalp, nostrils, and eyes filled with blood; the hemorrhaging continued until it seemed that every last drop of blood had been purged from my system. My body began to swell and the skin grew so tight that fissures tore open my flesh.

Would death ever rescue me from such suffering? Or had I in fact died in the night and been thrust into Hell, the hospital assistant no more than the ghastly ferryman himself? I had not lived a life free from sin, but surely no creature deserved this cruel fate! My thoughts began to whirl with remembrances and images from the past, and I felt the first cracks in that fragile barrier between sanity and madness. It seemed that the end had finally come when my heartbeat rose to a frightening, thunderous rate, plummeted to an irregular thud...and then stopped.

And yet I lived. The agonizing pain had disappeared, and although my senses were dull, I could still feel the rain-soaked cloak on my face and the chill of the mud beneath my body. Terrible groans filled my ears, and I realized that they issued from my own mouth. My breath returned in shallow, painful gasps. I moved my limbs, which cracked agonizingly back to life. Just then, my cloak was yanked back and the filthy, wizened face of a burying party worker appeared above me.

"Got a live one here," he exclaimed, though whether that were true or not I hardly dared imagine. He tied a white rag to a stick and planted it in the ground at my head to signal what few hospital workers remained.

I struggled to sit upright, but was too weak and lay back down in my erstwhile grave of mud. The rain had subsided and a weak wash of sun was attempting to break through the clouds. Far from a cheering sight, however, the sunlight produced such a painful reaction that I rolled over into the mud to escape it. Everything around me appeared muted, as if drained of color and dimension, and yet my sense of smell was unusually acute. The odors of rotting flesh and gun smoke overwhelmed me, and the smell of blood filled my entire being with some maddening desire, some overpowering need… I buried my face in my cloak to escape the morbid case of nerves that my ordeal had brought upon me.

My body had grown even weaker by the time I was finally carried from the hill to an ambulance wagon. Most of the wounded had already been evacuated, and the wagon contained only two other men. One had undergone amputations of both arms and a leg. The other had suffered a terrible head wound and lay shrouded and silent on his stretcher. We were the last of the survivors, if one could apply the term to such a forsaken lot.

Shortly into the slow, jolting journey, the smell of blood began to madden my senses once more. The hunger had grown into a monstrous thing beyond my ability to control.

I used the last of my strength to rise from my stretcher, and I suddenly recalled how my leg had been broken in the fall from my horse. I pulled up my trouser to examine it, but there was no sign of injury. I next lifted my tunic, but I already knew what I would find: the skin was as smooth as if nary a scratch had been made. I swooned on my feet with the feeling that I was caught in a waking dream, but this sensation was soon replaced by a much stronger one—the rabid desire for blood.

Not knowing what I was doing or why, I approached the amputee. He was a young boy, no more than seventeen years, and I now saw that the battle had also taken his right eye. The hair on the left side of his head was still soft and golden, but on the other side, where the muskets and shrapnel had done their work, it lay dank and crimson with gore, like a broken halo. I touched the golden side and leaned toward him; his remaining eye looked back at me with such suffering and despair that I had to turn away. And then I smelled it through the blood: the thick, sickening stench of infection. It had just set in and would not yet be detectable to the surgeons, but I could smell it, clear and unmistakable, from deep within the tissue. I had seen cases of surgical fevers before—evil smelling pus, infected blood, black and useless limbs. The worst kind of death: certain, yet cruel in its lingering.

In recounting what happened next, I still have to hold my hand steady over the page in order to transform the fantastical event into words. For beyond all rational thought or control, and without one moment's hesitation, I bent over the boy and fixed my mouth upon his neck; I pierced a large vein and drew forth the warm life-blood still within him. I drank and drank until the blood finally slowed, and then fell back, satiated at last. I watched the last of the boy's life leave him, then stared long at his face before closing the one remaining eye. And for the first time since that sabre entered my chest, I felt the life return to my body. My limbs surged with strength and vitality, my sight sharpened and the world again filled with color. I longed to feel the cool, fresh air upon my skin. I buried my face in my hands in joy, and only when they came away covered in blood did the fiendishness of my deed become real. I looked wildly about me in the wagon for the only witness to my crime, but the shrouded figure lay faceless and still.

I could no longer deny that something unnatural had happened to me on that hill in Sedan, something that had spared me from death by transforming me into a creature possessed of some great, diabolical power.

At the hospital, I allowed myself to be taken to an exam room, although I knew that the doctors would find nothing wrong. I waited for an opportune moment and slipped through the same doors that only moments earlier I had been carried through. By some instinct I knew the direction of my native land, and I walked northward for hours without tiring, through towns and countryside and forest. My strength seemed almost superhuman, for I could leap from cliffs and cross ravines as if flying!

I stopped by a lake to rest and wash away the filth of Sedan. Standing on a rock overlooking the water, I felt like Orpheus returned from the land of the dead with godlike powers; only I feared that I, too, could never look back. A small hare bounded out of the brush, and it occurred to me that I would soon need food. But strangely, I had neither appetite nor thirst, even though I had taken no nourishment since before the battle. It was early evening, and I considered taking shelter for the night, but I still felt no fatigue. My vision was sharp even in the growing darkness, so I decided to carry on. With my ears pricked for sounds and my nostrils quivering with the smells of the night, I felt more akin to the beasts of the forest than the man I used to be.

By the next evening, however, my strength had begun to ebb. My vision was again dull and colorless, and the sunlight burned my skin. By the third day, my limbs were weighted with heaviness, my movements slow and clumsy. My concentration began to fail, and my thoughts grew dim and confused. I knew that I must soon nourish my body or die. I came upon a brook and bent to drink, but the water produced a violent reaction and I immediately disgorged it.

I saw a small deer grazing farther down the brook, and drew my sabre; perhaps I could at least tolerate food. Her ears twitched in alarm, and I feared that I would prove too weak to overtake her; but suddenly the hunger rose up with a strength of its own. I was upon her before she even had time to draw her head from the water. Once again, without thought or pause, I found myself bending over the creature's wound, drinking greedily of her blood. I had enough strength to go on, but none of the power and vitality that I had felt after draining the boy.

I entered Prussia and found the Empire rejoicing in the victory at Sedan. My officer's uniform ensured my safe passage, though once in Berlin I knew that I would have to discard both my uniform and my identity papers for fear of being arrested and imprisoned for desertion of the colors.

Hanover was crawling with officers, and I lurked among the shadows in order to avoid the very men who mere days ago I regarded as brothers. When I passed a local *Kneipe,* the once-familiar smell of frying food, beer, and tobacco smoke now seemed strange, repugnant, even.

I crossed out of the city gates a few hours before dawn. My strength was quickly leaving me when I heard a traveler coming toward me on the road. He was alone. I stole into the brush to wait, and this time I could not feign ignorance of the treacherous act about to unfold. I made sure that no one else was about, then sprang like a wild cat and caught him about the neck, breaking it with one quick twist. And just as it had been with the boy, all of my strength and vitality returned. This, then, was the key to maintaining my own life force—the draining of another's through the precious blood running through his veins!

The traveler's knapsack contained a few personal items and a green leather book. His small case held the tools of an itinerant artisan: an assortment of silver and pewter pieces and an engraving kit. I undressed the body and removed my uniform, stripping it of medals and insignias. The traveler's clothes, though a bit small, created an acceptable enough appearance; I was, however, forced to keep my own boots. I rummaged in his pockets and studied my new identity: Franz Ernst, from the village of Thale. I bundled my own papers into my uniform, picked up the knapsack and case, and returned to the road.

Far from the gates of Hanover, I picked a desolate spot and trekked several miles into an area thick with brambles and underbrush. I arranged my papers and uniform among a pyre of brush and set it alight with a flint from the engraving kit. The flames burned my eyes and scorched my skin, and I scrambled backward to escape the discomfort. From this safe distance, I watched the fire consume everything I had once been. Perhaps it was this fiery obliteration which spurned the need to make a record, for I suddenly pulled the green book from the knapsack. It appeared to have been purchased recently—only the first few pages were written upon, a sales ledger of some sort. I tore them out and consigned them to the flames. I then decided to begin the book anew with this strange and terrible story. For how could I trust even my own recollections with the bizarre and astounding events unfolding like a dream? Without these words written on these pages, how could I tell madness from sensibility, shadow from substance?

The fire burned down and I turned a stick through the gray ashes. Nothing remained. I next gouged a deep hole in the ground and buried my medals and insignias; some sentimental impulse led me to retrieve only one before covering the last remnants of my former life with dark earth.

My family will assume I was lost at Sedan—an honorable death. I made a vow to renounce any traces of my ancestry, which must never bear the terrible weight of this thing that I have become. I looked up to the sky and searched for comfort in the heavens, but the heavens gave me no sign. I was alone in the universe without even my name. I picked up the once prized possessions of another man's life and headed toward the road. No more able to resist than poor Orpheus, I did look back, just once, but all that remained was a small pile of ash waiting to be scattered to the wind.

Hereafter, I will be called by many men's names and wear many men's clothes. But under that pitiless sky, I made a second vow: even if I am the last being on earth to remember, I will never forget that I was once a man known and loved as Verland!

CHAPTER 6

Elle laid the first set of pages aside. So the book was some sort of gothic fiction. And yet it was handwritten, like a diary or a memoir. Whatever it was, Elle could only imagine what it had to do with Kingman's own strange story. She picked up the next section and decided she might as well keep trying to find out.

17 November, 1870; Berlin

It has been over two months since my transformation, and I am still learning the rules of this new existence. In some ways, my body is much improved by the change. I have ten times the strength of an ordinary man, and my senses are as acute as any beast of the wild, especially my sense of smell. I can now easily detect any trace of human sickness; in fact, certain diseases of the blood affect me so powerfully that I find it difficult to be near those so afflicted. Even though winter has begun to descend upon the city, I have little sensitivity to the cold, nor do I have any need for either food or water.

And yet I also have new limitations. The most profound and disturbing is that I can only fully nourish myself on the blood of my fellow human beings. After such a feeding, I can last from one to three days before the weakening begins. Then my skin becomes drawn and gray; I can no longer tolerate the sun; and my vision drains of color and depth. I am like a dying man with a sickness slowly spreading throughout his system. The faint smell of rot that emanates from my body confirms this sensation. When the weakening begins, I must take rest in a lodging house and enter into a sleep free of dreams, a deathlike condition that can last for ten, even twelve hours. When I awaken, I must feed.

01 December

I have become adept at living among the lost and for-saken, those unfortunate souls who have crossed into the shadow lands that lie beyond reach of civilized society. The members of this forsaken tribe include the lepers and pros-titutes, the tanners, skinners, rat-catchers, and charcoal burners—any of the unclean peoples cast to the bottom of the human heap. It is among this wretched new brother-hood that I go to feed.

21 January, 1871

This evening I inspected myself in the looking glass above my shaving sink, the first I have done so since the transfor-mation. Instead of the depraved visage of a blood-mad fiend, I was astonished to find the same familiar face gazing back at me. Every feature, every last detail of my appearance remains unchanged: same eyes, nose, mouth, even the same crescent-shaped scar above my right eye, the souvenir of a dueling mishap in my foolish youth.

And yet I cannot quite believe that the depravity of what I have become has not altered my external form. How can those rivers of blood have failed to stain my countenance? How can the haunted eyes of the murdered not reflect back from my own eyes? Why does my twisted soul not likewise twist my features into a mask of degeneracy? How can such a thing as I walk among ordinary men so naturally disguised as one of their members?

23 January

Further examination has shed light upon the ease with which I can tear open flesh: several places back in my mouth, the teeth have grown unusually sharp. I believe this also allows me to drain blood with such astonishing speed and efficiency, much like a vector insect designed by nature as a kind of syringe.

Although I have no way to affirm it, in the instant before feeding the teeth seem to grow even more sharp and lethal. I feel a tingling sensation deep in the roots and then a tearing pressure against the flesh, as if the imminent taste of blood triggers some kind of supernatural growth. It must be temporary, though, for when I reexamine the teeth, they are unchanged, and it is possible that the additional growth is simply a product of my own imagination.

Though not too obscenely altered, such fang-like teeth may cause alarm to an observant witness, particularly if revealed in a full smile. Fortunately, I suppose, I no longer have much occasion to smile.

18 February

After a feeding, my body comes alive again. The life that I have taken, concentrated in that precious red liquid, somehow transfers into my lifeless body and restores me from living death. My hair and nails begin to grow, my penis can become enlivened again, and a flush of health infuses the gray pallor of my complexion. But too soon, often with the first twenty-four hours, my bodily functions grow dormant once more. Depending upon the energy I expend, my strength and vitality begin to ebb within another few days. By the fourth day, I am in an increasingly weakened state. My world changes from the vivid, sharply drawn lines of a blazing midday sun to the half-formed visions of a weak and sickly dawn.

15 March

I am determined to measure the maximum amount of days that I can survive without human blood. To this end, I have spent the previous month slowly lengthening the time between feedings. Thus far, I can only sustain for four and half days. However, I am convinced that lack of will alone prevents me from further endurance. I have thus decided to dedicate myself to the task with the discipline of the soldier I once was. I shall henceforth keep a daily log to record my progress.

19 March

Day four. This is when the cravings sharpen. I begin to emanate a faint smell of rotting meat. My skin drains of life and slight tremors disrupt my motions. I can no longer tolerate even the mildest sunlight, and my strength is greatly diminished. I tire easily, and all bodily functions have ceased. I sleep ten to twelve hours each day.

20 March

Day five. A great pain has begun within my bones and radiates outward to every point of my being. My skin is that of a dead man's, and my eyes have sunken deep into my skull. My muscles have begun to spasm uncontrollably.

21 March

Day six. The pain has grown intolerable. I can no longer move without excruciating pain. A leaden heaviness has descended upon me, as if I am being turned into living stone. My joints have stiffened. My skin gives way with the gentlest of pressure. I have the appearance of a man three times my age. The smell of rot has grown overwhelming. I cannot keep the flies from gathering. I do not know how much longer I can endure such suffering.

22 March

Day seven. I grow too weak to write. My nails give way from my fingertips at the slightest touch. Hair falls out in clumps. Skin bursts open and tears away from body. Cannot go on…

23 March

My test is complete. I can endure seven days without feeding, and I have risked my very survival to acquire this knowledge. By the evening of the seventh day, I had grown almost too weak to find a feeding source. I dragged my stinking, decaying form into the alleyway beside my lodging house, where I drained a feral cat without even ensuring that I was unobserved. It wasn't nearly enough to restore me, and I thought I would meet whatever end now awaits me right there among the refuse and vermin. I was spared, however, by man's own vice. I had nearly lost consciousness when I felt hands reaching into the pockets of my coat and trousers. I realized that I was being robbed, and with my last remaining strength, I reached out and snapped the neck of my would-be attacker. I drained him with such force that his skin came away in my mouth.

I was restored, but my need was now too great. I took to the streets and fed twice more in quick succession, the first time I have killed more than once at a time. Though I now know the limits of both my body and my will, I must take care not to repeat this experiment—when I taste blood again, the savage ferocity of my hunger calls forth a recklessness which I cannot risk and a brutality which I cannot bear.

14 April, 1871

The city is awakening from the icy sleep of winter. My days drift in a blood-soaked monotony of feeding. This book is my only comfort, the only thing to prove that I still exist and think and feel. I am a shadow among living men, a shade whom no man greets in the street, for whom no one awaits at home as evening descends.

Wandering for hours down streets and alleyways, I pass brightly lit windows and smell smoke from cheerful fires; I peer into bar rooms full of laughing people, and I shake from head to foot with a need not satisfied by the blood. To simply breathe and move about—is that life? Or did I in fact die on that cursed hill in Sedan, condemned as surely as Virgil to wander in eternal denial of either Heaven or Hell? At such times, the voice of the hospital assistant returns to me, and against all reason, I answer the same: yes, I still wish to live.

30 June

Time passes. The city is in a constant state of movement and change, but I am like an insect in amber, with no purpose save that of my own frozen existence.

02 September

The Brandenburg Gate has been illuminated in honor of *Sedantag,* the day chosen to celebrate the victory of Sedan. It has been one year. At noon I joined the crowds of soldiers and civilians filling the market square, and although I should have shared their joy on this great day in German history, I felt no more sentiment for a flag than a beast of the forest which knows and cares for nothing more than the ground upon which it stands.

18 November

I have begun experimenting upon myself. Yesterday in my dark and gloomy room I was overcome by an unbearable malaise. I was imagining the scene of my transformation over and over when I was seized by a strange urge: I retrieved a shaving blade from the sink and drew it against my arm just as the hospital assistant had done. I felt no pain, only the pressure of the instrument and the giving way of flesh. The wound bled for several minutes before the flow lessened and then stopped. Upon cleaning the skin, I found no trace of the gash. I drew the blade again and held my arm over a basin, pouring a steady stream of water to clear the blood flow. I then saw the tissue stitching itself back together again as surely as if a knitting circle of demons had set to work with supernatural needle and thread.

20 November

I have been slicing open my arm each day in order to monitor my healing abilities. It has now been almost four days since my last feeding, and I was not surprised that this evening's cut produced no blood. The skin is now gaping open and will not heal. The ghastly thought occurs to me that the blood that flowed from my wounds was not really my own, but more properly belonged to my last victim.

21 November

The wound has still not closed, and the skin around the opening has begun to blacken and reek of decay. Have I damaged myself irreparably? It appears that my wounds can only repair themselves when I am suffused with fresh blood, although I seem to suffer no ill effects from the injuries themselves. I must feed.

22 November

My wound has healed without any scarring, and the health has returned to my skin. Emboldened, I decided to cut even more deeply into my arm. I severed through arteries and veins, separating skin from muscle in a sickening display of gore. The blade drew very near to the bone before I lost courage and withdrew. Remembering the sabre wound at Sedan, I grew curious about my body's ability to repair fatal wounds. If I cut straight through and amputated the arm, would it stitch back together somehow? If I put a bullet through my head in the age-old soldier's death, would my brain be capable of healing? Alas, in this regard, my desire to live proves stronger than my sense of inquiry.

24 November

I have been considering the capabilities of my penis. Within the first day of feeding, I can perform as a normal man, and yet I lose this ability quicker than any other function. I thus wondered if my sexual organs were more sensitive than the rest of my form, and decided to conduct further experiments in regard to this question.

I began by drawing back the foreskin and pricking my organ with a needle. As with my arm, I felt the pressure of the instrument, but no pain. I drove the needle deeper, producing no greater reaction. I then immersed my penis in a glass of ice cold water. The skin lost color and shriveled, but I felt no discomfort. When I repeated the experiment with boiling water, the skin blistered and began to peel away, but again I felt no pain, and my member healed as soon as I removed it from the water. So it appears that despite its greater sensitivity to the effects of feeding, my penis is as impervious to pain as the rest of my body.

27 December

I have been building my tolerance to sunlight. After a feeding, I can withstand a full day, especially in the weak and hazy light of winter. However, if further exposure occurs without the protection of the blood, my skin begins to burn away like sheets of paper, and I feel an agony quite absent in my other experiments with pain. Thus, my new form has an innate predilection for the shadows of twilight rather than the brightly lit world that most prefer. In addition, I have found that I cannot tolerate fire to the slightest degree; even drawing too close to the harmless flames of a kitchen stove produces a dreadful sensation that seems to threaten the very essence of my being.

09 June, 1872

Several days ago, I came across a woman begging in a forlorn spot just outside the city gates. Her skin was drawn into a death-like mask around the bones of her face, her body wasted with the unmistakable signs of starvation. I knelt and asked how she had come to such a wretched place, and she told me that she had been expelled from her town for bearing an illegitimate child. She had traveled to Hanover and been detained for illegal entry, then sent to Berlin, where she had again been denied entry.

She held out a filthy bundle of swaddling rags—the child that had been the cause of her cruel ruin. Her arms suddenly gave way and the baby threatened to drop to the ground. I reached out and took her burden from her, realizing immediately that the child was dead. Its legs and arms were swollen, its face already turning black. I had begun to draw the cloth over the poor creature's face when the woman's skeletal hand grasped my wrist. Her eyes were lit with the fever of imminent death, yet some primal strength rose from the dregs of her ravaged soul, and with her last breath she pleaded with me to take the child. I hesitated only a moment before assuring her that it would indeed have a safe and happy life; the instant my promise had been delivered, her body gave up its struggle. I took her arm and gently opened a vein. There was almost no blood, and within minutes, I had taken what little life remained.

I placed the baby within her arms and covered them with my cloak, and the image of the ruined boy in the ambulance wagon at Sedan rose unbidden in my mind. Sometimes, it seems, mercy can be delivered along with death.

07 July

Last night I lay with a prostitute. I had just finished feeding and was roaming the streets when I found myself at the Silesian Station, where the most weather-beaten and dissolute prostitutes congregate. I had, of course, visited many prostitutes during my military service, but those had been smooth-skinned ladies who hid the more unseemly aspects of their trade behind their beauty and charms. There was no such varnish on these creatures making rude gestures and whistling the melodies of obscene songs to the men passing by.

I caught the attention of a robust blonde with a missing front tooth and an elaborate hairdo held together with tortoise shell combs. She had no stench of venereal disease like so many of the other women, and I quite unexpectedly found myself desiring her. A new hunger rose in me, not for blood but for the warmth of human flesh against my own. She opened her hand to reveal a key, and I followed her around a corner and up a darkened staircase to a room almost as mean and barren as my own. There I took her with an intensity that still startles me to recall. The way that her nipples hardened beneath my touch, the softness between her legs—her body seemed like a miracle, and I explored every inch of it as if she were some newly discovered treasure. I wanted her again and again, and though I offered her all of the money I possessed, I finally exhausted the last of the poor woman's energy.

I lay against the pulsing warmth of her flesh and began to devise a way to take her as my companion. I let my mind drift pleasantly with these thoughts before startling to my senses—without even realizing it, I had begun to pierce the soft flesh of her neck! Even though I had fed mere hours ago, my craving for the hot blood coursing through her veins was more powerful than anything I had ever known before.

I dressed quickly and somehow managed to flee the intoxication of her body before taking her life; I walked the streets all night thinking about what had occurred. Had my sexual desire for this woman also triggered the desire to feed? Was my lust for her body inseparable from the lust for her blood? I do not know these answers, but I do know that I cannot allow such unchecked passion to overtake me again, as it seems that my need to take a woman's body can easily transform into a need to take her very life.

17 August

She continues to haunt me. I have not returned to the Silesian Station for fear that I will not prevent myself from seeking out her or some other woman.

20 November

I must now write about another set of experiments that ended with such ghastly results that my hands still shake with dread as I attempt to write them down.

It began near the Tiergarten Station, where whores of the lowest sort gather—women long-deranged by drink, insanity, or both. I was feeding in the bushes along the footpath when I was come upon by a whore and her customer. I feigned the motions of a tryst until the couple passed by, and when I again bent to the body, I noticed that she was still alive. My urge to feed was strong, and I quickly drained her of life, but an idea had occurred to me that was so simple and yet so powerful that I was stupefied I had not considered it before: could I feed upon my victims without actually killing them? Could I sustain my own life without the need to destroy another's?

I brooded on this possibility for days before luring an old beggar to my room. I drained him as I normally would, but this time I withdrew before the last of his life had left him. I then bribed him to remain with food and alcohol, and at first, he seemed unchanged. However, in less than an hour's time he began complaining of headaches and a fever; by the second day, his speech had grown slurred and his body had begun to spasm. Within twenty-four more hours, his mind deteriorated into a violent state of mania, and I was forced to bind him to the bed. He seemed to be undergoing lurid and disturbing hallucinations. He could take no food or water and lay foaming at the mouth and writhing in pain. I know I should have killed him then, but my perverse and selfish curiosity overrode my mercifulness. Would his condition improve? Would he survive his ordeal as I had at Sedan, and become a creature like myself? By the fourth day, I had my answer. His jaw locked shut, and he began choking on his own saliva. His body went rigid with paralysis, he lost consciousness, and by early on the fifth day, he was dead.

I have no doubt that my bite caused this man's slow and agonizing death. Thus, the grim reality remains that I must kill in order to feed. The only choice is between delivering an immediate death or one like that of the poor wretch I thought to spare. I will not soon forget the consequences of this folly.

01 January, 1873

The city celebrates a new year, but I exist in a monotony that obliterates the passing of time. Each new day, month, year holds nothing different from what has come before. If I cannot die, I tremble with dread at the thought of an eternity spent in this gray nothingness.

13 February

My grim predictions for the new year appear to have been in error, for an event has occurred which has changed everything: I have met another.

By the time Elle placed the last page at the bottom of the stack, the sun had set over the Pacific. Nyholm and Vita appeared as if by some prearranged signal, and it occurred to Elle that the room had a hidden camera in order to make sure that she followed the rules. For all she knew, the whole house was one big surveillance system—Kingman wasn't known for his trusting nature, after all.

"I'll show you the way out," Vita offered.

Elle followed her through the circular hall with its unsettling fun-house effect of seeming to always end up in the same place you'd started. At the doorway, Vita paused as if waiting for something.

"Will Mr. Kingman contact my publishing company for another meeting? Or who will I be hearing from?"

Vita looked up at Elle with swimming brown eyes filled with a sadness much older than Vita herself, and much longer lasting.

"I'm not sure. I think Eliot will tell me when to call you next." She paused again, lowering her head. "I really do love him, you know. People said it was for the money and everything, but I don't care about that. He's a brilliant man, a genius. People will see one day. Someday they'll understand everything."

"I'd like to understand, Vita. Maybe you can help me do that. Do you think we could get together and talk some time? It can be off the record."

"I'd like that."

Her acceptance seemed sincere, and Elle realized that she must be awfully lonely sealed up in this half-abandoned castle with Nyholm, her husband in prison and the press still yapping at her heels every time she stepped outside.

"But I have to make sure it's OK with Eliot."

"Of course." Elle had already seen that stipulation coming.

She drove down the deserted driveway through the wrought-iron security gates hanging ajar like the battered remains of some long-vanquished kingdom. She had to admit that Kingman's castle was the perfect setting for a vampire, imaginary or not. In fact, it came complete with a murder victim, and Elle reminded herself not to forget that last, most fundamental requirement.

CHAPTER 7

The evening shadows had deepened across the canyons, but as Elle drove home, she hardly noticed their beauty; her mind was in the dirty alleyways and forsaken places of nineteenth-century Berlin. The origin of the book puzzled her. Supernatural tales and "true life" memoirs had been popular during the 1800s, but this seemed different. It was too personal, too unpolished compared to the flowery language and elaborate style typical of narratives from that era. From the book's poor condition, it didn't seem as if the writer had intended it for publication. But then why *had* it been written? It seemed awfully detailed for some Prussian gentleman's weekend amusement.

As soon as Elle opened the door of her apartment, she was met by two cats outraged at the delay in their dinner. Biggy, an over-sized gray man-cat given to extreme displays of suffering, circled her feet with a steady stream of plaintive cries, and as she dished out their foul-smelling food, she considered the hours, maybe even years, of her life dedicated to feeding cats and then cleaning up the aftermath. With that image in mind, Elle figured she might as well call Sam and check on the contracts.

"I need you to come over tomorrow afternoon and go over some fine points before the lawyers get involved. Our old terms aren't going to cut it this time."

"OK, I can be there by one. Listen, Sam, let me ask you a strange question. Do you believe in the concept of 'the undead'? Of creatures that don't die, or at least don't die the way everyone else does?"

"What, like a zombie or a vampire or something?"

"Not exactly a vampire; and definitely not a zombie. More a creature that is like a living person in most ways, but that is… dead, technically. And survives on human blood."

"And that's different from a vampire how?"

"I guess it's not. It's just that 'vampire' sounds so cheesy. So, I don't know… Hollywood."

"That's because vampires *are* cheesy and Hollywood, at least in our day and age. The gypsies and peasant folk or whoever thought them up no doubt had their own versions, but nowadays we like them gorgeous and in high-def color."

"But what do you think about them? The real vampire legends, I mean, not the Hollywood stuff."

"Well, I'm not sure what counts as 'real' as far as vampires go, but I guess I don't think much about them either way; except maybe if a really hot one shows up baring his fangs at the West Hollywood Halloween parade or something. But everyone loves vampire stories. There's something about the whole immortal, blood-sucking thing that just gets people going."

The word jumped out at her. "Something totem."

"What?"

"Just something Kingman said. He was talking about universal things that humans share across time and place. Primal things, like the fear of death or a belief in a higher power. He calls them totem."

"Well, totem-scrotum, I'm not the one to ask about sharing things with my fellow humans. I haven't even had a date in the last six months."

"That's because Maxine scares them all away. Would you want to date someone whose pet parrot corrects your grammar and criticizes your choice of footwear?"

"Maxine is not a pet; she's an avian companion. And you're just bitter about those cowboy boots, which, by the way, really weren't you. Maxine does have impeccable taste."

"Except in owners. Listen, I've got some research to do. I'll see you tomorrow."

"Wait just a minute. What's with the vampire stuff? Do *you* believe in the bloodthirsty undead?"

"No, of course not. But I think somewhere along the line Kingman and his crew might have started to."

"Does it have something to do with the murder? Did anything exciting turn up at the mansion?"

Elle thought about the green book, the alleyways of Berlin.

"Nothing yet. One thing I am sure of, though—there's more strangeness to this story than what we've already seen. And that's a lot of strangeness, Sam."

Elle hung up and tried to figure out why she hadn't mentioned the book. Sam loved to hear about the stories she was working on, each little piece fitting together to form a whole. She always shared her research with him, but there was something about that book... She closed her eyes and pictured the cover, those weird faces that seemed to shift and blend... It wasn't any oath to Kingman or warning from Nyholm that held her back. She just needed to figure things out a bit more.

That had to happen before her next meeting with Sadie Lowe, the head of Greene Line Publishing. Sadie was the physical and mental powerhouse who had taken over Greene Line when it was on the verge of bankruptcy. In less than five years, she had transformed it into one of the top independent publishing companies in the country. She often reminded Greene Line's writers that she had done this by paying attention to what the readers want.

"Number one: a villain." She ticked off her list on a set of lacquered fingernails in need of a deadly weapon permit. "Next, you need a victim. Photos of happier times, everyone smiling at the camera. Then *boom!* Murder, rape, destruction of the good life. And then you need the reassurance of the law. The police, the courtroom, the mug shots. A nice big prison. The bad guy gets caught, justice is served. That's it—you stick to that, you'll be all right."

Her last bit of advice had proved the hardest for Elle to follow: "And don't spend too much time on the 'why.' People don't care about all that psychological stuff."

But Elle always became too involved with the killers and victims, the family and friends, the cops and lawyers all bound together by violence and loss—they stayed with her long after the interviews were over, restless to tell their stories, to be given a voice. Sometimes Elle felt as if entire worlds inhabited her head, all swirling in an endless, disorienting panorama of the human condition. *No wonder so many writers drink themselves to death,* she often thought while reaching for another Dogfish.

"Public interest in crime stories lasts only as long as the next psycho turns up," Sadie always told her. "Remember, you're not writing *Ulysses* here."

Even though Elle didn't stick to the formula, her sales were solid enough to pay the rent and keep Sadie happy, and that was more than enough for her. She suspected that another reason Sadie gave her some leeway was because they shared something that went deeper than the bottom line: they both had been one of those family members whose smiling pictures juxtaposed with the stabbings, shootings, and strangulations. Sadie's fourteen-year-old brother had been gunned down when Sadie was only nine, and sometimes when they were discussing a story, an understanding would pass between them. Sadie knew business and she knew how to make a profit, but she also knew that for the people behind the stories, the scars last a lot longer than a spot on a bestseller list.

Elle sat down at the computer with the sincere intention of doing some research, but instead she found herself typing "Verland" into the search engine. Nothing turned up but a string of genealogy sites. She added "Prussia," and then "1870." Nothing. She tried a few other combinations without really expecting to find anything that might help her identify either the book or its author. She supposed she could track down the Prussian companies that had fought at Sedan, maybe even compile a list of actual people who might fit the diary entry. But that level of historical research was out of her league, and she wasn't being paid to write a book about nineteenth-century Prussian officers with a blood fetish. And yet that enticing little box kept goading her. She typed in "ver" and "prefix" and hit the search button. A long list of vocabulary sites by enterprising high school teachers appeared on the screen. She tried one called "Mr. Hanno's Greek and Latin Prefixes" and scrolled to *V.*

Root Meaning   Examples

ver	true, truth	verily, veracity, verisimilitude

She tried the same search with "German," and found another chart:

Prefix Meaning   Examples

ver	bad, awry, lost	verfahren (go astray, get lost)
		verkommen (go to ruin, become run down)
		verlassen (leave, abandon)

"One Roman's truth is another German's ruin, I guess."

She ran a few more searches, but this time, it was more to avoid the pile of transcript copy that awaited her than to track down elusive Prussians. When Elle had first started at Greene Line, Sadie had told her that people couldn't get enough of police procedure, forensics, court rooms—all of the dramatic law and order stuff from television and movies. In real life, though, detective work often means mind-numbing amounts of paperwork and hours of desk time, and trials are mostly legal jargon, repetition, and dull, often inarticulate testimony only occasionally punctuated by smoking gun evidence or a primetime-worthy witness. The Kingman trial had over ten thousand pages of transcript, and it was part of Elle's job to shift through every one of them in search of the entertaining, the scandalous, and the gruesome.

"Blood velocity and impact angles. There's some sexy forensics for you," she told her black cat, Bagera, who had jumped up to claim her lap. "What's not to love about simulated blood splatter?"

The defense had made a lot of noise about the lack of blood on Kingman's clothes, so the prosecution had cited several cases in which lack of blood hadn't equaled lack of guilt. One involved a man who had caved his wife's head in with a brick and only ended up with two spots of blood on his jeans. Elle often looked worse than that after shaving her legs.

She found the part midway through the trial where one of Kingman's lawyers had questioned the 911 operator. The call had been problematic for the prosecution; the police had never determined the identity of the caller, and Kingman's team had used this loose end to float the "third-party" theory in a bid for the ultimate trump card of reasonable doubt. They maintained that because of the size and layout of Kingman's property, it would have been impossible for someone outside the grounds to have witnessed the crime. So whoever had placed the 911 call must have been on the property, maybe even inside the mansion. In fact, it may have been the actual murderer himself, out to frame Kingman all along. And since Kingman had used the murder room for entertaining, forensics had collected enough physical evidence for an entire courthouse of suspects.

Elle flipped ahead to where the prosecution had presented the layout of Kingman's estate. In anticipation of most jurors' penchant for finding the rich and famous innocent even if proven guilty, the DA had taken every precaution to dismantle the third-party theory. They first demonstrated that there were only two ways to get off the property: through the gated front entry, which was controlled by a code that hadn't been deactivated before the police arrived; and down a set of private-access stairs at the back of the property that lead to the beach. Like most of the houses in Malibu, Kingman's mansion sat right on the edge of the cliffs that drop 125 feet to the beach below. Since the cliffs are a highly effective natural security system, most of the access stairs are primitive wooden affairs with no more than a locked gate at the top, and Kingman's property was no exception. If a third party had gone down the access stairs and escaped across the beach, it meant that Kingman had provided the gate key. The only other way off the property was straight over the cliff, where the police would have easily found the third party, broken legs and all. So either Kingman was the murderer, or if there had been a third person at the scene, Kingman knew who it was and was concealing it from his own defense, which didn't exactly broadcast his innocence, either.

In the end, the prosecution had been saved from the reasonable doubt of the 911 call by a fluke of activism. By law, beaches in California are public property, but the wealthy residents in Kingman's neighborhood had gotten around that by buying up all of the land with proximity to the beaches. So even though people had every right to be *on* the beaches, unless they planned to parachute down and be airlifted out, they had no way of actually *getting* there. Beach-access advocates had been suing over this loophole for decades, and the courts had finally ruled that a staircase had to be built to provide public access. Much to the residents' dismay, it went up in view of some of the most exclusive property in Malibu, including Kingman's. The prosecution had proved that there was one spot on the staircase where a witness of a certain height could have had a clear view into the room where Klee's murder had taken place. The jury had been asked to believe that a witness whose identity had never been confirmed *could* have seen the crime if he had been at least five feet ten, standing in precisely one spot, at precisely one angle, on a beach staircase at three o'clock Monday morning in one of the most exclusive neighborhoods in Malibu. A highly unlikely set of circumstances, but then again this was California, and in light of a dead body with only Kingman around to vouch for it, the possibility had been enough.

It was getting late and Elle was worn out. She flipped through a few more pages until a name caught her eye: Zor Pithador, the Necromancer, also known as Brian Williams. The prosecution had taken every opportunity to remind the jury of Kingman's bizarre obsessions and outlandish behavior in the years leading up to the murder, and Zor had been a landmine. Apparently, the two had made numerous visits to the county morgue and had regularly conducted late-night séances in cemeteries. She stopped at a place where the prosecutor was hammering Williams about a hundred thousand dollars Kingman had paid him about a year before Klee's death. The prosecutor was obviously implying that some kind of blackmail had been going on, but Williams wouldn't budge even when threatened with contempt. All he had been willing to divulge was that the money had been for "services rendered." Curious, Elle ran a search, and his webpage came up right away.

Welcome to the Necromancer's Lair

Zor Pithador

Portal to the undead and advisor to the rich and famous

488 Siguerro Street, Los Angeles, CA

Hours: 4:00 PM–8PM, Tues–Thurs.

Or call our **toll free** number for a **free** consultation and appointment time.

We are the key to the hidden truths that lurk behind the shadowy doors of the brightly lit world of illusion most call reality. Between this thing we call life and the cold chill of what we understand to be death are the Necromancers, the link between the living and the dead. We are the true bearers of the dark message of the dead. **We are The Necromancers.**

Elle scrolled through the pages and tried a couple of links. Apparently, Zor was a jack-of-all-trades kind of necromancer, offering everything from communication with the death to uncovering past lives, tarot card readings, and psychic visions. He also had a mind-boggling array of spells for everything from the usual love and money concerns to warding off a pack of wolves on a night of the full moon, which Elle hadn't realized was a common menace in downtown L.A. She jotted down the address before shutting the computer down. Tomorrow she would have to tackle Sam and his legal contracts, so she might as well add Zor and the undead to the list. With Maxine thrown into the mix, she wasn't sure which option was more intimidating.

CHAPTER 8

Sam lived in a cozy bungalow on Highland that actually belonged to Maxine, a gray parrot with a downright unsettling grasp of the English language. One of her favorite tricks was to greet visitors with the innocent enough question: "How are you today?" If they answered, "I'm good," Maxine would proceed to correct their grammar with the high-handedness of a British governess. Elle had once delivered a stern lecture on the use of *to be* as a linking verb, and Maxine had listened placidly, blinking her shrewd parrot eyes while Elle proved her grammatical superiority to a bird; by the end of the conversation, it was clear who the fool really was.

"Hello, hello—how are you today?"

Elle eyed the gray parrot with suspicion. She wasn't falling for that one again. "Sam, is that a straw hat on Maxine's head?"

"It is indeed. Doesn't it make her look tropical? I found it in a craft store the other day, and it was just her size. Only thing is, it falls off every time she moves, but I'm working on that. Do you think a little bit of elastic would do the trick?"

"Sam, you really need to start dating again."

"Well, let me know if you have any spare blond surfer gods stashed away somewhere. How is Gary these days, by the way?"

"Gary is Gary. The same."

"Well, that's a good thing in his case. I've told you a hundred times that you should start thinking about a real relationship with him instead of this flim-flam thing you've had going on for…how long now? Please."

"And I've told you a hundred and one times that this flim-flam thing works just fine. For both of us."

Sam snorted in disbelief. "That's what you say, but when some twenty-five-year-old babe with cellulite-free thighs and a faltering acting career comes along and snaps him up, your good thing will be *gone.*"

Elle sighed. "Don't think I haven't thought of that. What is that tyrant of a parrot doing?"

Maxine had swooped over to an end table and was opening and closing Sam's phone. Elle was always a little disturbed at what that bird could do with no more than a beak and some claws.

"Oh! Good bird, Maxie, good bird! She's practicing her newest skill."

"Which is, let me think…destroying expensive technological devices?"

"Please. She's not *destroying* it. She's making a *phone call.* You see, I read this story about a woman with epilepsy, and she had a fit one day when no one was around. Sad story, right? But no! It's a happy story, actually, because she had trained her golden retriever to use his *paws* to dial nine-one-one. That dog ended up saving her life. Amazing, isn't it? And Maxine is so much smarter than some golden retriever."

"But you don't have epilepsy, Sam."

"Hey, my cholesterol is through the roof, and I've been ten pounds over my target weight for about, oh, half my life now. Laugh if you must, but that parrot could end up a hero someday."

"From the looks of things, Maxine isn't ready for stardom just yet."

"Hmm. Opening and closing the phone is no problem, but she's having some trouble with the buttons." Sam put his hand in front of his mouth and assumed a stage whisper in order to spare Maxine's feelings. "*Big beak, you know.* Anyway, so far she's only managed to hit redial. So if you get a strange call in the middle of the night from a woman with a croaky voice and a limited vocabulary, don't panic. It's Maxine. Now, much as I know you'd rather spend the afternoon with my bird, business must come before pleasure."

It was early evening by the time they'd finished going over the contracts, and the beginning of a headache was tapping around Elle's temples. Despite Sam's best efforts, she couldn't stay focused on things like grant of rights and reserves against returns. Anything past the basics was for Sam, Sadie, and the lawyers to sort out.

Elle disentangled herself from the freeway and headed downtown. The Necromancer's Lair—the silliness of it all didn't in any way interfere with her desire to meet Zor, and not just for the sake of the story. Something about the idea of black magic and communion with the other side, even when it came from charlatans with toll free phone lines, was compelling. Elle agreed with Kingman about one thing, at least—the uncertainty of death gave it a terrible, fascinating power. After her mother's murder, those kind of dark preoccupations had taken hold of her and never really let go. She'd spent years dabbling in religion, philosophy, folklore—anything to make some sense of questions that didn't seem to have any answers. The only conclusion she had ever come to is that from the moment we're born, we're hurtling along a one-way path toward a destination we know nothing about, including whether or not it even exists. As Kingman had pointed out, who would buy a ticket for a ride like that?

Elle thought about how the loss of his father had caused death to take hold of Kingman, too—shoes set out for a day that never came, the psychic shock of someone being *right there*, making tea in the morning, leaving the dirty cup in sink just like always, and then in the instant it takes for a phone to ring, *not there*. Elle pictured a lone hawk hovering high in a blue Southern California sky...she gripped the steering wheel and willed the image away. She had to go into this with a clear head or she'd probably end up in a graveyard with Zor, communing with the dead to the tune of his no doubt very costly courier services.

The Necromancer's Lair was surprisingly nondescript. A neon "Open" sign flashed in the window, and the effect was more seedy Laundromat than chamber of the undead. Despite the shabby exterior, though, the interior was a shopper's paradise for the dark and creepy set, with one oddity after another crammed into every last inch of space. One wall held voodoo kits made with tarot cards, chicken feet, and colored powders in little cellophane packets; every shelf was stacked to the ceiling with jars of powders and herbs, rows of candles and crystal balls, and resin figurines of things like Death holding a globe in one hand and a scepter in the other. A collection of cloth dolls with their eyes and mouths sewn shut hung from a rack in the corner. Elle was examining a stuffed three-headed weasel when Zor himself appeared from behind a faded purple curtain.

From the trial coverage, Elle knew that Zor worked hard to live up to the image of what a good Necromancer should look like. In addition to the shaved head and paper white skin, he had shown up in court wearing an all-black tuxedo complete with floor-length velvet Dracula cape. Since then, he had upgraded even further by shaving off his eyebrows to match his head, which called to mind a cadaver awaiting autopsy. His fingernails were long and filed into sharp points, and he was wearing contact lenses that turned his eyes yellow. Elle wondered if the dead had a taste for the jaundiced look.

"May I help you?"

In light of the Nosferatu look, Elle hadn't been expecting such a mild, melodious voice; the juxtaposition was as jarring as the rest of him.

"I'd like to talk to you about Eliot Kingman. My name is Elle Bramasol."

"Ah, Mr. Kingman told me I might be hearing from you."

Of course. Elle was beginning to feel like a chess piece being moved around by an opponent always three steps ahead. Zor bowed and swept his arm toward the back of the shop.

"Follow me."

He led her into a small room lit with candles, and she caught her breath. Along the back wall sat a life-sized effigy on a gilded throne. The figure was draped in an elaborately patterned cloak, but it was the face that drew Elle's attention—or rather, the *lack* of a face. Its head was painted metallic black with two round mirrors where the eyes should have been; each mirror was etched with cracks, so that standing in front of it threw her broken double reflection back at her. Every inch of space around the throne was piled with objects: photos, plates of food wrapped in plastic, figures of saints and the Virgin Mary…a six pack of beer, a twenty-dollar bill, stuffed animals and toys… Elle noticed a stapler in the shape of a bee sitting on a stack of books, a full leg cast, a set of cooking pots… A lone man occupied one of the folding chairs arranged in rows around the shrine.

"A place to leave offerings for the dead," Zor explained. "Do you have anything you would like to leave? It's free."

Elle's mother skittered at the edges of her mind.

"No. No, I don't."

"Don't communicate with your dead?" He gestured for her to keep following. "Come then, let's leave him to his conversations."

They entered an even smaller room at the back, where the seedy Santeria décor transformed into a high-tech command center. Rows of computers stood ready to fax, phone, print, and transmit any spell or prophecy at the press of a button. She noticed a bank of security monitors displaying every angle of the storefront and shrine.

Zor sat down and rolled his chair over to one of the terminals.

"Quite sophisticated, isn't it? The dark arts have gone high tech like everything else. Here, take a look."

He hit a few keys and an elaborate astrological program appeared. "This can collate an incredible amount of information into a personal star profile. It's way beyond time of birth and sun signs these days. This program can factor in everything from the name of your cat to the color of your living room walls, and then formulate a completely personalized readout."

He rolled his chair over to another screen filled with streaming numerical configurations. "Numerology, the most important new growth area in the business. Did you know that numerologists predicted the last recession? The numbers are lining up for more bad juju, maybe within the next year. That's some free advice if you play the market."

"I don't."

"Oh. Well, you'd be surprised at the number of so-called legit economists that follow this stuff. Not my specialty, but I like to stay current. Here, have a seat."

Zor clasped his hands in front of him, looking more like an anxious schoolboy than a portal to the dead.

"You know, as a rule I never, ever discuss my clients. Privacy and discretion are fundamental to my business."

"The Kingman trial must have been a problem, then."

"Ah! Those fascists subpoenaed everything. My whole life went on hold for months. Of course, the publicity was fabulous for business. Profits were up one hundred and fifty percent for almost six months after the trial. It put me on the map, I'll give them that."

"Why violate your secrecy rules and talk to me about Kingman, then?"

"He wanted me to talk to you. You're writing a book about him, aren't you?"

"Yes, I am. How did you get involved with him?"

"Eliot first came to me when he was making his vampire film. What was the name of it?"

"*By Night*."

"Right. I never watch horror films myself. Anyway, he wanted to know about the occult, black magic, vampire lore. That sort of thing. Somewhere along the line, his interest went from the professional to the personal. It happens a lot, actually. People start out with a mild curiosity, maybe coming in with a group of friends for a laugh or something to tell the folks back at the office on Monday, and it goes from there. Did you know that there's a group right here in L.A. that meets twice a month to explore the dark arts? Séances, tarot, rituals, spells…a subset of the group is particularly interested in vampirism. The drinking of blood, the undead…"

"Was Kingman a part of this group?"

"Oh, no, no. Kingman's not a group type of person. Though you'd be surprised at some of the names that are on that list."

"I'm getting to the point where not much surprises me about this town."

Zor threw back his head and let out a deep, rolling laugh. "Oh, my girl. So you may think, so you may think."

"How did Kingman end up at the county morgue?"

The prosecution had gone over that again and again, painting a devastating picture of Kingman as an unstable, ghoulish man. Elle remembered a trial from her reporting days where a kindergarten teacher had taken an ax to her cheating husband's head right on the front lawn of their suburban home. It had ended in a mistrial because one juror had decided that anyone who worked with little children couldn't have really meant to murder anyone. For your average citizen, skulking around morgues chatting up dead bodies definitely doesn't qualify as sympathetic behavior.

"Eliot was interested in communicating with the dead. The most powerful connection takes place within the first half hour after death. After that, the soul begins to leave the body. Eventually, it's just a shell of flesh and bones. All signals gone. So my contact at the morgue would call me the instant they received a fresh one."

"How did you find this contact?"

Zor gave her a pitying look. "My dear…with enough money, you can find anything you're looking for. I have many contacts, not just with the coroner, but with the police, the major newspapers, the paparazzi… Even parking enforcement, a much maligned but very important source of information, believe it or not. We Los Angelinos love our cars, and spend a good portion of our lives getting ticketed in them. Sure, I lost a good contact because of that trial, but I had two new ones before the verdict was even in. One of life's great certainties is that there will never be a shortage of overworked, underpaid public servants looking to, shall we say, creatively supplement their income. Advantageous consequence of the capitalist system."

"No offense, but this place doesn't seem like much of a capitalist success story."

Zor laughed again, rich and musical. "It's really more of a hobby at this point. I started out over fifteen years ago with not much more than what's here now, minus the tech stuff, of course. Sentimental, I suppose. Plus, look around—the location keeps me in touch with the seedy side of the city in all of its glory. That comes in handy in my line of work, believe me. But the real money comes once the shop door closes. I own a three-quarter million-dollar home in the Hills and have almost as much in the bank. I do quite well for myself, Ms. Bramasol, humble little shop and all."

"One hundred thousand dollars of which came from Kingman."

"Ah, the mysterious hundred thousand dollars. Those fascist lawyers and cops turned themselves into pretzels trying to connect that money to blackmail."

"Was it connected?"

"My dear lady, I may be a renowned master of the black arts, but I don't trade in blackmail! And I certainly had nothing to do with the Kingman murder. If you communed with the dead, would you ever risk *killing* someone?"

"Then what was it for? That's an awful lot of money for a séance or two, fresh corpses or no."

"Immortality. That's what the money was for. Quite a reasonable price for such a product, don't you think?"

"Kingman paid you to make him immortal? How exactly does that work?"

"Well, perhaps I oversold myself a bit. Kingman paid me for the *chance* to become immortal. For the possibility."

"I'm going to be honest with you, Zor—that seems like a very expensive maybe."

"Ha! Did you know that right now, in a town twenty miles from downtown Detroit, there are ninety-two corpses in cheap sleeping bags suspended upside down in vats of liquid nitrogen at minus three hundred twenty degrees Fahrenheit? They've had the blood drained from their bodies, antifreeze pumped into their arteries, and holes drilled into their skulls. There they hang, waiting for technology to come along and defrost them back to life. Almost two thousand dollars to join, fifty-five thousand for the deep freeze, plus additional fees for transportation and legal documents. Talk about a lot to pay for a maybe!"

Zor leaned back and gave an expansive sigh. "Ah, immortality. Mankind's greatest quest. The Holy Grail! We search and we grasp like Tantalus for that most ultimate of all prizes—"

He paused for dramatic effect and swirled his hands into the air.

"And yet it forever slips out of reach."

"So you don't believe in immortality? Even though you're willing to sell it? Or at least the *possibility* of it?"

"It doesn't matter whether I *believe* it or not. The only trick is finding it. Come, let me show you."

He rolled to a computer at the far end of the room and began typing elaborate codes. A series of files appeared on the screen, and Zor opened up a map of L.A. County.

"Look at this. This is called digital mapping software. An acquaintance of mine in the FBI installed it and showed me how to use it."

"Another underpaid civil servant?"

"Ha! You catch on quick. See those flashing red dots? Those indicate the location of murders that fit my profile requirements for this particular little project."

He hit more keys and a series of red circles appeared. "Now, depending on what parameters I put in, the program can also come up with what police call an 'activity radius.' That's the region where the suspect is most likely to live and operate."

"What are the color-coded icons?"

"Those represent possible sources of information—witnesses most likely to have seen something or come in contact with the victim. Or the suspect, for that matter. Here, I can organize the map based on the dates of the crime. Blue indicates the oldest crime scenes; yellow, the middle range; red, the most recent."

Elle leaned closer to the screen; there were circles everywhere, from Hollywood to Sylmar, some all the way out in Antelope Valley.

"Based on this, it doesn't look like your suspect followed much of a pattern."

"He didn't follow the typical 'comfort zone' pattern. But with the marvels of modern technology, you can find a pattern anywhere if you know how to look."

Zor typed in more information; some of the flashing dots reconfigured, others disappeared altogether. Looking at it this way, a pattern did emerge—messy and fragmented, but a pattern nonetheless. The dots were clustered around specific areas of the central region, occasionally fanning out into the San Gabriel mountains. Zor hit some more keys and new dots appeared at random places throughout L.A. county.

"Those are instances where he strayed fairly far from his consistent radius."

An image of Verland wandering outside the gates of Berlin surfaced in Elle's mind. She shook her head to clear her thoughts. Zor and his computers in service to the dark side were beginning to get to her.

"And what's the connection between these murders? I mean, how can you be sure they were committed by the same person?" Elle couldn't help but feel some kind of a con coming on.

"I told you that my profile requirements were very strict. Believe me, I worked this program out to include everything from wound patterns, victim type, methodology—everything. Most important, all of these deaths fit one most fundamental criterion." Zor paused for effect. "In every case, the bodies had been significantly and inexplicably drained of blood."

Elle sat staring at Zor, who produced a smile that fell somewhere between enigmatic and oily.

"You're not telling me you think a vampire killed these people…"

"Once again, my dear, it doesn't matter in the least what I think. I began this project when a member of our little group became convinced that we had a vampire in our midst right here in sunny L.A. She has a lot of good connections in the underground, not to mention a lot of money. I'd just installed this mapping software, so I told her I'd give it a go. False sense of modesty aside, I worked up a profile so precise it would put the FBI to shame. I then used my contacts to track crime reports and autopsies that fit the profile. I went back five years, but my client wasn't as interested in finding out where he had *been* so much as where he *was*."

"To track him down?" Elle couldn't imagine how you'd strike up a conversation with a vampire even if you did find one. It wasn't exactly like making small talk with the cute guy at the local coffee shop.

"My role was strictly desk job. I never ask my clients what they intend to do with the information that I give them. Professional ethics, you know."

"And did you give your client all of this vampire-murder stuff?"

"Nope. And why do you think that was?"

"Because this is L.A., where everything is for sale to the highest bidder. Kingman was willing to pay more for it."

Zor roared with laughter, clapping his hands. "Bravo! Too much fun. When it became obvious that Mr. Kingman was interested in the more unusual aspects of my work, I told him about the project. He offered me one hundred thousand dollars on the spot for all the info I could produce, which ended up being over thirty pages' worth, maps included. Not a bad fee, eh?"

"More than I get per page, I'll give you that."

Zor let loose another roar. "The only condition was that I had to update him whenever I got any new information. Oh, and I had to swear never to share any of it with anyone else, ever. How or if he ever found the elusive vampire, I don't know. That's between Kingman and the powers that guide him. Or the money, whichever the case may be. Anyway, two years later, he was on trial for murder, and now he's in prison."

He waved his hands in the air like a magician performing a disappearing act. "Ta-ta! There goes one of my best clients."

"But you're still in contact with Kingman?"

"Oh, yes. You'd be surprised what you can get past the prison censors with the right incentives. I still update him whenever I get any new information. In fact, he's more interested in the program than ever."

"Were any of these murders solved?"

"No idea. That had no bearing on our interest in them. Most of them were homeless people, criminals, that sort of thing. Anyone who wouldn't be missed much. A few higher-profile cases here and there, but most of them were people on the fringes. You know, on the margins."

"Those unfortunate souls who have crossed into the shadow lands that lie beyond reach of civilized society."

"What's that?"

"Just something I read once."

"Now you have to understand that my narrow parameters eliminated a lot of maybes, some of which probably did belong to our vamp. But I needed to be as precise as possible. You also have to figure that with the types he killed, many of them probably weren't reported with all that much accuracy, let alone autopsied. Did you know that the County of Los Angeles won't pay to bury unclaimed bodies? They cremate them, and if you want the ashes, you have to reimburse the county for the costs.

They keep unclaimed ashes for three years and then dump them in a big common gravesite at Evergreen Cemetery near downtown. Last year over three thousand unclaimed souls went down together in afterlife anonymity. I went there once to visit the mass grave, and do you know what? After wandering up and down that cemetery for the better part of two hours, I never did find it. I keep promising myself I'll go back and make an official enquiry or something, but I never do. I think I'm afraid I'll find out that it doesn't really exist. Horrible to consider, isn't it?"

"That is pretty horrible."

Elle had an absurd image of a cleaning lady vacuuming up heaps of ash at the county morgue and emptying them out with the trash each night. She forced her attention back to the computer screen. With Zor, she had to avoid making wrong turns down one of his many twisted side streets.

"So if you're still giving Kingman updates, you're saying murders that fit the profile are still happening?"

"For about a year it's been nothing but a few scattered hits here and there. No pattern, no regularity. But then this turned up smack in the middle of his old kill zone."

He zoomed in on a red dot in the center of the map, and the location was instantly familiar. The wrong end of Sunset, less than four blocks from The Bradbury.

"Hollywood."

"A perfect place to pick off the underbelly, don't you think?"

Elle felt a tightening in her chest that wouldn't let go. "When did it take place?"

Zor switched back to the database. He leaned back and gave her a look that did nothing to quiet the fist hammering around beneath her ribcage.

"If we do have a vampire on our hands, it looks like he's back in town. That murder occurred last night."

CHAPTER 9

Dogfish, air conditioner, research. The city was baking in the summer heat, and hiding inside with the shades pulled down was the only escape. The messages were piling up from Gary, but Elle had been avoiding his calls. She had considered asking him about Zor's latest vampire murder, then decided against it. Asking questions about a murder in her neighborhood right on the heels of the Kingman story would set off his cop alarm bells, and she didn't want that kind of scrutiny just yet. She needed some time alone in her armchair with only her cats and a Pale Ale for company.

Elle could just imagine what Gary would think about Zor and his communion with the undead. Whenever either of them needed an escape, they would take a bottle of Pinot and sit late into the night in a deserted lifeguard stand at Santa Monica. The combination of the wine and the dark, crashing waves facilitated a lot of intense conversations, and Gary had once told her about his first few months in uniform, when it had really hit him that he could get hurt or even killed in the instant it took a call to go wrong. For the first time, he had stared into the abyss of his own mortality. But unlike Elle, Gary wasn't a dweller, and he definitely didn't have a penchant for the dark side; she sometimes sensed his bewilderment at the shadow that always seemed to hang over her like a rain cloud ready to break. Gary had been born to ride the crest of a crystal-clear wave all the way in to shore—why would he want to risk getting pulled out to sea by darker, more turbulent waters?

Elle stared at the stack of work in front of her. She had read through most of the trial transcripts and should have been outlining the book, maybe starting on the first chapter, but she was restless. She kept thinking about the murder so close to her own apartment—a coincidence, of course. But there were so many odd aspects to this story, and she couldn't shake the feeling that Kingman was grand master of some game that she didn't even know she was playing, let alone what the rules may be.

She went to the window for what must have been the twentieth time that day. No one in the streets except an ice cream vendor and a group of high school kids banging around on skateboards. *What did you expect, an unusually pale man in a Prussian uniform skulking on the corner with a blowsy-looking harlot on his arm?* She had just resigned herself to the blank pages she needed to fill when the phone rescued her. Nyholm Quinn, the last person on earth she'd been expecting to hear from.

"Mr. Kingman is ready for you to continue the book."

"And I suppose you do mean right now, as in this very moment."

Nyholm's voice came through the phone like a flick to her ear. "You're not ever *required* to come. But this particular offer is for today only."

Elle couldn't get over these people; they were demanding even by Hollywood standards. Then again, it wasn't like she'd been accomplishing much anyway.

"Get the reading room ready; I'll be there in an hour."

Nyholm answered the door this time. Vita was nowhere in sight, and without even one word he led her to the library, where three stacks of paper were already laid out.

"These are the next sections."

"I can't just read the rest of it all in one go?" She wondered how many trips it was going to take to finish the whole thing. Malibu wasn't exactly a short hop across town.

"No, only in sections. That's the way Mr. Kingman wants it." So that's the way it would be.

"I'd really like to meet with Mr. Kingman again. I haven't heard anything since our last meeting."

"That's not up to me."

That closed the issue as far as Nyholm was concerned, and he shut the door behind him without another word.

What, no offer of tea this time? Apparently, she'd worn out her welcome already. She picked up the first stack of paper and glanced at the top page. She let her mind drift back to the dark and dirty streets of Verland's Berlin, where he had been about to introduce her to "another"...

19 February, 1873

I have scarcely had time to think let alone write down all that has occurred. Beyond my wildest hopes or imaginings, I have found another like me, a woman—but I must not get ahead of myself. I must start at the beginning.

I was wandering on Charlottenstrasse. Evening was approaching, and I was in a particularly dreary frame of mind. I had turned back toward my lodgings when I was suddenly overcome with the strangest sensation. My thoughts grew confused and I staggered about in much the same state as drinking too much liquor in my previous form. Panic seized me, and I cast about for some shelter, but just as suddenly as the confusion had come, a clarity as sharp as a bayonet's edge cut through the disorder of my mind. I stood face to face with a woman. She had dark skin and magnificent ropes of tangled black hair streaming across her shoulders and down her back. For the first time since my transformation I saw recognition in the eyes of another. She spoke only two words: "Follow me."

She led me through a maze of narrow alleyways until we finally emerged on the brightly lit avenues of the Tiergarten. Smartly dressed couples promenaded around the grand hotels and bustling cafés, and I stood in a dazed stupor. After living for so long among the low and forsaken, such lively, cultured creatures startled me as surely as a wild beast let loose from its cage after long confinement. Crouching and flinching from the crowds and lights, it seemed impossible that I had once moved with perfect ease among men such as these—that I had once *been* a man such as these.

We arrived at a cottage near the opera house and she ushered me inside. We sat before a once-great fireplace now cold and black from long neglect. With no formality or introduction, she caught me by both hands and told me her story, which I shall set down as accurately as possible in her own words:

"My given name is Kazamira Anushka Narva. I am a daughter of what your people call the Tartan hordes, those fated to forever wander the harsh and lonely places of the earth. Many years ago, my people were traveling through Nerchinsk, a land far from both the great cities and the sea, surrounded only by mountains and forsaken by man and Allah himself.

"I had long since reached the age of marriage, and several times a husband had been chosen for me. But I was an unwilling bride, and each refusal made me a less desirable one. I knew that my family would soon force an arrangement rather than be burdened with a willful, unmarriageable daughter.

"The snow had been falling for many weeks and we had to set up camp near the silver mines, evil places where serfs and convicts are sent to work to their deaths at the very center of hell. My people would watch the transports come into camp, the hands of each half-starved man chained to the feet of the man in front of him. They came by the thousands, day and night; in less than a month's time, their skin would turn gray, and it is said that they would slowly turn to silver from the inside out.

"One day, some soldiers came to our camp looking for liquor and women. After many bottles of vodka, they began to tell strange and terrible stories in the way that soldiers do. Among them was an old guard named Vasily who told a story about a prisoner who had worked the mines for so long that no one could remember when he had come. Most men survived only two years at Nerchinsk; many did not live to see the end of a month, or a week. Some did not last even one day. The soldiers jeered the old man, but he would not be silenced.

"'One day,' he said, 'a loose-tongued guard told the other prisoners of a convict named Aslan who had been at the mines longer than any man before. Like you, they at first did not believe. But they kept watch on this Aslan just the same, and that's how they came to think that he could not die. What took other men to their graves did not affect him—not hunger, not cold, not sickness or fatigue. The peasants became afraid and fled their posts. We guards just laughed, but the tales grew more wild and fantastic, and some of the prisoners began refusing to go into the mines with this Aslan. This brought much trouble from our superiors, so one night three of us decided to fix the problem ourselves. Who cared about one more convict lost in the mines? He was as good as dead already as soon as he set foot in this hellish place.'

"'We caught him alone outside the barracks and cut him from the belly to the throat with a butcher knife. 'So, he dies like any other man!' we said, laughing as his stinking blood stained the snow. 'Fool peasants and their superstitions!' We celebrated our success with a bottle of vodka and threw his body to the wolves.'

"'The next day, we went looking for it, but it was gone. 'The wolves have taken it off,' we told ourselves. But apart from the stain where the body had fallen, no blood went away from that place, not one drop. It didn't take long for the story to spread through the camp, and ever since then, the prisoners say that his ghost walks the mines, traveling only at night and looking for revenge. Some even claim to see him running up in the mountains like a beast or a devil.'

"Vasily took a long drink from the vodka bottle before going on. 'That was one year ago today. Since then, both of my comrades from that night are dead. One was ripped to pieces by a pack of wolves in broad daylight, right outside the barracks; they couldn't even find enough of him left to bury. The other just went missing from his post one night; no one's ever found the body to this day. We can't keep a peasant on the job for more than six months anymore, and the prisoners say that men just disappear in the night without a trace.'

"His tale finished, Vasily fell into silence. The soldiers still jeered, but their hearts were no longer behind their laughter, and they, too, soon grew quiet. Some returned to their own camp, while others who had taken too much vodka or found a woman for the night drifted away to tents of their own.

"But the old man's tale had worked a strange magic on me. I stayed behind, watching him from the shadows of the fire. He sat staring into the flames for a long time before staggering to a tent on the far edge of camp. I followed him and crouched beneath a pile of animal skins, waiting for something I did not know or understand. My eyes had fallen shut with sleep when a great burst of cold flooded the tent and awoke me with a start. I could see the outline of a man against the sweep of stars and black sky, as wide and strong as an ox. He delivered a vicious kick to the old man's side. Vasily groaned and sat up, and quick as a flash the ox was beside him, gripping the weather-beaten old face in his huge hands.

"'Do you know who I am, old man?'

"Vasily tried to fall back to the ground, but the strong hands held him fast. 'I know who you are,' he finally said. 'You are Aslan Radev Movladian, the devil of Nerchinsk who cannot die. And you've come to kill me, like the others.'

"The man called Aslan threw back his head and laughed with the delight of a wicked child, tossing Vasily to the ground like a rag. 'You are right about three things, old man: I am Aslan Radev Movladian; I cannot die; and I did kill both of your murdering comrades just like you tried to kill me. But you are wrong about one thing—I am not here to kill you.'

"And then the devil of Nerchinsk sat down next to Vasily and spoke with almost a lover's tenderness, were it not for the cruelty of his words. 'No, old man, you will live, and you will return to those mines and tell my tale again and again, until the day you draw your last stinking breath and your own rotting carcass is tossed to the wolves. You will tell them about Aslan Radev Movladian, the man who conquered death and who lives forever in the mountains of Nerchinsk, the man who feeds upon the blood of all the wicked who pass through this cursed land.'

"He reached down and again took hold of Vasily's face. 'You will live, old man, to tell my tale. Say it!' He shook the crumpled face with savage violence. 'Swear upon your mother's soul, for if my name should die before you do, I will return to drain every last drop of blood in your worthless old body!'

"Vasily swore his oath, and the man called Aslan released him. He was at the entrance of the tent when he suddenly turned and looked straight at where I lay. I longed to burrow deeper beneath the skins, but I dared not move, dared hardly to breath. But my efforts were in vain. He came and slowly lifted the skins one at a time, as if he were playing a game with a child.

"I begged for mercy, and the old man struggled to his knees and shouted out, but with one quick movement the devil named Aslan scooped me beneath his cloak and carried me out into the blackness of the night.

"It seemed only a moment's time before we came to rest in a sheltered hollow deep within the mountains, many miles from the camp. I knew that he was going to kill me, and I prayed only that he spare me suffering or dishonor. He drew a small, curved blade from his belt and knelt by my side.

"'This will be quick, but not without pain,' he said, and drew the blade across my neck.

"I felt his cold lips upon my skin and made my peace with Allah, but he shook me to my senses. I then watched in horrified amazement as he flayed open the veins of his own neck.

"'You will die very soon,' he said. 'If you drink of my blood, you will become a creature like me. You will not die, and you will live as my companion. We will leave this place, and you will never see your people again.'

"I closed my eyes and began to pray, believing that in the final hour of judgment I was trapped between paradise and hell, frozen to this cursed piece of ground by the devil himself. He shook me angrily.

"'Do not look to the heavens for an answer! Your gods cannot follow you here! Only you can choose, and choose you must, or die like a dog without purpose or will!' He shook me harder, shouting, 'Choose, girl, choose!'

"And so I did. I reached out to him, and he placed his massive form upon me. This then, was to be my bridegroom, this my wedding night! The blood from his torn neck stained my face, filled my eyes and mouth with his wet, choking heat."

She leaned back and closed her eyes, and I thought of the medic's question: do you still wish to live? And I had chosen as she had—but had we chosen to *live*? Or had she realized the truth while lying in that icy grave—that she *was* now trapped between paradise and hell, incapable of neither death nor life?

"I could sense his presence all around me—*in* me," she resumed. "When the agony finally left my body, I did not have the strength to even stir from where I lay. That is when Aslan came to me. He lifted a goatskin *bota* to my lips, and I drank with a thirst so terrible that I feared never to quench it. But when I arose, I felt a power greater than anything I had ever before imagined. I stood in that forest knowing that I would never again suffer hunger or cold or weakness, would never again be helpless at the hands of men. I threw my head back and howled with pleasure at the magnificent creature I'd become.

"I left my people forever, and Aslan taught me the ways of our kind. In the mines, he had fed without restraint upon the sick and the dying, and this had left him with a terrible hunger that could never be satisfied. We would travel for days without rest in search of a clan of Tartans or gypsies, fur traders and Cossacks on the trade routes from Yakutsk. Then he would feed with a frenzy that still makes me tremble to recall. No source of human blood was too sacred or too innocent to spare. In Nerchinsk, his hunger had grown into a beast that could never be satiated, consuming his every thought and robbing him of even a moment's peace.

"We crossed the great wall that protects the people of China and spent many years wandering the Oriental lands. We then journeyed through the Ottoman Empire, and in the deep forests of the Bulgarian territories, we came upon a gypsy encampment. It had been several days since our last feeding, and the hunger proved too great for Aslan—he left no man, woman, or child alive.

"It took two days for the rest of the gypsy clan to overtake us. I had just finished bathing in a brook and was drying on an outcropping of rocks while Aslan rested below. He must have sensed danger, for he rose to his feet and called out—but it was too late. He was surrounded by a group of gypsy men who brought him down with their daggers and bound him with ropes.

"Aslan showed no fear. He had told me the many ways men had tried to kill him, but always they failed; always he rose again. This time should have been the same, but this time there was a difference—the gypsies knew the stories of the undead, and they knew what had to be done. They lashed Aslan to a tree and spread hawthorn branches at his feet; still he showed no fear. The gypsy women chanted '*vampir*' and '*mulo*' and began casting signs; one very old woman made the sign of the cross with one hand and pointed at Aslan with the index and little finger of her other hand. The men gathered torches and began to light the hawthorn. Only then did I see the realization come to his face, and he threw back his head and let loose a howl of rage that rings in my ears to this day. The terrible sound went on and on as the flames crept closer to him, and the gypsy women chanted louder and louder, their cries mixing with his in one maddening wail of terror.

"I clapped my hands to my ears and tried to turn away, but I could not. I watched as the first flames touched his body, and he began to…how should I say? To *come apart*…he did not so much burn as slowly disintegrate before my very eyes. As his howls of rage turned to howls of agony, I began to feel his suffering as surely as if I was lashed to the tree with him. I knew that I could not stifle my cries for much longer, but the suffering soon ended. All at once the remaining shell of his body filled with a crimson light that seemed to come from the very center of his being, and he imploded into a thousand embers that burned hot and bright before turning to black ash and falling to the forest floor. The gypsies screamed in terror and fled. In the instant Aslan disappeared, I felt my own essence flicker like a candle in a draft, and then fill with an emptiness that has been a part of my soul ever since.

"I stayed cowering among the rocks for days. When hunger finally drove me out, I saw that the gypsies had covered the trees around the place where Aslan had died with amulets of blue and white circles—the evil eye. They clanked and clanged in the wind, marking the spot as forever after contaminated with evil. I searched the ground for some remnant of Aslan to carry with me, but found nothing, not even a trace of ash to mark his existence.

"I was still filled with fear and traveled only in the darkest hours of night. I fed only upon animals and grew very weak. Outside the province of Pomerania, I met a merchant who took pity upon my wretched state. From him I learned the ways of the Prussians, your laws, customs, and language. I also learned how much easier it is to feed in the great cities, where thousands live and die each day without notice.

"One day the merchant went on a trip and did not return. I soon found myself on the streets of the city, where I learned that the world holds no place for a woman alone. I was easy prey for the men who look for such lost women—though a great many of them ended up as prey themselves!"

She laughed, and I will admit that there was something quite unsettling in the sound.

"In Posen I was arrested on charges of idle wandering and impertinent begging, though I had never begged so much as a *thaler*. The prison was damp and full of vermin and scabies. We slept on straw bedding, and those who misbehaved were tied to the Spanish Goat and given lashes to the back. But I laughed at their punishments, and thrived with life among the sick and dying!

"The authorities did not know what to do with me. One prison would release me and send me to another province, where I would immediately be imprisoned for illegal entry, expelled as an undesirable, and sent back to the very place from whence I had just come. There I would be arrested for illegal entry, and so it would begin again. Foolish laws of men! Eventually, a merciful solicitor arranged for me to be sent to a rich farmer in a distant province. I still have the contract; here, I'll show you."

She then produced a dirty, tattered paper that showed she had been made the legal ward of a farmer in Mecklenburg. I noticed that in place of her signature, she had simply marked + + +. The clerk had recorded the mark as a legal substitute for her name, noting that the prisoner "has no knowledge of writing." I wondered why she kept such a grim memento, but she resumed her story before I could ask.

"The farmer was a strict man with a cruel wife who beat me as soon as I arrived. They put me to work like a beast of burden and sent me to sleep in the barn among the cows and the goats. I was curled up, alone and wretched in the darkness, when I felt the warmth of a living creature; a small white goat had nestled in the folds of my skirts. I was growing sick with hunger, and leaned down to open its throat…but it looked up at me with such trusting innocence that I hesitated. What bitter irony, this lowly beast's tenderness in contrast to those tyrants asleep in their soft beds, their heads filled with the untroubled dreams of the righteous!

"And in that moment, I decided. I kissed the soft, silky white fur and went to the farmhouse. I killed the old man, his wife, and three servants. I drank their spilled blood, and in that moment I realized that I cared more for one little goat than a hundred men, women, or children." She then smiled with a cruelty that seemed more akin to those she despised than the blameless beast she had spared.

"Of course, I had to flee from what I had done. The greedy farmer had a bundle of gold coins hidden beneath the floorboards of his slaughterhouse—I had heard him whispering with his wife when they thought I was too far away to hear. Ha! They knew nothing of a wolf in woman's clothing! I took the gold, cut off my hair, and dressed in one of the servant boy's clothes. Thus disguised, I obtained a false journeyman's pass and entered the gates of Berlin, where I have been ever since."

She asked me my own story, and I began with the hill in Sedan; by the time I had finished, the sun was blazing outside our darkened room. We sat in silence for some time before she spoke.

"In Berlin, I learned that I did not have to live like a beggar in the streets. I learned the ways of money and power—how a woman's charms can open many doors. I can see that you have forgotten these things. You have lived too long without the many pleasures and fine things that make life worth living. But it is time for you to remember. Yes, we are creatures unlike any other, but that does not condemn us to live like despised outcasts. No! We can use our gifts to live any life that we desire, and I will show you! It is time for you to find your way back from the shadows—back to the world of women and men."

CHAPTER 10

Elle stared out at the Pacific, but instead of blue waves and white sand, she saw a cruel smile and blood-stained hands; instead of seagulls' cries and the roar of the surf, she heard the curses of gypsies and the screams of a devil that almost could not die. The sun glittered across the water and sand; such a picture-perfect scene seemed almost purposely designed to deny the ones written in the pages in front of her. She angled her chair away from the windows and picked up the next section.

21 March, 1873

The cottage in which Kazamira lives belongs to a stage actor. His craft demands long and frequent travel, so thankfully we are often spared his presence. I pass the time reading books from his library or playing the piano, pleasures which I have not indulged for quite some time. Some days I sit for hours observing the people on the streets hurrying from one place to the other in their fine clothes and carriages. In the evenings, we attend the theater or the opera, or visit one of the many salons that Kazamira favors.

We feed at two or three day intervals, which she considers a great sacrifice. She prefers to feed every day, and hunts with an alarming lack of caution; she will often set upon a drunken gentleman who has wandered too far from the Tiergarten as casually as she would a beggar or a prostitute. I told her about my experiments extending the time between feedings, but she just laughed and called me a priggish Prussian. Perhaps—but I fear her boldness may one day prove to be her undoing. After all, Berlin is not like the outposts of Siberia or the Orient, and a society gentleman or lady is quite a different matter than an isolated peasant or fur trader.

I will confess, however, that I share with her one motivation for a more zealous feeding schedule: on the nights that we feed, we make love with an intensity that I could not have even imagined in my former life. We stop only to rest in each other's arms before beginning again and again until exhaustion finally overtakes us.

09 April

From Kazamira, I have learned how easily a print worker can be bribed to prepare false papers, how quickly a master crafts-man will issue an identity certificate for a price. It seems, then, that she was correct—with enough knowledge and resources, a man can choose any life that he wishes.

15 April

When the actor is here, Kazamira returns to his bed. This does not inspire the jealousy it once would have, for I can see that she regards him much like a child regards an amusing play toy. In the bohemian way of actors and artists, he does not seem to mind my presence. Once he even asked me to join him and Kazamira in their bed chamber; suffice it to say that I did not hesitate to decline.

19 May

This evening, we attended Madame Blucher's salon. I was in a peevish mood and retired to a corner in order to avoid any company. From this vantage point, I could not help noticing that among such well-bred ladies and gentlemen, Kazamira stood out like the unlearned savage that she in fact is. She knows nothing of art or literature or music, nothing of social manners or delicacy of speech and feeling. I could furthermore see that everyone in attendance knew this. A fury rose in me as I observed how the ladies condescended to her, how the men's lust for her was fuelled by their very contempt. She was no more than a specimen on display, a crude and exotic novelty for their entertainment.

I made my way toward her, eager to leave such a poisoned place—but then, just as if she had read my thoughts, she turned and gave me a smile so sublime that it stopped me where I stood. I realized that she knew perfectly well how she was regarded in that room, knew the inseparable desire and hatred that she inspired in those fine ladies and gentlemen. And I also realized that she did not care in the slightest, that some part of her even reveled in the power she held over them, the perverse fascination she inspired. I could not prevent myself from laughing aloud at the absurdity of the situation: creatures like Kazamira and myself, surrounded by the most beautiful and well-bred of Prussian society, mutually feeding off of one another for no more than our own amusement.

07 July

I have been schooling Kazamira in the ways of society. She is a quick and eager student with a gift for music and languages, though she still resists any attempts at literacy. The salons have taught her the importance of good breeding, and she has utilized my own background as a source of inspiration: she has fashioned herself into a Russian countess, and I am to be her aristocratic gentleman escort. She shows great imagination with such inventions and would no doubt make a fine stage performer.

She has also had her hair styled in the ways of the most admired ladies, and the actor brings her the latest fashions from Paris. She is more beautiful than ever, but alas, the clothes do not make the lady, and she still has much to learn.

22 August

I never tire of her eyes, the way they deepen or change shade with a shift of light or mood; the gray-green is so startling against the darkness of her skin. I once told her that I had not thought such coloring possible among the darker-skinned races, but she said that it is not uncommon among her people, who descend from a curious mixture of Asian, Mongol, and Caucasoid blood.

30 November

I have come to a café to secure a few hours of peace. We have been denied an invitation to the Christmas ball at Countess Margaret's country palace. It is considered the event of the season, and Kazamira is inconsolable that we have been overlooked. She has spent the last several days alternating between despairing moods, in which she weeps without end, and fits of rage, which threaten to bring down anything foolish or unfortunate enough to cross her path. Last night, she fed in a sort of frenzy, three times in a row, in order to console herself.

She does not understand the limitations that prevent us from rising too high. First, we face the insurmountable obstacle of dining, the foundation of all social life. How many times can we refuse an invitation to dinner or a weekend soirée in order to avoid a simple bite of food or glass of liqueur? There is also the matter of our fantastical identities. How long can we turn the conversation from our rank and titles, our family estates and ancestral connections and all of the thousand details so important to the aristocratic classes? No, Kazamira does not understand the ways of this world, does not understand that we can never truly be a part of it.

I must take her away somewhere, perhaps to the more open societies of Paris or America. Not long ago, Kazamira revealed a collection of jewelry supposedly given to her by various admirers, though I suspect she may have stolen more than a few of the pieces. She will hate parting with such treasures, but along with what is left of the gold, the profits will sustain us for many years to come. We must now leave this land where I have spent all of my life, the land which I have always called my country and my home.

01 August, 1874; Stockholm, Sweden

We have been traveling through Europe, and Kazamira's gaiety appears restored. Only one incident threatened to mar her happiness—in the northern regions of Finland, we came upon a Lapland woman telling fortunes at a roadside stand. Upon crossing her path, she began making the sign of the evil eye and uttering oaths. It seemed as if Aslan had been summoned from his grave to haunt us in these northern lands, his scattered ashes buried deep in the earth beneath our very feet.

30 May, 1875; Paris, France

We have been in Paris for three months now. Kazamira has begun an affair with a writer whose society consists of debauched gentlemen and their mistresses, absinthe and opium addicts, and decadent estate-supported bohemians. Last night, we were in a seaside cottage occupied by an Englishman and his friend. The owner of the place was purported to be an English lord who concealed his identity under the name of his own mother's lover. There was a big monkey gamboling around the house that had been trained to play obscene tricks upon the guests. A drunken streetwalker lay sprawled in a corner, her breasts bare and her chemise hitched up over her knees. She would occasionally lift her head to either vomit or let loose a string of obscenities.

Late into the evening, the Englishman unveiled a photographic collection depicting every sexual act imaginable—and some better left unimagined—in every possible combination. His friend was dead drunk and kept fondling the fingers of what appeared to be a mummified hand being used as a paperweight. Upon leaving, I noticed an inscription over the door and bent closer to read it: Dolmancé Cottage.

Kazamira seems amused by such company, but I grow more weary with each passing day.

11 February, 1876

Yesterday I spent the evening with a group of writers. One was recovering from a long illness, and the conversation turned toward mortality, a subject which seemed to preoccupy them all. They then began a morbid game of one-upmanship in regard to the terror death possessed over each of them. The first revealed that each time he occupies a new lodging house, he immediately picks out a place where his coffin will eventually stand. Another described his mania for affixing his monogram to everything he owns, so that through his household items, at least, he can achieve some kind of perpetuity. But the undisputed winner recounted the story of his mother's death, how her coffin would not fit down the staircase of his home and had to be lowered out of the upper floor window of the room in which she died. Ever since then, neither he nor his wife can look out of their own bedroom window without wondering whose coffin would be the first to go through it.

All of them were paralyzed by death's unbreakable hold, and for the first time, I felt the full reach of my power—for I now knew why the wretched beggar in Berlin had come to such a horrid end. I had begun the transformation by opening his veins and drinking his blood, but by denying him my own, I had failed to perform the last, most crucial step.

Neither Kazamira nor I have ever transformed another, but sitting among those gifted men whom the grave would too soon rob from the world, one could not help considering it.

[undated]

We are on a train after being forced to flee Paris. Here is what happened: Kazamira's lover had taken her for an excursion in the countryside, whereupon he informed her that he had decided to marry, and that after today they could no longer see each other. Naturally, he wanted to make love one last time, and they proceeded to roll among the mud and vegetation in a frenzy of lust. He was on his back at the moment of orgasm when she tore open his throat and drained him, staying in the position of lovemaking and gazing into his eyes as the life left his body.

She arrived home in a state of great excitement, and we made love right in the entranceway with the dirt of the forest still on her before she finally recounted what she had done.

21 December, 1880; Törbel, Switzerland

For some time now, we have been living in the remote alpine mountains. Chastened by her recklessness in Paris, Kazamira agreed that we would subsist for a time only upon animals. However, this restraint has also taught us the limits of such options—after too long without a proper feeding, we grow weaker and weaker no matter how much animal blood we consume, and the rot and disintegration begin their slow but inevitable advance. Only human blood can reverse this.

We wait as long as we can and then venture far from our lodging to a remote outpost or hunting lodge. We choose our prey with utmost caution and make sure to drain every drop of blood. I have tried several preservation methods, from mixing in salt and herbs to cooling it in the snow, but so far, only freshly drawn blood seems to suffice.

As a result of these irregular feedings, we no longer possess the vitality that comes with the blood, including the kind of lovemaking to which we had grown accustomed. But we have gained a peace of mind missing for many years now.

19 April, 1881

I spend my time hunting or improving the lodging that I built for us with my own hands. Kazamira gathers flowers or tends to her little family of goats. She is inordinately fond of the beasts, insisting that they sleep inside when the weather turns cold. She even forgave them for eating her wardrobe, saying that she no longer needed such fine clothes now that she has returned to being a simple country girl.

In fair weather we swim by moonlight in the lake near our cabin. On some nights, white cranes fly overhead like mysterious talisman from some secret, aerial world of beauty and grace.

07 June, 1882

I must write about an extraordinary event that occurred earlier today. While hunting high in the mountains, I saw a hawk tracking its prey in the canyon below. I became absorbed in the creature's hypnotic circling, and after a time I began to feel the sort of light-headedness one experiences before a fainting spell. In the next instant, I found myself at a dizzying height, seeing what the hawk saw, feeling the sensation of the wind as it dove, the solid grip of the prey in its powerful talons. I was still with it as it soared upward again and came to rest in the branch of a towering pine. It tore into its prey, and I, too, felt the tearing flesh, the taste of blood… The hawk suddenly gave a piercing call, and I broke free of the spell. A sickening vertigo overtook me, and I crouched to the ground and closed my eyes in order to regain my composure. In my mind's eye, I could see the hawk take flight and come to rest on a branch directly in front of me, and when I opened my eyes, it was there. I held out my arm and it came to land, piercing the flesh with its talons. We gazed into each other's eyes, and an obscure, animal understanding passed between us. I knew that the hawk would obey my will, and that I, in turn, would always be its protector. Once it seemed satisfied that I understood, it took flight and called out one last time before disappearing over the mountaintop.

When I told Kazamira about what had happened, she said that she had often seen Aslan communicate with wolves, and that sometimes he could even command them to do his bidding, a prospect that greatly intrigues me with its possibilities.

02 July

Since the incident with the hawk, my attempts to re-create the experience have yielded interesting results. So far, with varying degrees of success, I have been able to enter into the consciousness of many different animals, including beasts as

great as the lynx and as humble as the marmots that burrow
in the meadows. Once, I even forged a strange and fleeting
connection with a black salamander I found sunning itself on
a rock by the lake.

Kazamira has also been practicing this newfound skill, and
it came as no surprise that her bond is with the goat kingdom.
Here is how it is done—we only need fix on the animal in
question and enter into a meditative state in which the mind
is cleared of every trace of self-awareness. If any such thought
intrudes, the connection is broken. However, once the link is
established, we can see what the animal sees, experience what
it experiences, and command it at will. The amount of control we exert depends upon the animal—placid and agreea-
ble beasts like the alpine deer do our bidding quite willingly,
while others, like Kazamira's goats, require a more diplomatic
approach.

The experience is most powerful when we connect with
those creatures meant especially for ourselves, and hawks seem
to be my chosen guides. When I connect with these great birds
of prey, I feel that I actually *am* the hawk, and that the hawk is
me—that we become one, somehow. With them, I do not need
to employ the same effort required with other animals. Our
bond is natural, ever present, and with practice, I can now call
it forth with only the slightest effort. Sometimes I am able to
travel for miles and miles, seeing what the hawk sees, feeling
what it feels.

There is one limitation, though. As with all of our powers,
we can only link with the animal kingdom within the first few
days of a feeding. After that, the connections grow weak, as if

the animals are calling to us across a deep divide that we can no longer cross.

08 November, 1884

Kazamira dreads the coming of winter. She has been refusing to feed and has grown weak and listless, staying indoors for weeks at a time and neglecting even the care of her goats. Although I have been unwilling to admit it, I know how to make her happy again. I know that she misses society, the life of gaiety and leisure that we enjoyed in Paris and Berlin. Although I feel as if I could stay in these mountains forever, perhaps we both need to return to the society of men for a while, lest we lose their ways entirely and become fit only for the company of birds and beasts.

11 November

Winter has come hard and early; this morning we awoke with the cabin halfway buried in snow. Although I promised Kazamira that we would leave Switzerland, the roads are no longer passable. I have consoled her with the promise that as soon as conditions allow, we will travel to London, which she has been longing to see for some time now.

22 March, 1885

Spring has finally arrived. As we make preparations for our departure, we both feel the sadness of leaving a place where we have spent so many close and happy hours, free from the din and chaos of society.

Coming over the hill after an evening's hunt or a walk in the mountains, my heart aches to see our home standing there so solid and steady, Kazamira inside awaiting my return. How difficult it is to leave the things one has built!

31 April

We have settled the last of what small affairs we have here, and our passage to England has been arranged. We sold the goats to a family in a nearby village, and Kazamira wept bitterly at their parting. Soon, the sea will separate me even farther from my homeland.

31 September; London, England

In London, the air smells of coal. A dismal fog mixed with the foul smog of the factories transforms day into perpetual twilight. Like Berlin, the city teems with the poor and the downtrodden, the workhouse and the prison in the shadow of the great cathedrals and monuments to progress. In short, a city like every other, and the faces of the people streaming by seem the same faces over and over again, filling the same streets without end.

17 June, 1886

Kazamira has returned to feeding every day; we frequent a part of the city known as the East End, where ramshackle buildings sit so tightly packed that a man can stand in an alleyway and spread his hands from one side to the other without even stretching. The people are just as compressed into these wretched streets, and a constant influx of immigrants, beggars, and whores ensures that the population is never exhausted, and never accounted for.

20 January, 1887

Several days ago while browsing through a bookshop in the Lake District, a curious title caught my eye: *The Vampyre.* Superstitions about our kind have of course existed for many years, but I was surprised to find such folktales refashioned in the form of a modern novel. The vampyre in question was an aristocratic gentleman disguising himself among human society, and for a moment I had the uncanny sensation that the author had somehow spied directly into my own life. I admit that I also felt an unexpected thrill at the thought of our kind securing a place in literature, small and forgotten though it may prove to be. I suppose the book called forth in me some need to have one's story told, to leave behind some record, some evidence of one's passing; perhaps that is what this diary represents to me.

I almost purchased the book, but when I skimmed ahead to the ending and found the suave vampyre brutally feeding upon his young bride on the very night of their wedding, I decided against it.

22 August, 1888

I had a most strange encounter while feeding in the East End last night. At the dead-end of a narrow alleyway, I came upon a prostitute and her client; I attempted to withdraw, but the man caught sight of me and flung the whore to the ground with a startling viciousness. He then rushed past me, and as our eyes met, I felt a sickening sensation, a malevolence and ill-will that filled the alleyway as surely as a physical presence.

I knew that this man had intended to kill the whore, and the hair on the back of my neck stood up like an animal whose hackles rise in the face of a terrible foe…or a terrible rival, for it did not escape me how easily I could have stepped in and finished what he had begun. The dazed and wretched woman would have been easy prey, but I was overcome with a nameless dread and fled as quickly as possible.

In retrospect, a perverse irony reveals itself: while an encounter with one predator had nearly ended the prostitute's life, an encounter with *two* predators had saved it.

17 September

The entire city is fixated on a series of grisly prostitute murders in Whitechapel. A citizen's committee has begun paying unemployed men to patrol the streets from midnight until four in the morning, and house-to-house inquiries are conducted daily. A local shoemaker, a Jew, was arrested on the basis of evidence no more compelling than rumor and an unfortunate nickname.

Kazamira is most agitated by the gruesome nature of the murders. When I mentioned that perhaps we were in no position to cast judgment, she grew enraged, saying, "There is more savagery in feeding upon a man while he is still alive than after he is dead."

I asked what she meant by this, and she replied, "I have seen men torn apart on the rack, broken on the wheel, and

roasted alive on the pyre; women beaten and violated worse
than the lowest of beasts; the smallest of children, starving in
the streets—thousands of people breathing, moving about, but
not really *alive*. Such an existence is not life—it is a walking
death in the long shadow of starvation and sickness and suffering. And do the rich and powerful pick the flesh from their
bones less than we do? We kill to feed, to live, no worse than a
wolf of the forest or a leopard of the jungle. But mankind kills
for greed, for power, and also, it seems, for perversions of the
most unimaginable kind. No, do not ever compare what we are
to the brutal savagery of your so-called humanity!"

Alarmed as I was by the fury of her words, I could think of
no adequate reply.

03 October

The mood of the East End has grown thick with fear and
paranoia: neighbor watches neighbor; wives look at husbands
with suspicious new eyes; and every butcher, surgeon, or dock
worker makes sure to account for his every action.

I have told Kazamira to limit her feedings and go nowhere
near the East End; we can afford no risks until this madness
passes.

12 November

I have discovered that far from avoiding the East End,
Kazamira has in fact been going to Whitechapel for over a
week now, and probably even longer than that, though she
won't confess it. I uncovered this deception while reading her
an article from the *Times* about a series of fresh murders. The

police assured the public that they had not been committed by the same man responsible for the mutilation killings, citing differences such as the drainage of blood from the bodies and the fact that the victims had been the clients of prostitutes rather than the women themselves—I then stopped short, for I *knew* that Kazamira was responsible.

I could not understand why she would specifically choose to feed in what is now the most scrutinized area of the city, and she eventually revealed her strange motive: "Any man out roaming the streets at night in Whitechapel these days has to be either the killer himself or some savage just like him. So I am doing a great service to the women of the East End, including, no doubt, their long-suffering wives and children."

I must have looked as astonished as I felt, for she added, "You are the one who reads the newspapers, filled each day with so many murders the police cannot even keep track. Body parts floating in the Thames, a torso propped up by the railway station like a forgotten piece of luggage! And almost *always* the victims are women! You are the one who torments yourself about the deaths of innocent people—so why not feed upon men who despise women so much that they carve them up like a side of meat on a butcher's block? Are they not more deserving of death than the derelicts and prostitutes *you* justify feeding upon? No, my conscience is no less clear than the high-and-mighty Verland!"

Her eyes had a wild, desperate look that I had never seen before, and in that instant, I believe that she hated me as purely and completely as she hated those men in Whitechapel.

I am convinced that this horrible business has eroded her mind just as it is has the rest of the city. It is imperative that we leave London until Kazamira regains her mental fitness.

17 January, 1892; Dublin, Ireland

We have settled in Ireland, where I feel quite at home among the dark waters, the mists that shroud the hills, the language and the poetry of the people…the Irish seem a race in constant struggle with the contradictory forces raging within them: pagan roots grown into a peculiar, hybrid Catholicism; an inherent melancholy interrupted by an equally innate liveliness; ancient oppression fueled by rebellion against it—a people whose nature is in some ways quite akin to our own.

17 August, 1894; London, England

We have returned to London after a terrible incident in the Scottish Highlands. Kazamira was wandering in the Culag Woods, outside the village of Lochinver, when she came across a hunter scouting water fowl. She says that she watched him to make sure that he was alone—but, in fact, he was not. She was soon surprised by the rest of his hunting party, her face covered with gore, the still-warm body of their friend in her arms. They shot her on the spot as a deranged and brain-sick madwoman. Terrified of discovery, Kazamira fought to keep still as they dragged her deep into the woods and set to work. Though she dared not open her eyes, she heard the sound of metal against earth, and realized that the men were digging her grave. She could hardly resist fleeing, but she knew what had to be done. She let them lower her into the grave and cover her with shovelful after shovelful of suffocating earth.

Fortunately, the fresh blood of the hunter coursing through her gave her strength enough to claw upward one agonizing inch at a time. It took almost three days to free herself, and I still shudder to think of what horrors she must have endured during those endless hours! When she finally made it back to our lodging, she was filthy, her hands in tatters, so weak and half-starved that she collapsed into my arms the instant I opened the door. I fed her continually until she was restored, but I could feel the danger closing around us every minute, and we fled the country as soon as she was strong enough. Fate has been quite cruel to my poor Kazamira lately, and I have brought her back to London in the hopes of reviving her spirits with the bright lights and society that she so loves.

In the modern world, it seems that a man can be more alone among thousands of men than in the most solitary countryside.

01 December, 1894

Kazamira has thrown herself back into society with renewed vigor. Her beauty and peculiar charm, in which the ancient Tartan forms a half-savage, half-civilized hybrid with the modern lady, ensure her no shortage of admirers. For my part, I do not wish to return to the sort of life we left behind in Paris, and no longer accompany her on the rounds of parties and music halls and social events that so occupy her time. She is more cautious than before, but during these last few years, some dark and furious seed seems to have grown deep within her, always threatening to burst to the surface in some new form of recklessness. Something in her has changed; I cannot quite put it into words, but it is as if she has withdrawn the most essential part of herself, has hidden it away from anyone else's view—including my own.

It is not unusual for weeks to pass during which we see each other only briefly, superfluously, like two acquaintances passing in the street who can't quite recall how they once knew each other.

01 June, 1897

Today I read a review of a new novel called *Dracula*. Imagine my surprise upon finding another story about a bloodthirsty member of the undead—I had thought that little book in the Lake District to be the first and last of its kind. The reviewer declared the book "a classic of Gothic horror" and went on to praise the "gloomy fascination" of such a terrible tale.

And so it seems that the modern reader has quite an appetite for the macabre mysteries of our kind.

16 November, 1897

I finished *Dracula* in one sitting. Certain particulars of the author's imagination amused me—for instance, although I can commune with the bat kingdom, I have yet to change into one entirely. However, I could not help but be taken aback by some of the details, and his portrayal of the creature's power curtailed by his wretched isolation moved me deeply. A thought then occurred to me that sent a tremor through my entire being: had this Bram Stoker discovered one of our kind? Had he drawn forth his secrets in order to transform them into the fantastical story now filling the imaginations of thousands of ordinary people?

I sat the entire night pondering the implications of this possibility. I confess it filled me with a mixture of dread and excitement to consider what would happen if all of mankind knew and understood the ways of our kind. Would it mean our inevitable destruction, as it had for the creature in the novel? Or could we somehow find a way to live openly among them, to feed in some way less loathsome and treacherous? Would exposure lead to our salvation, or our doom?

01 January, 1900

The city is celebrating the turn of the century. The newspapers say that it will be an age of machines and progress unrivaled in all of history.

Curious how at such times of looking forward one is also compelled to look back—had that French Cuirassier come over the hill a minute earlier or a minute later, or had his sabre missed its mark by mere inches, I would now be enjoying my old age, surrounded by a wife and a happy troupe of children and grandchildren. Or perhaps more likely, I would have died a soldier's death on one battlefield or another, the way I should have at Sedan. As it is, I stare at my face in the mirror on this cold, gray first day of the new century and find myself, as always, unchanged. And fated to remain so…for the beginning of how many more new centuries?

CHAPTER 11

Elle stood up and went to the window; the floor-to-ceiling view made it seem as if she were balanced at the very edge of the Pacific. Her head was whirling with a jumble of images…a small, lonely little cabin in the Swiss Alps; the foul streets of the East End; a beautiful woman clawing her way out of her own grave. She closed her eyes to try and clear her thoughts, and when she opened them, a tremendous golden hawk was sitting on the walkway railing behind Kingman's mansion. It was staring right at her, and she stared back. *No.* She shook her head and made herself say the words.

"There are no hawks on the beaches of Malibu."

And then the hawk that wasn't there let out three powerful cries before disappearing across the water. Elle pressed her body against the window, seized by some powerful urge for flight beyond her control. She was so close to the glass that the crashing waves seemed ready to sweep her out to sea. The world tilted, and she closed her eyes again and sank to the floor in order to stop herself from going right over the cliffs—because in that moment when hawk and water and air had collided, Elle knew that it had happened. She knew that she had begun to believe.

She sat back down and picked up the last stack of paper, following Verland into the twentieth century. It had indeed been unrivaled in history, though probably not in the ways those enthusiastic newspapermen could have imagined.

20 January, 1901

Today I read that Kaiser Wilhelm II has come to England to visit the dying Queen. A strange and unsettling reminder of the past, this man who would have been my king.

20 January

Queen Victoria is dead.

06 April, 1904

Britain has signed an agreement with the French Republic. I went straight to an international newsagent, and sure enough, the German papers are full of talk about French revenge and foreign encirclement. One illustration showed John Bull turning his back on a Prussian officer in order to sneak off with the harlot Marianne in her Tricolor dress. The tip of a saber was protruding from beneath the officer's overcoat, aimed straight at England and France.

11 July, 1905

The newspapers produce a steady stream of hand-wringing over German militarism and aggression. One article even suggested that German bakers are putting arsenic into their bread to weaken the population for the coming invasion. The people are being whipped into a state of fear and paranoia, and today I overheard a conversation in which two perfectly reasonable-looking gentlemen placed blame for Britain's entry into the Boer War on German and Jewish financiers.

January 01, 1906

The new year begins with tension and unrest. Most of the British are convinced that conflict with Germany is all but inevitable.

02 September, 1907

Britain has signed a treaty with Russia.

03 February, 1910

An article in the *Contemporary Review* made the extraordinary claim that England is infiltrated with over 350,000 German spies. I wonder how they find time for espionage after baking sugar and sewing footwear in the East End for twelve hours every day?

13 August, 1913

Anti-German sentiment has grown intolerable. There are reports of German-owned stores being looted, and in some areas, gangs of youth assault anyone they even suspect of being German. Fears of spies and sabotage have encouraged rumors that the British government may eventually imprison all German males between the ages of sixteen and seventy. A scare-tactic, no doubt, but it cannot be long before all enemy aliens are forced to register, at the very least. Even with an assumed identity, my English is not fluent enough to eradicate all traces of my heritage, and I have told Kazamira to prepare for the possibility of leaving England should the situation grow any worse.

02 September, 1913

For the last month, Kazamira and I have been quarreling constantly. She does not understand the difficulties that may arise if the crisis brewing in Europe escalates into a major conflict. In such times, one cannot simply skip from country to country switching identities, and even we will be forced to submit to the restrictions imposed by war.

29 June, 1914

The archduke of Austria and his wife have been assassinated in Sarajevo. I have made arrangements to return to Berlin with identity papers naming Kazamira as my wife. She does not wish to return to Germany, and I have repeatedly assured her that we can make further arrangements from Berlin, but right now we must leave England as quickly as possible before it is too late.

[undated]

We have gotten out in the nick of time—Austria-Hungary has declared war on Serbia. It is only a matter of time before France enters the conflict, with Great Britain sure to follow.

02 August; Berlin, Germany

War declared on Russia. In the early morning hours people began gathering outside the Kaiser's palace. When war was announced, the crowd struck up the national anthem, cheering and waving banners. A mob gathered at the Russian embassy, and the ambassador and his party were attacked and beaten with sticks. Innocent people are being seized on the street and shot as spies. Kazamira's dark skin and Eastern accent will put her at great risk, and I have implored her to conduct herself with the utmost caution until some order is restored.

03 August

War declared against France.

04 August

Great Britain has entered the war. Soldiers now stand guard at every bridge and railroad, stopping anyone even remotely suspected of espionage or questionable activity.

06 August

I must finally write the words that until now I could not bear to set down, as if by not recording them I could make them less true: Kazamira and I have decided to part. Upon returning to our lodging house one evening, I found her sitting calmly in the foyer with a bag by her side. She had been in a state of agitation ever since our return to Germany, and a part of me was not surprised when she told me that she had made up her mind to travel to America. She then made it clear that she would go either with or without me, and I did not doubt her for a moment. With her little bag in hand, the foolish woman thought she was going to just walk down the street and find passage from Berlin to New York during the outbreak of war!

I persuaded her to at least let me make the proper arrangements, and in a voice trembling with emotion, she asked whether they would be for one or for two. In that moment, a part of my heart closed, for I knew that I would not go with her, and I could see that she knew it, too. I said something about my heritage putting us at risk, making travel difficult, and so on; but of course this was untrue—we could have gone to any far corner of the world, assumed any identities we wanted. But how could I tell her the deeper, more complicated truth? I knew that I should leave Europe with her as quickly as possible, but how easily the passions of the soul override the sensibilities of the brain! For I could not deny the deep, instinctual need to remain in my homeland at this time of crisis. The man I had been, the oaths I had once sworn—though long dead and buried, I felt them stir to life once more.

Kazamira wept terribly and begged me to come with her, but neither for as long nor as fervently as she once might have. Perhaps the conflict tearing through Europe has also torn down the veil that for some time now has been obscuring the distance between us, a space so far and wide that neither of us seems capable of crossing it any longer.

10 August

At great expense and risk, I have obtained Kazamira a new set of identity papers and have made arrangements for her safe passage to America. I have made sure that she has enough gold and currency, and though I have no doubts as to her resourcefulness, I worry how she will manage in a world full of a thousand practical concerns about which she still knows so little.

Her ship leaves from Hamburg in two days, and we have been carefully moving around each other, as cautious as a surgeon who keeps his fist closed tightly round the heart lest the slightest unclenching let loose the fatal flow.

12 August

She is gone. When the time came, the full realization of our parting overwhelmed her, and at first, she would not board the ship. However, I took her hands in mine and told her that it was now my turn to give life back to her as she had once done for me. I saw the resilience that had carried her through so many hardships rise within her, and her tears dried for the last time. She promised that someday, once the war had ended, we would be together again, that she would remain in America and retain the same identity until I had found her. I know that her heart was sincere, but mine does not depend upon this promise. The ancient blood of the Tartans, the blood of a nomadic, restless people destined to wander the earth forever, will always run through Kazamira's veins. And yet the ancient blood of *my* people runs just as powerfully through mine, tying me to my homeland just as surely as hers has driven her from it.

15 August

Without her, a terrible void has opened up, and I have decided to fill it the only way that I know how: on the battlefield, where neither the past nor the future exist, only each passing second of the present. I knew immediately what role I must play—I volunteered for the medical corps and have been assigned to the Eighty-eighth Infantry of the Twenty-first Division of the Eighth Army. I do not know how well the conditions of my existence will lend themselves to war, if at all, but I will soon find out. In two days, we leave for the Western Front.

18 August

In every town, the people cheer and throw flowers as we march past. Everyone says that the war will be over by Christmas—I wonder if they will still be throwing flowers by then.

Initially, I thought it would be difficult to serve without rank or title. I had been groomed my entire life for the officer corps, and now I would be taking orders from a fresh-faced lieutenant not yet born while I was commanding regiments. But the transition proved easier than I had expected. I feel no desire to socialize with the officers, and have even found some degree of pleasure in the role of an ordinary soldier who gives no orders, who makes no decisions, who is not even required to think from one moment to the next.

It is altogether more strange to once again be in such intimate contact with mortal men of any rank or station. When my comrades gather at mealtimes or go out for a night of carousing, I sometimes forget myself and think to join in. But always the shadow of what I am rises up as surely as any wall made of concrete or stone.

20 August

Yesterday, I spoke with a soldier who had been at Tannenberg. He described how the Eighth Army had forced a Russian cavalry brigade into a lake to drown, and the screams of the soldiers had been so terrible that the officers had ordered machine guns turned on them to shorten their agony. The men and horses were packed so tightly in the water that they had remained upright even after they were dead. As the soldier told me this story, his face took on that familiar haunted look of one who has already foreseen his own doom. He could not have been more than twenty years old.

[undated]

Our first engagement with enemy forces outside Tintage. Now these young men, so full of bravado, have seen what war really is, which up to now they have only known from books.

28 August

Today we engaged in a fierce battle made more difficult by a hill that prevented our advancement. Only once the fighting subsided did our location become clear to me: Sedan. I was overcome with the dreamlike sensation that time had somehow turned back upon itself, that I was once again a mortal man leading my squadron up that cursed hill. When we entered the village, this impression was reinforced by the scene that lay before me: the same burning houses, same choking black smoke, same streets littered with the dead and dying. Same terrible cries of suffering. In every way, the past had come back as the present, as if not only I had remained unchanged through the years, but the world and all of its terrible suffering, as well.

[undated]

In Raucourt, a group of soldiers got drunk after looting a wine cellar and began fighting among themselves. Several officers went to quell the commotion and found the body of a soldier with his head smashed in. They knew another German soldier was responsible, because the blood-splattered rifle was still lying next to the body.

Lieutenant Kennor then went out of the house and accused the townspeople of having murdered a Prussian soldier. Under Colonel Pruder's orders, all of the inhabitants of the nearby houses were arrested. Pruder shouted, 'Kill this whole crowd immediately even though the innocent will suffer with the guilty!'

Whether he intended for the order to be carried out or was simply trying to flush out the actual killer, no one had the chance to find out. As soon as the words were spoken, the soldiers opened fire on the men and women and killed them all on the spot.

The next day was a Sunday, and the chaplain's sermon was based on the following passage: Love thy neighbor as thyself.

19 September

The war creates conditions that require me to feed every day, sometimes more than once. The prolonged exposure to sunlight taxes me greatly, and although I can tolerate proximity to fire much better than I used to, the bonfires that result from the looting and razing are a constant concern. In addition, achieving any kind of deep, isolated rest is out of the question. Constant feeding is the only way to counteract these conditions. The dead and dying, of course, are never in short supply.

However, the memory of Aslan serves as an ever-present reminder: first, if I am caught in even the most minor shelling or conflagration, I know that I will perish without hope of rescue or regeneration. Second, no matter how much the war demands of me or how plentiful the dead, I must remain as disciplined as possible in order to avoid developing the same insatiable bloodlust that brought Aslan to his ruin.

[undated]

Our fourth day in the trenches. Men half-starved, disheartened. Raining in torrents, trenches half-filled with water. In these hellish mazes, a soldier has two options: leave the trenches and get shot or stay put and drown to death anyway.

March 1915

The meadows are just beginning to turn green.

[undated]

The trenches are so shallow that it is impossible to walk upright. We are forced to crawl along the rotting bodies, which are so numerous that we can no longer bury them all, and must throw them in front of the trench line like sandbags. The cries of the dead seem to rise from the bowels of hell itself, until one realizes that they come from soldiers who have been buried alive right where they stood in their shelters. Impossible to describe the men's suffering.

It has occurred to me many times how easily I could desert or arrange my own death; the fact that I have not done so has forced me to consider a more sinister, and more selfish, motivation for joining this madness than duty alone. Did I enter the war with the secret hope that I would be killed? That men and machines could accomplish what neither my courage nor my will has thus permitted? And yet despite this vague and passive desire for death, some essential part of me still wishes to live—always to live on, in spite of all else, rather than face one's own extinction!

[undated]

In transport to the Eastern Front. Upon crossing into Russia, I thought of Kazamira, but forced her image from my mind. I could not otherwise continue to go on.

April

Yesterday Lieutenant Daucher took a bullet in the abdomen. Before the war, he had been a student at a music seminary in Leipzig. When we first crossed into France, he had come upon an upright piano in a farm house, and played Chopin's Nocturnes so beautifully that even the enlisted men had stopped their looting long enough to listen. He was suffering immensely, and as I tended his wounds, we both knew that he could not be saved. Teeth clenched in agony, he begged me to kill him quickly, and suddenly a voice from the past whispered that fateful question into my ear: *Do you still want to live?*

I looked at this gifted, gentle boy dying far from home on a filthy, blood-covered field, and for the first time since the war began, I desperately wanted to offer the choice. The words were on my lips, but as I bent toward him, I felt the warmth of his skin and smelled the powerfully *human* scent of his sweat and fear and *life*. I knew then that I could only end the suffering of his body. I could not transfer it to his soul.

24 May

A curious situation has developed. Ever since reaching the Eastern Front, the men have been infested with lice and fleas. No amount of powder eliminates the problem, and even the highest-ranking officers constantly scratch and squirm at the mercy of these pests. I, on the other hand, have remained entirely free of infestation, and there isn't a man in the regiment who hasn't bribed or badgered me for my secret.

[undated]

Today I came upon a soldier who had lain down next to his dead comrades and would not move even once the shelling started. Many men go mad in the trenches, singing and laughing among the corpses or going stone deaf and sitting on the ground, speaking to no one and staring ahead in stupid oblivion.

30 September

Three hundred men remain out of a thousand.

8 October

Our unit has been sent replacements of boys scarcely eighteen years old and men over forty with gray in their hair. There are even cripples among them, men who lost an arm or a leg and got sent back to the front just the same. Those too disfigured to fight are put to work burying the dead. One poor soul missing both a leg and an eye told me that at Vimy Ridge, they had buried four thousand corpses a day.

February 1916

At Verdun, warfare of a magnitude beyond imagination— every conceivable engine of war gathered in one place. An individual man, or unit, even an entire regiment or division, mean nothing at all in the face of such force. To retreat was just as dangerous as to advance—the only choice was to be swept forward in the faceless, terrible new warfare of machines.

[undated]

Our regiment has been broken apart and mixed with other regiments. The war is lost; now it is only a matter of how many more deaths are required to justify defeat.

September 1917

I have been transferred to the auxiliary corps and assigned to Berlin, which now functions as the medical center for all military operations.

[undated]

It appears that the civilian population has been suffering nearly as much as the soldiers. There is a severe coal shortage, and tuberculosis has spread with alarming speed; the people survive on little more than dandelion soup and turnips. Rationing has become so bad that it is now considered a criminal offense to bake a cake.

18 November

At the hospital where I've been assigned, wounded men routinely refuse operations in order to avoid being sent back to the front. Here, the worst horrors of war reveal themselves on every bed and stretcher: boys barely out of puberty shot through the groin; men without limbs and stomachs, faces turned to lumpy mounds of misshapen flesh; gas victims swelling up so grotesquely that they no longer resemble the human beings trapped inside their misshapen forms…

01 December

An extraordinary occurrence today—I was making my rounds at the hospital when I came across the record of a young officer who bore that name once more valuable to me than my own life. With trembling hands, I drew the curtain from around his bed and gazed at features so like my own that I had to steady myself to prevent being overtaken by emotions that I cannot find the words to describe.

If he recognized anything familiar in my countenance, he did not show it, though as an officer he naturally took little notice of a common orderly. Once I had gathered my wits, I said, "Sir, I know your family name. Tell me, did any of your kinsmen fight at Sedan in eighteen seventy?"

He replied, "Indeed! In fact, one of my great uncles was among the many who gave their lives for our nation's triumph that day." He then asked, "Did you also have kinsmen at Sedan?"

A most natural question, yet quite extraordinary for me to answer. I finally replied, "Yes… I, too, had kinsmen at Sedan."

I longed to ask of people long dead and places long changed, but all I could do was commit to memory everything about this young man who in an instant had brought back to flesh and blood that life now so lost to me.

04 December

I take every opportunity to attend to my kinsman. I cannot explain why, but I feel a strange comfort in simply looking at him and being near his side.

09 December

Today I stopped by his bed and he was gone. I learned from the desk nurse that he had been discharged early this morning. I began pressing her for information about his unit when I was struck by the inexplicable, yet certain, belief that I had seen my bloodline for the last time. I made no further inquiries and will probably never know if fate grants him the increasingly rare good fortune of surviving this war.

21 January, 1918

Yesterday in Alexanderplatz, I happened upon a building called the Nachlass Bureau. Curious, I stepped inside and discovered a jumble of boxes containing an extraordinary array of items: crushed and bloodstained cigarette cases, a lock of hair tied with a dirty ribbon, scraps of photos and letters, monogrammed handkerchiefs—even a broken set of dentures. I inquired as to the purpose of cataloguing such items, and learned that the objects were retrieved from battlefields and saved in case anyone should ever wish to find them. The clerk then showed me the storeroom, where row after row of boxes were stacked as far as the eye could see, every one of them filled with the once-treasured refuse of the dead.

07 February

Today I passed a banquet hall filled with a group of high staff members dining on champagne and pheasant. Two of them left the feast and were walking just ahead of me when I overheard one say to the other, "If we can convince command that the soldiers no longer need butter with their bread, next time we'll have three birds apiece instead of two." His comrade replied, "If the casualties are as bad as last month, those that are left can have their butter and we'll *still* end up with three birds apiece!'

They found this little joke very amusing, and without hesitation, I followed them down a side street and killed them both right where they stood.

This marks the first time that I have killed men of such importance in such a reckless manner. It also marks the first time that I have killed out of hatred and revenge. I confess that I have felt not one moment of guilt or regret.

10 November

The Kaiser has abdicated. Riots breaking out everywhere, mobs smashing things to bits. High-ranking officers are being thrown into the Spree, and many more have chosen suicide rather than face defeat. To add to the misery, the country is in the grip of an influenza epidemic. The papers report that three hundred people die each day in Berlin alone. The food shortage grows more and more severe, and it is not uncommon to come across a group of people fighting over the corpse of a horse, which they cut to pieces so thoroughly that almost nothing of the poor beast remains.

30 November

The soldiers return home with haggard faces, each and every one wasted from hunger and deprivation, reduced to almost nothing from endless days of terror and courage and death.

January 1919

The city has fallen into absolute chaos. Rioting and looting day and night, senseless shootings everywhere…ordinary people have taken to walking around with Mausers and machine guns, firing from rooftops at anything that moves.

March

A few days ago, street fighting broke out between revolutionary groups. I was caught in a crowd of people when the riflemen on top of the Brandenburg Gate started spraying bullets to control the mobs. Everyone around me went down, so I quickly dropped among the dead and wounded. A group of Freikorps members began throwing the bodies into the canals, which these days are permanently clogged with corpses. I found myself grabbed about the feet and hands and unceremoniously tossed into the putrid water.

I floated for quite a ways before reaching a spot desolate enough to swim ashore without attracting notice. While wringing out my clothes, I noticed that the back of my shirt was riddled with holes. Upon examining myself, I felt five hard, round fragments just under the skin's surface on my stomach. It seems that after lodging in my back, the bullets kept traveling through my body inch by inch, pushing their gore-covered way to the surface like deep-sea creatures struggling toward the light.

Eventually, my body expelled them entirely, and they now sit in a saucer on my dresser like some sort of macabre holiday souvenir.

21 July

Today I came upon a retired general rummaging in the streets for scraps of food. In broad daylight, scavengers take away anything that might fetch a price on the black market—door handles, mailboxes, garden rails, roof tiles—anything that can be torn down and carried away.

May 1920

The city has descended into a perpetual state of madness and despair. Crime and prostitution are the only means left for survival. Last night, I was feeding near Schutzenstrasse when I was interrupted by a tall, lean-faced fellow in a tattered cavalry coat. At first, I was alarmed, but his nonchalant, almost cordial manner reassured me that he had no intention of alerting the police. In fact, I soon realized that he was in the alley for the same reason that I was. He gave me a rather charming smile made grotesque by the circumstances, and said, "Don't mind me, friend, there's enough to go around. What's your racket?"

In response to my baffled silence, he reached into the pockets of his great coat and produced two amber-colored jars packed tight with pieces of meat. "Just label them goat's meat or preserved pork and they go for a fortune on the black market."

13 November

Vigilante groups roam the streets and commit violence at will, clubbing and beating anyone accused of unpatriotic activity. It is easier these days to kill a man than to buy a loaf of bread. Surrounded by nothing but death and depravity, I struggle more and more each day to remember what worth a human life is supposed to have.

19 August, 1921

Currency has become all but useless. Today I saw an old woman attempting to buy a potato with a wheelbarrow full of mark notes. A man who spent his whole life scrimping and saving now finds his one hundred thousand marks worth less than a few cents. It is not uncommon to hear of desperate people withdrawing their entire savings for one last tram ride across town or for one stamp to place on a letter to a loved one before committing suicide. I am beginning to think that instead of lurking in the shadows like a fiend, I would do better to take out an ad in the paper advertising my services: a quick and painless death compared to hanging or throwing oneself into the Spree; cheaper than morphine or the price of a pistol; and much safer than taking a chance with the street thugs, who might break a leg or crack open a head without properly finishing the job!

December

This evening I went to feed by the abandoned glassworks where the most desperate of the prostitutes gather. I made my attack quickly, from behind, and only when I turned the body over did I realize that she was a girl of no more than thirteen years of age. She was still wearing her school uniform, with a return bus ticket stuffed in the front shirt pocket.

I must leave Berlin before I become lost in the madness, before I am pulled down into an abyss in which violence and depravity and death have become so mundane, so ordinary that one can scarcely remember a time when law and order existed, when hopeful young girls and confident young men dreamed of a bright and sure future…can such a future exist, with over a million of those boys now rotting on already forgotten battlefields, and the cheeks of those same girls now sunken with sickness and starvation?

I do not know the answer to such questions, but of one thing I am certain: if I wish to retain any part of the humanity I once knew, I must renounce my homeland. I must escape from the madness of a people being tossed and torn in the battering winds of a dark and foreboding storm—for experience tells me that far from being over, this particular storm has only just begun.

[undated]

I have smuggled aboard a ship bound for South America. Surviving on rats in the cargo bay. Very weak, but no desire to feed upon the crew. A strange contentment burrowed here among the vermin. No need to think about streets full of the starving and the broken. No soldiers with haunted faces and ruined bodies, no black market full of the fiendish profiteers of human tragedy; no morphine and cocaine addicts with raving, desperate eyes; no street gangs, revolutionaries, or uprisings. No young girls barely out of childhood selling themselves for the price of a bus ticket. No suffering. No death. Except for the rats, who seem to understand and even accept it.

[undated]

Have set down in Brazil. I plan to travel northwards toward the United States, where perhaps I shall find Kazamira—though I fear that there is very little left to recognize of the man she once knew.

[undated]

In Colombia.

[undated]

Adrift without thought or purpose, like a stone moving slowly along the bottom of a river—attached to nothing, ignorant of where it has been, not caring where it is headed.

[undated]

After such a long time of wandering, here is what happened: while trekking through the mountains of the high country of

Guatemala, I found myself on a narrow footpath leading to a nearby Indian village. The day had been hot and humid, followed by a rapid cooling at dusk, and a thick, dense mountain fog was now making its way into the lowlands.

I was moving cautiously along the path when I felt a sensation that I had only felt once before, but had never forgotten: that disorienting light-headedness followed by the knife cut of clarity—the same sensation that had overtaken me when I first encountered Kazamira. I felt a rush of joy that we had found each other, and her name was on my lips before I froze—it was not possible that I had stumbled upon Kazamira in the middle of the night on a treacherous mountain road in the wilds of Guatemala. Such things only occur in children's fairy tales, and this was no fairy tale. But then who—or what—was waiting for me down that path?

I peered ahead as far as I could, but the fog had grown too thick to see more than a few feet in front of me, and the moonlight and mist were playing tricks with my eyes. Filled with apprehension and uncertain how to proceed, I put my hands out in front of me like a child feeling his way through the dark. Just then another's hand reached through the mist and found my own. Our fingertips touched for only an instant before the rest of him emerged from the fog, and this time I knew what I had found. I was surprised when he spoke in my own language. "My name is Gideon," he said, and for the first time in many years, I spoke the name now almost forgotten. "My name," I told him, "is Verland."

CHAPTER 12

The spell the diary had cast over Elle lasted until the phone call from Sadie. Elle knew that with a story as big as Eliot Kingman, there would be a lot of pressure coming her way, and Sadie wasted no time getting started.

"I don't have to tell you that this book is worth some serious money. We're looking at having it packaged and on the shelves in nine months, *max*."

"I really need another meeting with Kingman. A big part of the story involves his claim that he didn't kill Klee, so his version of what happened is really critical. But so far, he hasn't given me anything. He hardly even talked about the murder."

"Well, what did he talk about?" Sadie wasn't the kind of person you talked to about universal totems.

"Esoteric stuff, mostly. Death, mortality. That sort of thing."

"We can't use that kind of crap! Our readers want *details*. They want a good *story*. Kingman's made millions in the biz; he should know that."

"I don't think he actually cares about the book one way or the other. I'm not sure, but there's something else going on with this thing—"

"And I don't care one way or the other what *he* cares about! *I* care about *this book*." Sadie sighed. "I'll try to set up another meeting, but I'll straight up admit it—he may be a convicted murderer, but he's still Eliot Kingman. He's got a team of lawyers that make our legal department look like first-year law students. He's directing this show as surely as one of his block-busters. We're *all* just hired hands as far as he's concerned."

"What about his wife?" Elle couldn't shake the feeling that there was more going on there than the usual Hollywood buy-a-wife routine.

"I don't know about that, but I can guarantee one thing—no one's talking without Kingman's say so. Listen, this guy is a notorious control freak. He's got an appeal in right now, and I'm guessing no one in his camp believes he'll be in prison for-ever; so, naturally, everyone wants to stay on his side. I wouldn't be surprised if he does get his conviction overturned, which is another reason why we've got to get this book out *now, now, now.*"

"I know. That's also why it's important to include his ver-sion of what happened."

"I'll try putting some pressure on his people to get you another visit. In the meantime, you're on a strict timeline with this one."

That should have inspired Elle to put in a few uninter-rupted hours at the computer, but thinking about Kingman always lead to thinking about Verland, and that was something she'd been doing far too much of lately. Gary had left a message saying he had the day off, and suddenly her apartment felt a little too claustrophobic. Gary's house, on the other hand, was a hidden gem from L.A.'s golden era of 1920s architecture: part Mediterranean adobe, part clean-line modernity, the past and the present jumbled together in irreverent Southern California style. Tucked into a hillside in Los Feliz that had once been an olive grove, it had lush gardens and an unbeatable view of Griffith Park. Compared to the neighborhood standard, Gary's house was on the small side, but there was still no way his cop's salary could have covered even a quarter of the mortgage let alone the taxes and upkeep. He had never mentioned it, and she had never asked, but she knew it had to have come from his family. It wasn't hard to understand why Gary rarely had any of his cop friends over—their modest three-bedroom stuccos in the Valley meant years of overtime and missed vacations. Just one more way Gary's background kept him a little bit separate from most of the people in his life.

"Where's Bosie?"

Gary had a yellow Lab who usually bowled her over as soon as she walked through the door. Not long after they'd met, Gary's explanation of why he'd named his dog after Oscar Wilde's lover had convinced her that in addition to having good taste in reading material, he might prove interesting in bed.

"Bosie can run around checking out rear ends in a way his namesake never could. That seems like historical justice to me. In fact, maybe Bosie is a reincarnation of the original."

"Well, then you've castrated Lord Bosie, Gare."

"Whoa! I didn't think of that. Well, it doesn't interfere with the rear sniffing, and he doesn't seem to mind the loss."

Gary beckoned her into the kitchen, where it looked like he was actually attempting to make lunch. "Come on in. Lupita has Bosie out back."

Lupita was a retired nurse's aide and a source of endless energy who looked after Bosie and pretty much everything else in Gary's life. With his long and irregular work hours, Lupita was the only thing standing between him and complete domestic destruction. Her favorite subject was when Elle and Gary were going to get married, which she returned to as soon as she brought Bosie back inside.

"Elle! How are you? You know, Gary just broke up with one of his day-spa ladies."

That was Lupita's term for the high-maintenance women who spent more in a day at the salon than she had earned in a week changing bed pans and giving sponge baths.

"So that means he's available. How about you? Are you available right now?"

"Well, I'm not dating, if that's what you mean, but available…I'm not so sure about that."

"She sure hasn't been available to me lately," Gary chimed in. "I can't even get her to return my calls."

"Oh, come on now, you are both two crazy people," Lupita said, clucking her tongue in disapproval. "One of you living all by himself in this beautiful house and the other one living right across town in a little apartment with nobody but some cats! So why not get married and live here *together*? Doesn't make sense to me, no sense at all."

"I'm not all by myself. I have you and Bosie."

"You may forget it sometimes, mister, but Bosie is a dog, not a person. As for me, I hate to tell you, but I'm not always gonna be around to take care of you."

"Lupita, don't leave me. I swear there won't be any other women."

"Ha! Always the same with you men. In fact, I'm leaving you right now. My son's new wife is coming for dinner, and I have not one thing ready. So you two go ahead and do whatever it is that young people do when they're alone together. It's been too long for me to remember."

She bustled out the door, and Bosie wagged over to honor his namesake. Gary flashed her one of those thousand-watt smiles that could disarm day-spa ladies and reluctant witnesses alike.

"So what do you say? Want to get married?"

"Sure. We can make it to Vegas in eight hours, at least if you do the driving."

"I always figured you'd want a white wedding. The rebel-outcast types always do in the end."

"Not this rebel-outcast type."

"Seriously, Elle, don't you ever think about getting married?"

"Nope. Wedlock is a padlock, as a wise woman once said. Why, are you getting tired of the bachelor life?" When Elle had imagined Gary getting married again, she hadn't thought it would be this soon.

"I don't know. You start thinking about things differently when you get older, you know? When you're young, all you want to do is run around, have some adventures. Then you get more serious about things—get a job you care about, maybe prove yourself a bit. Prove you're good at something that matters. Then the years roll by and before you even realize it those things don't seem so important anymore. And in the end what you really want is someone to share it all with."

He stood and paced around the room. "I mean, don't you get tired of being alone all the time? Of your life being nothing but work, hanging out with some friends now and then, checking in with the family once a year at Christmas…" He sat down again, agitated—a rare thing for him. "Think about how it could be, the two of us living here."

"You're serious, aren't you?" Elle had not seen this one coming; she felt little pulses of alarm lighting up all over the place.

"Think about it. Without having to worry about money all the time, you could write whatever you wanted for a change. I know you write better books than most of the assembly-line crap that Greene Line puts out, but still. No way should you just do crime stuff for the rest of your life."

Like most writers, Elle had a secret nest of unwritten novels stored away for future use, and sometimes when she was feeling ambitious, she talked to Gary about moving beyond Greene Line. But unwritten novels didn't pay the rent. She had gotten into crime writing in order to make a living, and somewhere along the line, it had become a life.

"I know, Gare. It's just that writing for Greene Line is easy, so I guess it's easy to stay with it."

"But that's what I'm talking about," Gary said, resuming his pacing. "Aren't you tired of always just doing what's easy? Of just letting one easy year after another go by? That's what I spent the whole first part of my life doing, and I know how fast it can wear out. When I became a cop, my life had purpose for the first time in a long time. Next I made detective, and that was even better. But I've been at this for a while now, Elle. I can feel it starting to slide. I can feel it become sort of like going through the motions. It's like something should come next, something different."

He paused. She had never seen him look so earnest.

"You're thinking of quitting the force?"

Elle knew how much Gary loved his job, and she couldn't imagine him giving it up. But it was still a less alarming topic that the other direction he had been heading in.

"You know how the job can get to you. I don't want it to run me through like I've seen happen to so many other guys… totally burned out, used up."

"But what would you do if you left the police?"

"I don't know. Maybe become one of those smooth private investigators like in those movies you always watch. But whatever it is, I want to do it with you along for the ride. We're good together, Elle."

"Gary, I…" She could not think of one thing to say.

True to his usual charm, Gary eased her through the moment with a laugh.

"Hey, don't look so shaken up!" He turned his pockets inside out and stood flapping them at his sides. "I don't have a ring hidden in here ready to spring on you!"

"Good. I thought you were about ready to go down on one knee there for a minute."

Elle was grateful for the shift in tone. She would have to spend some time thinking about this latest turn of events—life was just one surprise after another these days.

"Come on," Gary said, good humor restored. "Let's go work some of this fat off of Bosie."

They hiked to the top of Griffith Park and stopped to rest at Dante's View; from here the city looked like a tiny kingdom of glass and steel surrounded by a moat of smog. Working up a sweat on the trails, Elle had felt her mind clear for the first time in days. But as she looked down on Los Angeles like some modern-day Zeus, her thoughts drifted back to those flashing red dots on Zor's computer screen—unsolved murders where the victims had been drained of blood...and one practically right on her own doorstep. Surrounded by Bosie, Gary, and the warm sun, Verland and his dark shadow world seemed as impossible as one of Kingman's blockbusters. And yet she realized that she had been scanning the skies for hawks all afternoon.

"You're a million miles away," Gary broke in. "Is it because of what we talked about earlier?"

"No. Well, yes. Sort of. I'll admit you totally caught me off guard, Gare. I knew you'd been restless lately, but...not *that* restless! But, no, it's more than that. This Kingman story...it just doesn't feel right. I can't explain it, but...there are strange things going on."

"Don't do the story if it doesn't feel right. No book is worth going against your gut feeling. If one thing for sure came out of the trial, it's that Kingman is one disturbed piece of work. Promise me you'll drop the story if it gets too weird."

"Oh, I don't feel threatened or anything like that. It's just that..."

Just that what? That there's this nineteenth-century vampire running around Hollywood, and Kingman has his diary, and for some reason, he wants me to read it...

"It's just that I'm not totally sure what Kingman is up to. I'm not going to tell Sadie, but I don't think he ever intended to cooperate on the book."

"Then why contact Greene Line in the first place?"

"I'm not sure." Vampire or no, Elle really hadn't come up with an answer to that one yet.

"Well, if you want my guess, it's got something to do with the appeals his lawyers have going on. Kingman may be loony, but he's nobody's fool, and I think he learned his lesson the hard way. He'll play it smarter next time around, and he'll use anyone or anything to do it."

"You're probably right." Gary's theory made sense, but then again, he wasn't factoring Verland into the picture.

"I don't want you mixed up in anything like that, Elle. I'm serious. Trust me, these kinds of people will plow down anything in their way to get what they want."

A light breeze brought his musky-sweat smell toward her, and she felt an unexpected jolt of desire. Without even checking to make sure they were alone, she guided his hands down the front of her shorts, and he slid his fingers inside her. Gary closed his eyes, and with his head thrown back and his hair gilded with sunlight, he looked like a sun god straight out of some ancient myth. What would it be like to wake up next to that for the rest of her life? Right now, it seemed like a pretty marvelous prospect. He started to withdraw his hand, but she held it in place, moving against him until she climaxed right there among the sage with Bosie dozing at their feet.

"Jesus. I'm going to ask you to marry me every day if that's the result. I need you right here, Elle. I'm serious. I'm in agony."

"I can see that," she teased. "But I'm not that bold yet."

"Okay, but this is going to be the fastest descent ever recorded in Griffith Park history."

They made love until the soft shadows of late afternoon gave way to evening. The night jasmine opened, and the air was sweet and cool; Elle was beginning to think that maybe she and Gary should move in together for a while, see how it went. She was just about to bring it up when Gary called her over to the front window. He pointed to a brown sedan parked down the street.

"That car has been out front for two hours now. I don't want to do the paranoid cop thing, but they've moved twice so far, always in range of the house."

"Maybe it's someone's guest or something." Through the years, Elle had gotten used to the paranoid cop thing.

"Sitting in the car in eighty-five-degree heat? I don't think so. Is Kingman having you followed?"

"Why would he have me followed?"

"I don't know. But I've got the license plate number, and you can bet I'm going to run it. If Kingman's following you, he's going to have some serious interference to deal with."

"Calm down, Gare. I'm sure there's some explanation."

What she did not need right now was Gary jumping into the mix with the full weight of the LAPD behind him. Before he could answer, Elle's phone rang. It was Sadie, who had made good on her promise to get her another interview with Kingman. It looked like she would be heading back to Delano tomorrow afternoon, and this time, she intended to get some answers.

CHAPTER 13

With Gary on high alert over the sedan, Elle had decided not to tell him that she was going to see Kingman again. When she woke up the next day, he'd already left a message to call him back, which meant he'd run the plates before she'd even gotten out of bed.

"It's Kingman all right. The plates are registered to his private security team, which he kept on the payroll even after his conviction. Lots of ex-military, a couple of retired feds. Some real heavyweights. I can pull a few in on something and find out why the hell they're following you."

"No, not yet. Let me talk to Sadie first. She might know something about it that she just forgot to mention." Elle absolutely did not want Gary getting involved. Not yet, anyway.

"Okay. But I'm keeping my eye on this thing, and that's nonnegotiable."

Elle made the long drive to Delano alone this time, and she used the empty miles to think. So much had been happening with the Kingman story, and now Gary had thrown a hand-grenade into things with the idea of marriage. Elle's instincts had always been against getting too serious with someone as good-looking as Gary. She considered herself attractive, sure, but Gary was in a different league altogether; that meant trying to either even things up a little or resigning herself to the discrepancy. Besides, living with someone day after day was a big leap forward from a beer-and-pizza tryst every now and then. But she had to admit that the biggest obstacle to moving in with Gary had nothing to do with him—it had to do with how much it would change her own life, and Elle had learned a long time ago to be afraid of change.

Right now, though, Gary would have to wait until she figured things out with Kingman. Why in the world was he following her? It had to have something to do with Verland… *Verland*—Elle realized that he had slipped into her thoughts on a first-name basis, like Sam or Sadie or any other real-life person. *And do you actually believe in an immortal being that feeds on human blood?* She could believe in Verland as long as he stayed in the background, elusive and insubstantial as the shadows he preferred; but if she tried to draw him into the light, he vanished like a dream that she could no longer remember the moment she awoke from sleep.

Kingman came into the interview room with the same assumption of authority as before, but this time Elle wasn't giving him complete control. One thing Gary could be sure of was that she *would* walk away from this story, no matter how much Sam and Sadie and the rest of her career might depend on it.

"You have some questions for me, no doubt."

"You bet I do. For one thing, I'd like to know why you're having your security team follow me."

Kingman held out his hands like a preacher calming his flock. "One thing at a time. I promise you'll have your answers, but a good story must proceed in its natural order."

"This isn't one of your stories, Kingman."

"Of course it's a story. Everything's a story, after all. You've read some of the book by now?"

"You know I have. What does the book have to do with anything? What is it even supposed to be anyway?"

"It's exactly what it appears to be—a diary. A very old, very unique one, but a diary nonetheless; and written for the same reason thousands of other diaries have been written throughout thousands of years."

"Which is?"

"To make a record of one's life; of one's self. Remember our last conversation? The need to tell stories—perhaps the most powerful need of all is to tell one's *own* story. And what else is a diary except telling one's own story?"

"Only this is a vampire's diary."

"Do you believe it?"

"Of course I don't believe it." Elle forced herself to tamp down her anger and play along. Confrontation wasn't going to get her anywhere with a man like Kingman.

"When Zor first told me he was tracking a vampire—you've met Zor, haven't you?—I didn't believe it, either. I'd been researching vampires for my film, and I'd already put in a lot of money and effort and hadn't turned up anything even remotely credible. But I didn't have anything to lose, and ultimately, Zor and his silly voodoo shop brought me the real thing."

"And so you actually met a vampire?" Elle was more convinced than ever that she'd stumbled headlong into a lunatic's fantasy, and yet it was disconcerting how sane, how reasonable Kingman seemed. And yet perfectly convinced he'd found a vampire.

"Oh, yes. Numerous times, in fact. Once my people used Zor's information to pinpoint his location, all I had to do was take it very slow and establish contact. And do you know why he kept meeting with me?"

"Why?"

"For the same reason you do. Verland has a story to tell. The need to tell one's story, Ms. Bramasol—now *that's* totem."

"So he wanted you to do what—make a movie about his life?"

Kingman laughed. "Verland is more a connoisseur of literature than film. But he has an interest in how vampires are represented in popular culture going all the way back to John Polidori, if you remember, so yes, he had an interest in my work."

"And he decided to tell you his life story?"

"No. But I took every chance I got to talk about the nature of telling stories, creating myths. I talked a lot about the vampire legend, how it has changed through the years. What it means to people. From these conversations, I realized that he had been keeping some kind of a record of his own story—and that he just might want it told, which is where I could come in."

"But you ended up in Delano instead."

Kingman shrugged as if they were discussing a college prank gone wrong instead of first degree murder. "The problem was that while I was more than happy to tell Verland's story, I also wanted something much more."

Elle had one of those rare moments when a half-formed idea springs Athena-like into a fully formed conviction. "You wanted him to turn you into a vampire."

Kingman threw his arms above his head and looked at the ceiling in mock relief. "And there you finally have it!"

Elle said it again just to make sure that she hadn't gone insane along with him. "You wanted to become a vampire."

"Of course I did. Let's forget about all the moralizing bullshit for a second and tell me— who wouldn't? Did you know that Henry Ford believed in reincarnation? And do you know why?"

"No."

"Because he was honest. He once told an interviewer that most religions offered him nothing, because the greatest accomplishments in the world don't mean one thing if we can't take anything with us. Only after he discovered reincarnation did he come to believe that we *can* take it with us; he thought genius, for instance, wasn't some kind of a special gift, but the built up experiences of many lives. Once he figured that out, he said felt at ease for the first time in his life."

"But you don't believe in reincarnation."

"No. I've tried every belief system out there, but none of them work. None of them go back together again once you take them apart and look at the thing. But like Ford and every other thinking person who's ever lived, I wanted answers."

"Well, vampires supposedly don't die, so they can't actually provide any answers about the afterlife per se."

"That's the point. If no one can find out what happens after death, then there's only one other way to win the game—not die in the first place. Immortality!"

"But that only works as long as there are still some mortals around to feed on."

"I never said I was interested in immortality for the entire human race. That wouldn't be desirable even if it were possible."

"But it's desirable for yourself, of course."

Kingman smiled as if he were talking to a silly child. "Do you know how people always say, 'Being a parent is the greatest thing I've ever done?' Well, I have kids of my own, and for a long time, that kind of talk irritated me—how could something that billions of idiots all across the planet do every day be the greatest thing someone has ever done? But then I realized it's true. Any idiot *can* be a parent, and it probably *is* the greatest thing most people ever do. But only one in a million people can make films like I can, or cure diseases, or write a symphony."

"So not everyone deserves to be immortal."

"Of course not, no more than everyone deserves to earn a billion dollars or discover the radiation theory of black holes. Do you remember the place in Verland's diary where he reads Stoker's *Dracula* and speculates about whether or not vampires could live openly among mortals? Well, I came to believe that there was a way. I envisioned a group dedicated to things like science, the arts, technology—all of the best minds, the greatest talents brought together for the rest of eternity. Immortal talent and intellect combined with the powers that Verland describes—the result would be something unprecedented in all of human history."

"And how would this select group feed?"

"That's where the politically incorrect part comes in. You see, for thousands of years, people accepted the natural order of things: the great at one end of the spectrum, the base at the other, like a pyramid. And the base were put on the bottom in order to serve the great. That's the natural order of things, and only modern man with his illusions of equality has tried to pretend it isn't so. But look around—centuries after Jesus Christ, the gap between the great and the base is just as wide as it's always been. The meek have never inherited anything, and never will."

Elle was suddenly very glad that Kingman woke up every day behind bars. "So a class of slaves would be bred to feed the vampire elite?"

"Nothing as crude as that. Look at the way people worship celebrity. Look at how they prostrate themselves at the feet of the rich and famous—these days, even a no-talent idiot on some third-rate reality TV show can be headline news. Do you think we'd have any problem selling people on the idea of spending their lives among creatures more magnificent than their wildest imaginings, and then, before they could grow old and useless, sacrificing themselves to a cause so glorious that any other existence would seem meaningless? We'd get so many people lining up that we'd have to turn them away."

"And this vampire community was supposed to start with you and Verland?" It's no wonder Kingman's lawyers hadn't put him on the stand.

"At first, I was only after my own immortality. But I wasn't willing to skulk around on the margins of society like Verland, and that's when it came to me—why would I have to? Modern audiences have been obsessed with vampires for a long time, and it would take *nothing* for them to embrace the idea of an elite group of immortals living among them."

"And *off* them."

"Only on the *willing*. The rest of society would benefit beyond measure. Just imagine the things that could be accomplished!"

"But Verland wouldn't go along with it."

"We only ever talked theoretically, as if it was just an idea for a movie. But even then I couldn't get him to see the greatness of the plan, the potential."

"Unless there's something you haven't told me, he obviously wouldn't even turn *you* into a vampire."

"Things went wrong, I'll admit it. I made mistakes. But like I've told you, I'm a very persistent man."

"And you're also in prison."

Kingman's face darkened. "When faced with the possibility of eternal life, it's easy to forget that you're still living in the real world. I didn't have time for petty bullshit like police and lawyers, and that was a mistake. A big one. But I'll say one thing—getting convicted brought me back down to earth in a hurry. I sure as hell don't plan on staying in here forever, and I'm not the kind of man who makes the same mistake twice."

"Was David Klee's murder another one of those mistakes?"

"Klee's death was a mistake, yes, and so was my attitude toward both the investigation and the trial."

Elle noticed how he avoided the word 'murder.'

"And it cost me more than the nuisance of ending up here. It cost me Verland."

"Why?"

"For one thing, he disappeared. He was probably worried about exposure—and justifiably so, in this media-vulture world of ours—which is why I had to make sure that his existence stayed completely secret, no matter what it cost me."

"But no one would have believed in a vampire." Zor had been bad enough; Elle couldn't imagine what would have happened had vampires been brought into the picture.

"That wasn't the point. I couldn't take the risk of even the *idea* of a vampire causing the kind of media feeding frenzy that would drive him underground for good. I didn't want the press nosing around in *any* of it."

Not to mention that Kingman needed to keep the key to the vampire kingdom all to himself, at least until his own entry had been assured.

"So what happened with Klee?"

Kingman frowned. He clearly didn't like this subject, probably because it was one of the few times in his life he had miscalculated to such catastrophic effect. And as Kingman himself said, men like him don't like making mistakes.

"None of that matters anymore. The only thing that matters is reestablishing contact with Verland. That is *the only thing*."

"Is that where I come in? I'm guessing by now that I'm not actually here to write a book about you."

Kingman laughed, smoothing the rough edges back to their usual polish. "No, you're not. But you can see the need for the pretext. Couldn't exactly start off with the vampire bit, could I?"

"No, I guess not. But that still doesn't answer my question."

Kingman leaned forward, his face inches from hers. She almost couldn't suppress the urge to draw back, but she forced herself to stay still.

"I need you for two reasons. First, I believe that Verland still wants someone to tell his story; it's just obviously not going to be me. Which leads me to reason number two—he no longer trusts me enough to make contact, not even to get the diary back."

Elle didn't blame him. "I'm surprised he gave it to you in the first place."

"He didn't give it to me. I stole it."

"You *stole* it?" Elle had to admit, the guy had an impressive amount of moxie to steal from the undead.

"It wasn't easy, believe me. But I have some very skilled men on my payroll. When it became obvious that Verland wasn't exactly sold on my plan, I needed a bargaining chip. Some kind of leverage. I had to know he wouldn't just disappear one day and head for some god-forsaken corner of the world, never to be found again. Stealing the diary was a big risk, but I thought the time had come to force his hand."

Elle marveled at the kind of guy who thought that he could force a vampire's anything.

"And you're counting on the fact that he wants the book back."

"Oh, I know he wants it back; there's no doubt about that. After all, it's the only record he has of everything that's happened to him. In the end, we leave nothing behind but our stories, and the hope that others will tell them. That's pretty powerful stuff, even for a vampire. Maybe especially for a vampire."

"So why bring me into things?"

"Because I'm done trying to flush him out. He wants the diary back, but not bad enough to come and get it. Ending up in here wasn't part of the plan, but it's been good in one way at least. I've had no choice but to be patient, which comes in handy when dealing with a creature with no concerns about time. But I'm not a naturally patient man. The house has been on twenty-four-hour watch seven days a week, he knows the diary is there, and still not one trace of him."

Kingman smiled at her surprise.

"Oh, I know it seems like some deserted haunted house, but the truth is the entire property is loaded from top to bottom with surveillance, and I keep a full-time security team whose only mission is to wait for that vampire to turn up. I know he's still out there, watching. Waiting for the right time."

"So you want to draw him out? Is that why your men are following me—to draw him out and catch him?"

Kingman laughed, shaking his head. "Finding a vampire is one thing, but catching him is another thing entirely. Believe me, it's almost impossible to *catch* a vampire, at least if you want him alive. My men are following you for the same reason I keep track of everyone I work with—to find out what you're all about, what's important in your life. Gary Holland, age forty-three. Detective with the Los Angeles Police Department, Northeast Division. Divorced, one son, age sixteen, currently living with his mother in Andover, New York. Don't look so disturbed.

They won't be following you around wherever you go. I just like to keep tabs now and then. That's how I do business."

Elle decided to let his business tactics pass for now.

"So if you can't catch a vampire, what can you do? Draw him out with the diary, and then what?"

"That depends on him. It all comes down to quid pro quo. What he wants in exchange for what I want. He gets the diary back and, if he still wants it, another chance at what drew him in to begin with—the chance to tell the world his story. And that's where you come in. I did my homework in order to find a writer who I thought would be in sympathy with Verland and what he wants to say; a writer who would get where he's coming from. Plus, I've lowered his end of the deal. At this point, I don't care about the vampire collective thing. There'll be time for that later. I'll have all the damn time in the world once I'm immortal—me and Henry Ford! So there's only one goal for now: make me into one of them."

"And what if he still doesn't go for it?"

"Well, thanks to Zor, I'm positive he's back in L.A., so he must want something. And that something has got to be the diary. I'd like him to turn me willingly; he would make one hell of an ally. But this time around, I'll get what I want one way or the other. I promise you that above all else."

Kingman's smile made her glad that she wasn't on the receiving end of that promise.

"There's still one missing piece of the puzzle. What if I have no intention of going along with any of this?"

"It doesn't matter whether you do or not. Maybe you'll walk out of here thinking I'm completely insane and go on writing your meaningless little book. Maybe your involvement will help draw Verland out, maybe it won't. Either way, I lose nothing but time, which I have a lot of these days anyway. If it doesn't work, I'll try again some other way. But I think you will go along with it. Like I said, I always do my homework before I cast any role. You've spent half your life trying to figure out the mysteries of death—writing about it, thinking about it. Obsessing about it. You're not going to pass up this kind of a chance. Maybe when the time comes, you'll want to be turned as well. How's that for sweetening the deal?"

Kingman leaned back and went silent. Elle, relieved to finally have him out of her face, let him to his own thoughts until he was ready to continue.

"You know, I was shooting a film in South America some years back when I met this man who had been imprisoned under a military dictatorship. He had been given a death sentence, and every night he sat in his prison cell listening to the priest and the guards go from one cell to the next rounding up those scheduled to be shot that night. Every night he just sat there waiting for the key to turn in his door next. Lucky for him, a coup took place and he was set free—but he told me that sometimes he still woke up at night homesick for his cell in that death house. He couldn't make sense of it until he realized that the instant he had accepted that he was as good as dead, that the key would turn in his lock next, he had become a man without a shadow, dismissed from the ranks of the mortal for the first time in his life. He said it was the most complete sense of freedom he'd ever had before or since. Now imagine having that kind of freedom every day, *for the rest of time.* Forever! No one could walk away from an offer like that."

"You're awfully sure of that."

"I don't go after something unless I'm sure." He motioned for the guards and stood up, meeting adjourned. "Keep reading the book. Keep getting to know Verland. Hopefully before too long, you'll get the chance to meet the real thing."

CHAPTER 14

Vita called the next day. Elle wondered if she'd passed some sort of test proving she was insane enough to join Kingman's team. That was one game she had no desire to play, but she wasn't ready to walk away just yet, either. Kingman had judged her correctly about that part, at least, which made her wonder what else he may have gotten right. *Maybe when the time comes, you'll want to be turned as well…* And here she had been thinking that moving in with Gary would change her life.

On the drive to Malibu, Elle tried to return to at least some version of reality by sorting through the facts: while making his vampire movie, Kingman had come across Zor, who for the bargain price of one hundred thousand dollars had sold him a vampire—or at least the means to find one. Kingman had then tracked down some actual person claiming to be a vampire… had it been a set-up right from the start? Someone capitalizing on Kingman's bizarre obsessions in order to pitch a script or con more money out of him? Elle wondered if Zor had been in on the scam; with someone like Zor, it was impossible to tell, and probably irrelevant either way. But if "Verland" *was* a fake, no wonder he had backed off when Kingman started pushing to be turned into a vampire—even the best con man couldn't fake that part.

But Elle had saved the best question for last—what about the diary? It seemed like an awful lot of trouble to go through for a scam, but if Verland was a fake, then so was the diary. The only other answer slithered to life like a serpent whose half-glimpsed presence beneath the floorboards must be carefully denied in order to sleep at night: maybe the diary was real; maybe Kingman *had* found a Prussian vampire named Verland with a tale to tell.

Vita and Nyholm both met her at the door this time. As they passed rows of closed doors along empty hallways, Elle had to remind herself that the entire property was under sur-veillance. It seemed so deserted, and it crossed her mind that the forsaken look was intentional—easier to lure a vampire in that way. She was beginning to realize that Kingman could work his magic of illusion and make-believe just as effectively in real life as on a movie set. Given the role that Elle was supposed to play in his greatest project yet, she decided it would be wise to keep that in mind.

In the library, the next sections were laid out in neat stacks just like before. Vita and Nyholm seemed tense, as if Elle's knowledge of the truth had raised the stakes to an uncomfort-able new level.

"Look, now that I know the situation...about Verland, I mean..." She felt ludicrous, standing here negotiating about a vampire. "Maybe I can read the rest of the diary today. Or at least take it with me."

Beautiful as her reading room was, a tank of gas didn't come cheap these days.

"Oh, no," Vita said. "Eliot feels very strongly that you shouldn't read it all at once. It might be too overwhelming."

"Not to mention that he doesn't want anyone else having that kind of access to it," Nyholm added.

Vita smiled, but it didn't extend to her eyes. "Well, it's ridiculous to expect anything less, and we'll all be better off if we don't forget that."

Elle looked a little more closely at her hosts. Nyholm was even more haggard than when she'd first met him, and that was saying something. He was completely on edge—shadow-ringed eyes skittering around the room, body tensed like a fuse about to blow. Vita, on the other hand, was sharp and focused, as if Kingman putting the ball back into play had jolted her awake out in left field. It occurred to Elle that Kingman had probably promised Vita that she would be one of the first inductees into his vampire hall of fame—though Elle wondered if Vita would measure up to the stiff entrance requirements once the time actually came.

"In the next sections, Verland's in Guatemala; he just met Gideon," Nyholm said, turning his back on Vita. "The most important part of the diary, in my opinion, so read it carefully."

His eyes finally came to rest, meeting her gaze and holding it. Elle had the bizarre impression that since her first visit, Nyholm and Vita had somehow switched personalities like characters in a 1960s sci-fi show—he now seemed almost eager for Elle to read the book, while Vita had taken over the paranoid role. As usual in Kingman's haunted mansion, each new doorway seemed to lead to more doorways; for now, though, she would just have to go through the next one and see where she ended up this time.

August 1931; Guatemala

Gideon lives in a crude adobe hut at the base of one of the three volcanoes that surround the lake. The hut contains almost nothing apart from stacks of books filled with every conceivable subject, in every conceivable language, many of which appear to be quite old.

The surrounding region is breath-taking, with pine-covered slopes and a crater lake called Laguna Atitlán with emerald waters that reach over a thousand feet deep in places. The Indian villages scattered about are accessible by narrow paths fit only for walking or horseback. Gideon's hut is even more remote, without even a primitive trail to connect it to the nearest village almost two miles away. The only town even resembling civilization is Santiago Atitlán on the far side of the lake.

14 August

Last night we rowed to Santiago Atitlán in a canoe-like vessel that Gideon built himself. Since it is the only large town for many miles, it attracts a steady supply of traders and migratory workers, many of whom sleep out in the open and alongside the roads after drinking all night in the cantinas. Even so, the feeding opportunities must be limited in such a remote area and the risk of discovery great, so I will rest here only a few days longer before moving on.

[undated]

Even though I have told him my own story, Gideon has not yet told me his; so far, I have been unable to pinpoint even his heritage. His German is excellent, but his speech is layered with the remnants of many languages from many lands, and I cannot make out his native tongue. He is well educated, yet without aristocratic mannerisms. His hair is dark and curly like the Mediterranean races, and he wears it long, like a Bohemian. His complexion is also dark, and his nose somewhat difficult— long and narrow like a Roman's, but rather curved at the end. I have not wanted to appear ill mannered by pressing him for too much information, but I admit that I am uneasy living so intimately with one about whom I know so little.

12 September

Gideon has been living in his volcano hut for several years. When I expressed surprise that he should settle in such a remote location, he told me the strange story of how it came to be:

"Like you, I was weary from too many days in the mountains when I stumbled upon the village. I found an isolated spot right where this hut now stands and settled down to wait for darkness. But I did not rest long before I sensed someone's approach; I hid in the bushes and an Indian man soon appeared. I was surprised, for I knew that the Mayans feared the Guardians of the Mountains, the ancient *espantos*, or spirits, that lure hunters too far from home or seduce women while they're out gathering herbs. But most dangerous of all are the Guardians of the Volcanoes, who incite men to murder and then carry them off inside the volcano, never to return.

"The Indian who had come to such a dreaded spot, whom I later learned is called Tono, wished to offer a prayer to the Guardians of the Volcanoes. The village shaman had prepared herbs and incense soaked in chicken blood, and Tono performed his rituals while telling the espantos his story. He said that his sister, a good, hardworking woman, had died in childbirth along with the infant. Her husband, a man named Melchior, turned to drink and began taking advantage of his only remaining child, a daughter named Anita not yet fourteen years of age. Tono was worried that his brother-in-law's misdeeds would bring God's judgment upon the entire village—crop failures or sickness, perhaps even a great earthquake that would swallow every man, woman, and child into the earth. Even if God spared the village, Tono knew that his niece would eventually end up with child, destroying any chance for her to marry and have a happy life. Tono then offered all of his land and crops, his own life, if the Guardians would take Melchior into the volcano, never to return.

"I listened to Tono's story, and my sense of mischief stirred to life along with my hunger. I followed him back to San Pedro Laguna, and that night I did indeed take Melchior into the volcano, never to return. That should have been the end of the story—but I soon learned that there had been a silent witness to my deed.

"The next day, Tono returned. He knelt at the base of the volcano and said, 'Great Guardian who walks in the form of a man, reveal yourself to me as you did to my niece. You have done my people a great service. Reveal yourself, and we will be your protectors for all eternity.' And so after that kind of an offer, I stepped forward and revealed myself."

I could not conceal my horror at such recklessness, but Gideon just laughed.

"You see," he explained, "I had at last come to the place of rest I had been searching for a very long time."

When I asked how he managed to feed in such a remote location, he said, "I have a great deal of control over my feedings. If you stay here, I can teach you my methods." I must not have looked very convinced, because he then reassured me of a coffee plantation full of migrant workers less than a day's journey from the village. I suspect that he longs for the company of his own kind and is trying to tempt me into staying; I will admit that being here has been like waking from a long and terrible dream when I had not even realized I had been sleeping.

October

Gideon possesses abilities far beyond either Kazamira's or my own. At times he moves so quickly that he seems to disappear, then reappear elsewhere before I have even realized he is gone. More curious still, he is somehow able to go without feeding for weeks at a time. He says that his only secret is a combination of meditation, limited exertion, and prolonged periods of rest; he also claims that his record is twenty-eight days, though I am quite skeptical of this. Remarkably, the rot and decay only come upon him gradually, as if he has actually slowed the degeneration on a cellular level. Even more confounding, when he breaks his fasts, he calmly resumes feeding without a trace of the frenzied bloodlust that inevitably follows even my most successful efforts.

[undated]

Gideon has been instructing me on his meditative techniques, and after many failed attempts, I have completed ten days without feeding. The stench, however, was so terrible toward the end that Gideon forbid me from entering the hut. It seems it will take some time to master the preservation of the flesh part.

[undated]

I had determined to reach fourteen days without feeding, but after the twelfth day, my will broke. I went into the mountains like a raving madman and drained four wild pigs before rowing to Santiago Atitlán and feeding with a recklessness I haven't exhibited in many years. I have been painfully reminded that I still have much to learn, and must not let my ambitions outstrip my experience.

December

Yesterday we traveled to San Pedro Laguna. Most of the townspeople kept a wary distance, but showed no real fear or hostility; the only exception was the new mothers, who hid their infants and fled at our approach. Gideon explained that in Mayan culture, children are thought to be particularly susceptible to the spirit world, and those who possess dark powers can harm an infant just by looking at it.

As we were leaving the village, we encountered a young woman holding a small boy by the hand. Although she kept her eyes averted and hid the child in her skirts, she did not run away like the others had; instead, she gave us a charming half-bow, half-curtsey as we passed. When I asked Gideon about her, he told me that this particular young woman had a different regard for him than the other villagers.

"You see," he said, "that lovely creature was Melchior's daughter, Anita. After her father was taken by the volcano, she married a hardworking young man with enough land to provide her with a good life. That was their first child you saw, a boy she named Tono, in honor of her uncle."

February 1932

A great variety of hawks inhabit this country, including a magnificent species the natives call the crane hawk with jet-black feathers and a white stripe across the tail. Gideon told me that he once lived among an Indian tribe in North America that believed each person possesses a unique animal spirit, which the Mayans also believe. He said that the Indians communicated with their animal spirits in much the same what that we do, and a profound question occurred to me: what if our powers are inherent in all men, and have only been lost through ages of disuse and disbelief?

[undated]

For some weeks now I have tried every form of trickery to discover Gideon's spirit animal, and he finally grew tired of my pestering. I had imagined some great predator, perhaps the sly jaguars that lurk in the mountains and cause no end of terror to the villagers. So imagine my surprise to learn that the great and powerful Gideon is spiritually linked not with the jaguar, not with the wolf or even the coyote—but with the humble *ass*! This causes me no end of amusement, but Gideon just smiles, and says, "It is easy enough to laugh at the poor beast of burden, but think of the places he can go that the hawk or the jaguar cannot. After all, no one pays the harmless burro any mind, and prophets and kings alike have ridden the ass. Can you say the same about your jaguar?"

[undated]

When Gideon and I travel to distant villages to feed, we spend days roaming the mountains as free as any creature of the wild. As we run in the moonlight and swim through the rivers, we are something more than gods, who never know the pleasures of earth and flesh, yet more than men, as well, forever bound by their own mortality. We are something entirely new, something freed from the laws of both gods *and* men.

[undated]

This evening we found the body of a migrant worker on the trails. He had been attacked by a jaguar, but too much time had passed for us to feed. I lamented the fact that we have so little time before the blood becomes useless, and recounted my failed attempts at preservation. Gideon said that modern science now allows doctors to refrigerate blood for several days, and that they even store it in "blood banks" for future use. I became quite excited about the advantages such places could offer our kind, but Gideon stopped me, saying, "I once drained every sample in one of these blood banks in much the same hope. The result? Nothing. The smallest field mouse produced more effect than those neatly labeled bags of plastic."

I said that this was a very curious failure, and he replied, "Not really. You see, for us, the blood is so much more than a collection of cells and platelets and plasma to be transferred from one body to the next. We must connect to the spirit, the essence still moving through the body before it departs this earth. For us, the blood only has value when it's inseparable from the life it sustains."

July 25, 1933

San Pedro Laguna is celebrating the yearly festival in honor of its patron saint, and the roads are jammed with travelers coming to take part in the festivities. I mentioned to Gideon that conditions were perfect for feeding, but he said that he would never feed during the festival; it is very sacred to the Mayans, and a death during this time would bring bad luck and shame for an entire year.

July 26

The village is alive with traders and food stalls. The bands play marimba music while dancers in bright Spanish costumes reenact the conquests of centuries ago. Looking down from our lonely mountain hideaway, I measure the distance not in miles or years, but in the sound of the voices and laughter that float through the darkness and evaporate like the mist upon reaching our door.

[undated]

We have been discussing the ways by which our kind can be killed. Fire seems to be our most lethal enemy, though sunlight is more complicated. Gideon says that many must limit exposure even after a feeding, and some cannot endure it at all. He was surprised that I had developed such strong tolerance so soon after my transformation, and I told him about my experiments, adding that my years of service to the Prussian army no doubt also contributed to my fortitude.

He smiled and said, "The might of the Prussian army notwithstanding, the one who made you must have been very old." I asked him what importance this had, and he said, "During the transformation process, some essential part of the creator enters the one being created. Thus, the greater his or her powers, the greater yours will be, even when you are still very young."

He then told me that we can also die by decapitation—no surprise to find that even our powers cannot heal a wound such as this! I mentioned the old legends about driving a stake through the heart, and Gideon said, "Once in the great forests of North America, I sensed another's presence—close, but very faint. For some time I tried to draw her toward me without success. Despite my unease, I finally sought her out.

"When I found her, I realized why she had failed to come to me—she had been staked to an oak tree by a wooden spear. It had been driven through her heart and deep into the trunk of the tree. She was near starvation, and had the thick canopy of leaves not hidden the sunlight, she would have been gone already. When I drew the stake out of her body, layers of skin came away with it, and the wound gaped in her rotted flesh. I fed her with one wild animal after another until she was somewhat restored, but I could not forge even a basic connection between us, and she refused to speak. She was quite deranged in the mind, and I never found out how or why she ended up like that. But you see, the stake alone did not kill her, though make no mistake— it will immobilize and weaken us enough to finish the job, should our attacker know how to do it."

I asked him what would happen if our hearts were pierced by a thin blade or a bullet, and he said that the weapon must be substantial enough, or else the heart will either expel it or repair itself around the intrusion like a tree that grows with a piece of metal in its trunk. Likewise, if the weapon is removed, no matter what the size, the wound immediately begins to heal. But if a large enough weapon is driven through the heart and left in place, we are compromised enough for our pursuers to then chop off our heads, though it seems that many neglect to carry out this last, most crucial step.

October

The rainy season is particularly bad this year. It has been raining almost continuously since late August, and I believe I have now read every one of Gideon's books at least three times. He seems content to peruse his favorite, a very old portfolio filled with sketches, but I will admit that my nerves are beginning to fray.

10 November

We have come to La Antigua in order to escape the weather for a time. When we visited the abandoned monastery of Santo Domingo, I was hesitant to enter. I realized that I had not been near a church since my transformation, and I was plagued by the irrational yet persistent fear that God might strike us dead on the spot if we attempted to transgress sacred ground. I expected Gideon to laugh at this foolishness, but he instead told me the following story:

"A long time ago, I was making my way up a steep hillside in the Italian countryside when I came upon a trio of Cistercian monks struggling with a large chest. One of them called out to me for help, saying, 'God will reward you greatly for your service, my friend, as a most sacred relic rests inside.' Like you, I hesitated, but the monks were persistent, and I finally obliged them.

"At the crest of the hill, they stopped for refreshment, and the wine in combination with the drowsy heat of the day loosened their tongues. One of them unlatched the chest and revealed a mummified, headless corpse, which he claimed was the remains of a much-celebrated saint. He then explained that the pope had ordered the relic removed from the Cistercians and given to another order; outraged at this theft, the monks had cut off the saint's head and hidden it in a tabernacle behind their choir, and were now transporting the body to a secret location in order to prevent the transfer.

"It took another five hundred years for that much-harassed body to finally come to rest in a sarcophagus of gold and silver in Toulouse. The head finally got there, too—or at least some poor soul's did, since at least three other orders now claim to have the original. For all anyone knows, those remains belong to a humble beggar who would have been despised by the very people now kneeling before his corpse! Ever since then, the objects and places declared sacred by men can still fill me with awe and wonder, but never fear or dread."

We spent the rest of the afternoon in pleasant exploration of the ruins.

13 November

I've been reading the international papers, my first news of the world since the end of the war. A party called the National Socialists has come to power in Germany. The new chancellor has begun rearmament, and the French and British press are already sounding alarms about the "new menace of Germany." New! It sounds to me much like 1914, or 1870, for that matter—only this time, such news has no power to stir any sense of national duty or pride.

11 December

Gideon has been learning to drive. He is much taken with the activity, and drives around day and night in an awful, chugging contraption that crawls the earth like some giant, mechanized black beetle. Although I ride along with him and cannot help but be impressed by the ingeniousness of such a machine, I have no desire to operate one myself.

29 January, 1934

I am glad be back at our volcano after so many months away, and must now record an extraordinary incident that occurred as we were leaving La Antigua. We were feeding in preparation for our journey when a police officer came upon us. I sprang forward to silence him, but Gideon stopped me. The young man drew his gun, his hands shaking so violently that he was at far greater risk of shooting his foot than us. In a low, soothing voice, Gideon kept repeating, "Put your gun back in the holster. Turn around and go back the way you came. You saw nothing here and will remember nothing." I watched in astonishment as the officer repeated his exact words and then walked away as placidly as if he were taking a stroll through the park. At that moment, the idea occurred to me for the first time—do the powers that we possess in regard to the animal kingdom extend to human beings, as well?

When I asked Gideon about this, he said that it had taken many years before he could link with human consciousness, and that doing so is both difficult and unpredictable.

"You see, unlike the instinct-driven beasts and birds, the human mind is a swirling jumble of thoughts and emotions and memories and sensations of every sort. Even after long practice, I can only link with humans for a limited amount of time before being drowned out by the din of even the simplest of minds—never even mind the complex ones!"

When I asked him how difficult it was to command a human in the way that he had the policeman, he said, "The feeble-minded are easily led, but most require some degree of weakness or susceptibility, such as the officer's fear; even then there are limits to how far one can go. Each person is different, and it is not uncommon to find those whose minds cannot be penetrated at all."

[undated]

Gideon refuses to teach me how to connect with human consciousness. He maintains that it is far too dangerous to be undertaken by one as inexperienced as myself; however, I have concluded that it cannot be much different from connecting with the animal kingdom, and I have been crossing the lake to Santiago Atitlán twice a week in order to practice. I'm sure that Gideon knows what I am doing, but he has not tried to either dissuade or stop me.

September

I have thus far been able to form only weak and unsatisfying connections. Furthermore, I have not been able to command even the simplest of peasants to so much as scratch behind his own ear.

30 November

Several nights ago I finally forged a link with a villager. What followed was a flood so chaotic that I felt like a tiny vessel being tossed about on a heaving, storm-ridden sea, hopeless of ever reaching solid ground. Days later, my mind is still broken into fragmented pieces of confusion. Gideon is guiding me through a series of meditations to help restore my senses, and I am once again reminded that I cannot so easily acquire what has taken him such time and effort to master. I must have patience as well as discipline, and although I lack none of the latter, I confess that the former has never been one of my greater virtues.

03 December

Gideon has decided to help me connect with humans. I suppose that is one way to bend his will to my own: the threat of self-destruction. Base, but effective. We began by linking our own minds—an altogether frightening, exhilarating experience. Although Kazamira and I shared an awareness of each other's emotions, to become one with another in mind and essence is unlike anything that I have ever experienced before. It requires a level of surrender that would have been unimaginable to me before Gideon.

I told him that on the night we met I had sensed his presence through the fog on that treacherous mountain path, and only now did I realize how strongly he must have sensed me. He smiled and said, "I sensed you long before you ever set foot on that path. How do you think you ended up there in the first place?"

March 1937

For some years now I have been learning Spanish, and today when I sat down to write, for the first time the words did not come in German.

August 1940

In San Pedro Laguna, we met an American woman who has come to teach in the village school. She has all of the charm and confidence of this new race of conquerors, and it is startling to see how free and independent women have become. It does my heart good to think of Kazamira among these bold people of the future, so unencumbered by the cobwebs of European custom.

She also brought news of the war, now spreading like a forest fire beyond control; and so it seems that mankind is set to tear itself asunder once again.

17 September

The American woman is named Sally, and she comes from a place called Cleveland, Ohio. She studies languages and came here in order to improve her Spanish and learn the Mayan dialects. She was thrilled to discover that between Gideon and myself she could practice over a dozen languages, so we have begun meeting one evening a week in the grove of cypress trees near the lake. At first, we met in the town square, but the villagers cast such dark glances that we chose a more secluded spot.

31 September

Sally is one of the most cheerful and optimistic people I have ever encountered. She laughs easily and regularly—quite a breath of fresh air among the usually gloomy chambers of my own mind. She must be quite brave to come by herself to such a strange and remote part of the world, an unmarried *gringa* on her own.

17 October

For the first time Sally asked about our curious living arrangement on the volcano. Gideon answered quite convincingly, something about anthropological studies or some such thing—but my heart froze nonetheless. When Gideon asked her about the villagers' opinion of her friendship with us, she laughed, saying, "Oh, you must know their superstitions—they think the two of you are supernatural beings living in the volcano! In fact, they told me all sorts of horrible things that can happen to those who consort with the gods. So I guess I should find out—do you use your supernatural powers for good or for evil?"

She laughed again, but Gideon and I could only exchange dark glances in response to such jests.

23 December

The school is on holiday and Sally longs to visit Guatemala City. She cannot travel alone, so I have agreed to go with her. Gideon has chosen not to accompany us, and I know that he thinks I am becoming too close in my relations with Sally. I realize that I must be careful, and yet it has been so long since I have enjoyed the company of a bright and lively woman.

01 January, 1941

As I both expected and refused to acknowledge, Sally and I have begun an intimate relationship. I had not forgotten how quickly my desire can turn dangerous, but Gideon's teachings and the passage of time have effected a tremendous improvement in my level of control, and by holding back the full measure of my passion, I can keep the hunger in check. I had, however, forgotten the warmth and pulsing vitality that only the living, flowing blood can give to the flesh.

I know that she must have noticed the peculiarities of my appearance, the coldness of the skin, the lack of those subtle smells and textures one doesn't take notice of until they are absent. Perhaps like many Americans, she attributes my oddities to the general strangeness of foreigners. Or perhaps I am greatly underestimating both her sophistication and her nerve.

27 March

The social customs of humanity once again intrude upon an otherwise enjoyable companionship. Sally's bewilderment about why I have never taken her out for so much as a simple cup of coffee is turning to vexation. She has hinted several times for an invitation to dinner at our hut, but I highly doubt she would care to dine on the carcass of a freshly killed jaguar or the still-warm corpse of a migrant worker or two. How I loathe descending into such flippant sarcasm, but one does grow weary of the constant, impossible barriers!

April

A typhus epidemic is spreading through the village. Eight people have died so far, including four children and an infant. There are no doctors, so the people have only the shamans and the saints—poor protection, I fear, against the deaths that are surely yet to come.

07 May

Twelve more deaths in the village. The people make the rounds to the sacred shrines day and night, wild-eyed with desperation and grief. I am relieved that Tono has not showed up at our door hoping for some volcano-god magic that we are, of course, quite incapable of delivering. Our only magic is a relatively quick and painless end to the suffering, and any mortal with a sharp enough machete and a strong enough will can offer the same.

[undated]

Now I know why none of the villagers came to our volcano for help: they blame the epidemic on Sally. They believe that her relations with us have violated the taboo between mortals and gods and brought a curse upon the entire village. She showed up at our hut several nights ago after the village elders demanded that she leave San Pedro Laguna immediately. She tried reasoning with them, but then parents who had recently lost a child to the disease showed up and began making charges of *brujeria*—black magic. A mob gathered, and as is the way with humans, grief found outlet in blame. Sally, in fear for her very safety, fled the village and tried to find our hut; she no doubt would have perished of exposure had Gideon not sensed her presence and sent a burro out to investigate.

The donkey led her to us, and she told us her story before her courage finally failed and she broke down in exhausted grief. Our hut was woefully unfit to accommodate her for the night, so before she had time to protest, Gideon summoned three strong burros to take us to the nearby town of Solola. We spent two days there while Sally contacted her colleagues in America, and once she had finalized her travel arrangements, she was gone. We offered to accompany her to Guatemala City, but she refused; it was clear that she wanted to put the entire incident behind her as quickly as possible.

By now she is back in Cleveland, and we are back in San Pedro Laguna, where I look down at the villagers with a new resentment simmering as dangerously as the fire of their supposed volcano gods.

June

Why should a bright and free-thinking woman who brought nothing but goodwill to the village be run off in the middle of the night like some medieval witch hunt? Why must the ignorant persist in persecuting anyone different from themselves? Every night I pace the perimeter of our hut glowering with rage at these questions, and Gideon does not help matters—he persists in defending the villagers' beliefs, if not their actions. When I demanded to know if he, too, thought Sally's relationship with us caused the typhus epidemic, he said, "Of course not; and yet the villagers are not wrong in one thing: we *are* supernatural creatures, and can either of us deny that mortals would not be better off avoiding our kind?"

When I failed to answer, he added, "Perhaps the villagers, with their foolish superstitions, are wiser than those who forget or deny that which can't be explained by reason alone."

17 August

The incident with Sally continues to agitate my mind, and I have decided to travel north in order to meditate in solitude. Although I know Gideon does not wish me to go, he has not tried to dissuade or stop me. And so I leave with a heavy heart, not knowing when—or even if —I shall return.

CHAPTER 15

Elle laid the pages down and gazed out of the window. She thought about the hawk she had seen the last time, and imagined Verland seeing through its eyes. Had he been watching her then, sitting in Kingman's plush library reading a copy of his diary? Was he watching her now? She felt the serpent stir beneath the floorboards and then quiet. Kingman had also been right about another thing: along with the fear came the fascination, the overpowering desire to *know*.

The skies were perfectly blue and empty of even a single cloud. She sat down and picked up the last stack of paper.

30 August

I have been traveling up the coastline of Mexico reflecting upon my reaction to what happened with Sally. I harbored no illusions about our relationship, nor do I believe that the villagers' cruel treatment caused her any lasting harm. I now realize that what grieved me the most was that Sally had been added to the long list of things that I have been forced to leave behind. Even a brief, harmless relationship ends with yet another lesson about what our kind cannot have, and I wonder: how many losses can one endure before nothing remains worth acquiring?

[undated]

I find great comfort in the ebb and flow of the sea. It is not possible to feel overwhelmed by one's own existence when faced with such power, which reduces even our kind to nothing but grains of sand being swept along the bottom of the ocean.

[undated]

Today I ventured into the salty waves to float and dive as the dolphins do. Now, alone with the vast, dark waters, I find myself thinking of Gideon. Sometimes it feels as if he is here by my side; but when I turn to him, he is, of course, not there.

[undated]

I have now set foot in the United States of America for the first time. In a city called San Diego, I discovered an entire population of Sallys—confident, energetic people busily forging the future. I visited the naval yards, a reminder that the United States is now as entrenched in the war as the rest of the world. I occasionally pick up a newspaper and read the latest developments, but I find that the conflicts of men no longer have the same power to move me as they once did.

[undated]

I awoke today with an overpowering need to return. I must leave for San Pedro Laguna as quickly as possible, and will rest only when necessary.

[undated]

Last night I found myself on that path now so familiar to me that I could navigate it even through the thickest fog. With each step toward the hut I could feel Gideon's presence grow stronger, and I fully expected him to materialize in front of me as he had on the night we met. But he was nowhere to be found, and I continued my journey alone.

When I finally reached the hut, I found Gideon reading a book; he looked up when I entered, and in that moment, a sensation overtook me that I still find quite difficult to describe. A warmth began to spread throughout my body; my thoughts grew unfocused, abstract, as if my consciousness was not so much linking with his as *blending* with it entirely. The experience calls to mind the liquefaction process of candle-making, whereby layers of wax are melted into fluidity and then blended to form something new. I realized that we were connecting more powerfully, more completely, than ever before, as if our minds, our very souls, were becoming one entity separated only in body.

Later, when I told him that I had been expecting him to turn up along the path like he had when we met, he smiled and said, "No, Verland. This time you had to find your way on your own."

November 1942

Yesterday, Gideon and I were discussing the despair that overtook me after the incident with Sally. He broke off the conversation to retrieve the large portfolio that so frequently engages his attention. Unlike his other books, he had not yet shared this one with me, and as I leafed through the pages, I cried out in astonishment—there, in front of my eyes, were drawings made by the unmistakable hand of the most celebrated master of the Italian Renaissance; page after page of unknown treasures, including a remarkable series of sketches depicting Gideon himself.

He told me that he had once studied painting with the great master, and their friendship had flourished even though Gideon's talent had not. He then said, "Something that stayed with me, though, is the phenomenon called *pentimento*; it occurs when an artist draws an image, and then paints over it. In time, the original drawing begins to show through, blending with the new image to create a work of art quite different from what the artist may have intended."

I asked why this had impressed him so much, and he said, "You see, those stubborn, long-obscured images are like the layers of our own existence; we are the painters covering them over and over again, but that which appears lost is merely hidden. The old images bide their time and then rise to the surface to join with the new ones. Don't you see? *Pentimento*, Verland, transforms the perception of loss into the promise of reconfiguration."

[undated]

After Gideon shared his portfolio, I decided to reciprocate with this diary—a poor offering, but the only one I possess. My own eyes have been the only ones to ever look upon these pages, and I was surprised at the trembling of my hands as I placed the book into another's for the first time. He read it straight through and then told me how much it had moved him; I must confess that I was quite taken aback by how profoundly this response moved *me*.

[undated]

We have been discussing tales about supernatural beings that consume the blood or flesh of the living, and have concluded that they exist in some form or another in nearly every culture around the world. In addition to the European folktales, Gideon spoke of the ancient Indian goddess Kali and the Egyptian goddess Sekhmet, both of whom feast upon the blood of living men. He then described shards of pottery excavated in ancient Persia that depict a variety of blood-drinking demons. The Mayans also have a legend about a spirit named Cholero who travels the mountain trails killing people for food.

Gideon said, "Some years after my own transformation, I lived among the Aghoris of Northern India, a sect of Hindus who believe that supernatural powers can be acquired by consuming the flesh of the dead. For them, this is a means of converting matter from one form to another." When I dismissed such practices and beliefs, Gideon said, "Perhaps it would make more sense if I put it in this way: 'This is my body; this is my blood.'" I must have looked quite taken aback, for he then added, "What is the Eucharist, after all, but the world's most prolific blood ritual?"

This led to an even more astonishing discussion of cannibalism as a fundamental part of human evolution. He said, "Cannibalism surfaces throughout all of human history, from the literal piles of butchered human bones discovered at prehistoric sites to the symbolic stories such as Baba Yaga and Saturn devouring his son. Your own culture has its own rather quaint version called 'Hansel and Gretel,' I believe."

As if this wasn't disconcerting enough, his next theoretical turn went even farther. "Imagine," he said, "the first primitive tribes of men. Now imagine the most isolated of those tribes being forced to feed upon their own kind in order to survive. Captives from other tribes, their own weak or dying; maybe even willing sacrifices—the first cannibals. Centuries pass and mankind progresses. Societies form, men develop more sophisticated methods of gathering and producing food. The cannibal tribes are more and more feared, despised and driven to the most remote corners of the earth. Their numbers dwindle. But among those that remain, something deep within begins to mutate. The Mayans have a term for such things—*mala sana*. Worse even than *mala sangre*, the "bad blood" that causes most violence, mala sana comes from the very marrow, the very core of one's being.

"Now, consider that from this ancient mutation, this mala sana, a new species of beings emerge, creatures long sustained upon the flesh and blood of their own kind. Their survival eventually narrows down to one most essential thing—the life blood. Their numbers grow smaller and smaller as both enemies and evolution take their toll; but perhaps at least a few survived to ensure that you and I now sit here and puzzle out the riddle of our existence."

[undated]

I asked Gideon if he has ever transformed another, and he replied, "Yes, four times. Once out of curiosity, once out of love, once out of hatred, and once for no reason at all."

When I told him that I had yet to turn anyone, he took my arm and spoke with a most uncharacteristic urgency, saying, "I hope that you never do, my friend. Transforming another creates a connection that can never be broken; with the intermingling of the blood, some essential part of the life force that you have taken enters your own being. And then, by giving the blood back, a symbiosis occurs between creator and created, a dark alchemy forever binding the two. Although you are not yet aware of it, you are connected to the one who created you just as surely as he is to you."

I thought of the hospital attendant, but could recall nothing apart from that strangely compelling voice. "Perhaps," I said, "the one who made me no longer exists."

But Gideon had no such doubts. "Trust me when I tell you that when your creator is destroyed, you know of it instantly. No, the one who made you still exists."

I thought of Kazamira and Aslan and longed to ask him more, but he was lost to his own thoughts. He finally said, "The ones you create never leave you, Verland, but such connections are not like the one that you and I share. Those that you create will haunt your soul until your own moment of destruction returns to haunt theirs."

In all of our years together, Gideon had never requested anything of such importance from me, so without a moment's hesitation, I swore an oath that no matter what the circumstance, I would never transform another into one of our kind.

[undated]

Gideon has finally told me the story of his own transformation, and only now do I understand why his powers are so much greater than my own—but perhaps his tale should be told in his own words:

"It happened long ago, in the time of the great Jewish rebellions against the Romans. A man named Josephus, a descendent of many powerful priests and nobles, was given command of the lands of Galilee. Even though I was no longer a young man, I was burning to defend our people, and joined the rebel forces under Josephus's command.

"One blazing day in early June a thousand cavalrymen arrived at the gates of Yodfat, and it did not take long for the rest of the Roman army to join them. The siege lasted for forty-seven days; when it ended, many of those not already dead from thirst or starvation chose to take their own lives rather than surrender. The Romans slaughtered every remaining man and took the women and children into slavery, ransacking and burning the city until there wasn't a brick left standing.

"Josephus and a group of forty soldiers had escaped to a cave outside of the town—I was among those forty. We lasted three days before for the Romans discovered us and sealed the mouth of the cave, demanding our surrender. We argued among ourselves about what to do, and out of the darkness of that cave came the resolution to die by our own hands rather than let a Roman sword draw even one more drop of our people's blood.

"To our surprise, Josephus urged us to surrender. 'What of placing the sin of suicide upon our souls?' he asked. 'What of the moment when a man feels the cold steel upon his throat, and his courage fails?'

"But he saw that we could not be swayed, and finally said, 'If you choose to die, then I will die with you. But hear this first—rather than each man entrusting death to his own faltering hand, there is another way.'

"He told us that we must first form a circle; one man would be chosen to draw his blade against the neck of the man standing to his right. The blade would then be passed three times and the cycle repeated until only two men remained. 'In this way,' Josephus said, 'only one man will be required to take his own life—the last left alive by either luck or the hand of God.' Each man stood with his own fear deep within the heart, and each man agreed to the plan.

"The circle was formed and Josephus stepped into the center. 'All that remains is to decide who will die first. As your commander, it is my duty…' But his words were drowned out by our protests: 'Our humble deaths will be more glorious with our commander by our side! God willing you should be the last!'

"A soldier stepped forward, a thick-set man who had been a silk merchant before joining the rebel forces. He said, 'I request the honor of being the first to die.'

"Those of us already trembling with dread could only envy the firmness of his voice and the steadiness of his hand as he drew his blade and handed it to the soldier next to him, a young man not even old enough for his first beard. Josephus nodded and stood still for a moment, then turned to look each one of us in the eye before taking his own place in the circle.

"The merchant's courage held even as his young comrade's faltered, for the raised blade quivered so badly that the rest of us feared it may drop and break the spell that had thus far held us in its sway. But the boy mastered himself, drawing the blade swiftly across his comrade's throat. He did not flinch when the shock of crimson spray burst forth.

"The blade passed from one man to the next in steps of three, round and round like a mad kaleidoscope as the circle grew smaller and smaller. Some of the men went to their deaths without fear. Some prayed to God or wept; some urinated where they stood. Some found it more difficult to deliver death than to receive it—but not one man broke the oath. Finally, there were six men left, then five. Four, three, only two left standing—me and Josephus, the gore-covered blade now at rest in his hands. I knew that death would come quicker if I tilted my head back, and I soon felt the surprise of the steel, then nothing at all.

"The next thing I remember is being shaken awake. Josephus was hovering above me, still very much alive. He held a cup to my lips and said, 'Drink this, soldier. It is God's will.'

"I forced down the thick, foul liquid, and the agony began. When it ended, Josephus told me that we must surrender. I protested that this would be a sacrilege against our comrades, and he replied, 'No! *Our* deaths will be the sacrilege.'

"He held the blade up in front of my eyes. 'In the name of God, I swear that I used this against you. You felt the blade, felt death rise up to take you. Look at your blood-drenched tunic! Look at my own hands and clothes! And yet you live! God has spared you and broken the oath, and no promise sworn by men is greater than the will of God!'

"I was in no condition to argue against the will of God, so he helped me to my feet and we made our surrender. As soon as the guards seized us, Josephus told them what had taken place; the blood-soaked ring of corpses inside the cave was proof enough of his story. He then said, 'The instant I held the blade to my neck, God revealed a most profound prophecy. Yet I had sworn to die with my men, so die I must! But then an even greater miracle occurred: God returned this soldier from the dead as a sign that I must live and tell the prophecy. Understand this! I am now your prisoner, but I am also God's messenger. The future of the entire Roman empire will be decided within the next few moments—for it is your own commander's fate which God has revealed to me!'

"The solider in charge hesitated only a moment before leading Josephus away, and I knew that his life would be spared. He had spoken no word on my behalf, and I was seized by three guards who dragged me toward the reinforcement wall at the south end of the town. I knew the spot all too well: the Romans brought captured rebels here to be crucified, their slow, agonizing deaths an example to all. My only comfort was that in my weakened state, my suffering would not last long.

"What happened next took place as if time had slowed down, and I can still see each moment as if I were right there again among the dust and scorching sun. One of the guards paused to wipe the sweat from his brow. As he drew his hand across his forehead, I saw the skin catch on a ragged piece of metal sticking up along the rim of his helmet. He swore and shook his hand in pain, and a spray of blood flew forth and struck my face. In an instant, I was overcome by a hunger so great that it swept away my weakness and fear; I lunged for the guard and had his torn throat in my mouth before I even realized what I was doing. The remaining guards drove their swords through me, but I felt no pain. The blood was the only thing that existed, the only thing that mattered. I killed the last two guards, and by the time I had finished draining the bodies, I had the power and strength of a thousand Roman soldiers.

"I heard more soldiers approaching, and looked at the carnage around me as if seeing it for the first time. Overcome by the enormity of what I had done, I fled the city in fear for my sanity as well as my life. Only much later, when I had taken refuge among the Persians, did I begin to understand what I had become.

"For years afterward, I thought about what had happened in that cave. I came to understand that Josephus had planned the entire outcome as soon as he had realized that we would not surrender. I went over and over everything that had taken place, every word, every gesture. He had of course known that his soldiers would never permit him to die first, that at least one soldier would step forward to take his place. I remembered how he had paused before joining us, had slowly turned round in the middle of the circle to look each of us in the eye one last time. Only now I understood his real intention—to gain enough time to determine the exact place he needed to stand in order to be the last man left alive."

Gideon rummaged in his books and found a half-disintegrated piece of parchment paper with a series of equations scrawled across it. "You see? Once he knew who would be the first to die, he easily calculated who would then be the last. Basic mathematics, but genius in its application. He must also have realized that he needed some explanation for walking out of that cave over the dead bodies of his own soldiers—and so my own miraculous survival justified his own. He told me nothing of what I had become, and I would have perished on the cross had it not been for that one Roman soldier bothered by the sting of sweat in his eyes, that one sword that had struck his helmet and torn loose that one piece of metal that brought forth those drops of blood.

"Many years later, I learned the prophecy that Josephus had delivered to the Roman legate: 'I was sent by God himself to foretell of the greatness that awaits you. You will be master not only of me, but of the land and the sea and the entire human race.' This was of course high treason against the emperor, but the legate's ambition had been stirred. A military coup soon drove the emperor from the throne, and the legate came to power. The prophecy thus fulfilled, Josephus's life was spared, and he was given lifelong patronage from the Romans. He lived among them for many years afterward, writing the history of the Jews while Roman soldiers marched through the streets with treasures looted from Jewish temples and Jewish captives bound in chains."

[undated]

Gideon continues to amaze me with his fantastic theories. Yesterday after swimming in the lake, we sat watching a flock of sparrows, and he said, "All of those millions of years ago, when life crawled up from the sludge, imagine if what would go on to become the first humans had followed those sparrows instead of whatever poor slugs they chose instead. Look at them! Needing nothing more to survive than the berries on the trees and the seeds of the earth; no need to hunt or destroy each other in order to survive. I like to picture this might-have-been race of bird-men, glorious feathered things winging across the endless sky instead of forever fighting each other for these sparse patches of earth."

I told him that in order to survive, man had been made a predator as surely as the hawk or the lion, and he said, "Perhaps, but man just as surely was meant to evolve, no? Did you know that scientists now think entire species may have been wiped from the earth simply because they failed to adapt their diets? Some human beings have already chosen to eat like the sparrows, so who knows—maybe evolution will not favor those creatures who must feed upon each other in order to survive."

I told him I found this prediction rather unlikely, and he said, "Why so? Isn't it more practical to sustain oneself from the earth's bounty alone? And more merciful, too—after all, the gazelle wishes to live as much as the lion, and even the most skilled predators bring the terror of the hunt upon their prey, as you and I know too well. No, a creature's sustenance being dependent upon another creature's death is not the end point of our evolution, just one more transition to be made. And as it has always been, each creature must either adapt or perish."

When I pointed out that in this particular version of evolution, our kind didn't stand much of a chance, he replied, "Oh, certainly not. In fact, our kind would be the first to go."

I was reluctant to pursue this line of thought any further and instead chose to contemplate the sparrows in silence for the rest of the evening.

October 1954

For many years we have been almost completely isolated from human society, but the affairs of men now threaten to intrude even upon this remote corner of the world—the people's elected leader has been overthrown by a military junta. Guatemala is no stranger to political unrest, but this time the difference can be measured by the steady arrival of heavily armed foreign soldiers. A military garrison has been set up outside of Santiago Atitlán, and soldiers have begun patrolling the mountain trails, though so far none have ventured as far as our hut.

12 December

At the lake, Gideon pointed out a large boat docking at the town of Panajachel: "Foreign tourists." We watched the boat make its way back across the lake, and he added, "The soldiers have brought evangelicals with them along with their guns. Have you noticed the new church that went up in Santiago

Atitlán? The Catholics then brought their own priests, and some have already begun forbidding the *costumbre* rituals. The invaders have been competing for the salvation of the Mayan soul for thousands of years, not to mention ownership of their land. The masks on the faces may change, but the dance is always the same."

March 1955

We have been discussing the immutability of the soul. Gideon spoke of the self-immolation practiced by some Buddhist and Hindu sects, as well as warrior cultures like the Charans and Rajputs. He said, "History is full of stories of regeneration and rebirth through fire. During the Great Schism of the Russian Church, entire villages of Old Believers burned themselves to death in an act known as 'fire baptism.' In Santiago Atitlán, when the Spanish conquistadores came and slaughtered hundreds of Mayan warriors, the bravest sealed themselves inside a cave and self-immolated rather than face captivity. Pity we didn't think of that back in Yodfat."

I couldn't tell if he was joking or not, so I let him continue without comment.

"You see, with fire, the power to create is inextricable from the power to destroy. I once studied with a monk who told me the sutra of the Medicine King: in order to demonstrate the deathless nature of the soul, he set his own body ablaze, and the flames illuminated the world for a thousand years."

I told him about Kazamira's description of Aslan disintegrating in the gypsies' pyre, and said, "Ironic that a sacred form of regeneration is complete annihilation for us."

He then replied, "I suppose that depends upon your view of annihilation. In many ancient religions, the body is merely an instrument to carry the soul, and cremation in fact frees it from its earthly form. So looked at in this way, I suppose that our kind is no exception."

I must have looked skeptical, because he added, "Consider the fact that a belief in the immortality of the soul in some form or another is fundamental to every religion. And yet why, then, do most humans fear and despise death? Why do so many consider the universe so small, its energy so limited, that this one blip of time and space is all there is to it?"

I then asked him how creatures that do not die fit into this system of transfiguration, and he said, "That's just it, Verland— we don't. What if the Holy Grail of eternal life is actually a terrible disruption of the most fundamental cycle of regeneration? If that is so, then the immortality of our bodies is in fact the *mortality* of our souls. Imagine it! This strange mutation of a species trapped for eternity in this one biological form. No, I neither mourn for Aslan nor fear his fate; he has now become what you and I can as yet only imagine."

When I asked him what he thought that might be, he said, "That which comes next, Verland. Nothing more and nothing less."

1958

The fighting between the Army and guerrilla forces has intensified. Gideon said, "As it has always been, the poor will bear the worst of the suffering. The Mayans will become slaves on their own land, the villages will burn and the fields will be scorched. Thousands will die, and I fear that not even the most powerful of Guardians will be able to protect them now."

[undated]

Gideon spends more and more time staring at the volcano across the lake. Unlike our volcano, with its hard black lava cone and layers of ash, this one is active. Gideon told me that the Mayans call it Juan Noq, in honor of the supernatural being that lives inside. According to legend, his home burns down every night, causing the smoke that rises from the volcano's peak. Since Juan Noq must then rebuild again and again for all of time, he steals the souls of the dead to do the work for him. Once a worker has built enough houses, Juan Noq rewards him by releasing his soul from the volcano. However, whenever there is a shortage of workers, Juan Noq erupts in anger in order to collect more souls.

When Gideon finished this strange tale, he added an even stranger question: "Given how long I've been on this earth, I wonder how many houses I would have to build before Juan Noq would reward me and release my soul?"

August 1966

The conflict grows worse with each passing year. The government has launched a counterinsurgency against the guerrillas, and the country is now crawling with elite units of foreign soldiers and vigilante death squads. Many civilians have already been killed or have just "disappeared" from their *milpas* or villages, and I fear that the worst is yet to come.

January 1967

We must leave Guatemala very soon. The guerrillas have begun taking refuge in the mountains, and the army now conducts regular sweeps to drive them out of hiding. We are becoming extremely vulnerable here, yet Gideon refuses to leave. I have tried to reason with him, I have argued—I have even resorted to outright begging. But so far he hasn't shown even the slightest amount of concern for our situation.

16 January

I am only now able to write this. Yesterday Gideon told me that I must take whatever things I wish and leave Guatemala immediately. Relieved that he had finally come to his senses, I began making plans to cross the border into Mexico, maybe enter the United States or even return to Europe—but my chattering was a desperate attempt to stave off what I have most dreaded, what has been hidden behind so many of our conversations for so long now—Gideon has no intention of leaving Guatemala, not now, not ever.

Once he had confirmed my fears, he waited through the outburst that followed, and then said, "Verland, do you remember when we first met, how I told you that when I found this volcano I had found my place of rest? I knew then that I would not leave here—at least not in this body, which has already traveled across too many miles for too many years. Your coming here was a gift—one of the great gifts of my existence! But nothing stays frozen in time, Verland, not even for us, and the change that has come to this village, to this country, will bring much bloodshed and destruction. And yet I cannot leave here, cannot start anew in yet another place, with yet another life. No—this is the final destination for me."

I would not be consoled, and continued to rage and plead and rant until his patience finally failed him in a way I had never seen before.

"Do you think that we are simply meant to go on forever? That we alone among all creatures of the earth are never meant to know what else awaits us?"

Then all of the fire went out of him and he sank to the floor in silence. After what seemed like a very long time, he said, "I am tired, Verland. Tired of this form, this existence, these never-ending thoughts and memories and lives, the many I've known and loved and lost, forever and ever and ever the same."

He had never before spoken of these inescapable scars of time, the ones that go far deeper than mere flesh; and yet I could not deny that I often felt a great weariness inside of him, the terrible weight of all of those years pressing upon his soul. He closed his eyes and put his head in his hands; I wanted to scream, to weep, to shake him and comfort him at the same time. But all that I could do was sit down next to him in the darkness and take his hands in mine. We sat that way long into the night until a fragile peace formed, the kind stitched together from the frayed remains of a great, unwoven sorrow.

17 January

I asked Gideon what he intended to do once I had gone, and he said, "For years now I've been watching Juan Noq over there across the lake. I think it's time that I helped him out with those houses. So I suppose, Verland, that I am going in search of that which comes next. Nothing more and nothing less."

18 January

I cannot accept this—I will not! Please, God, whom I know long ago stopped listening to my prayers, please hear me this one last time! I get down on both knees and beg you to give me the words, the power to somehow change his mind!

20 January

I have decided that I will join him in his journey to the volcano. This is my only source of consolation. Then, whatever may await us, we will at least be together; that thought fills me with the only bit of comfort I've had in days.

22 January

Gideon insists that I am not ready to join him. We have been arguing nonstop, and I cannot argue any further. I do not know what to do, what to think. I asked Gideon what gave him the right to judge whether or not I was ready to leave this world the same way that he wished to do. He held up this book, saying, "For one thing, because you are still writing in this. You still have things to say, things that you need to tell. Your story is not yet over, Verland. Your story still remains to be told."

25 January

I cannot say that I have accepted Gideon's decision. That is not possible, and I would still do anything, without exception, if I thought it would change his mind. But his beliefs are strong and his heart is true. I know the weariness of his soul, the longing to break free of this world. To deny this would be to deny everything between us, everything we have shared so utterly and without restraint—everything that I know and understand to be Gideon.

30 January

I spent days sorting through his books, adding and taking away from the pile I wished to take with me, but in the end I decided to keep only one: his beloved portfolio of sketches. We gave the rest to the local school—the very one in which Sally taught, in what now seems like a lifetime ago.

Before we gave the books away, Gideon retrieved an elaborately drawn map from one of the oldest and most worn. He showed it to me and said, "Just over the Mexican border, deep within the jungles of the Petén Basin, lies the ruins of an ancient city called Calakmul. Many centuries ago it was the seat of power for what the Mayans called the great Snake Kingdom."

He then pointed out a series of concentric designs with a place marked along the outermost ring. "Among the ruins are many stone slabs carved with emblems and hieroglyphics. The Mayans erected them for commemorative occasions, and archeologists now call them *stele*. Along this outer circle there is a stele lying on the ground that no ordinary man could ever hope to move. You will recognize it by the large carving of a snake's head at the top of the stone—the emblem of the Snake

Kingdom. This marks the place where a chest is buried; the contents are yours if and when you should want them."

I took the map and tucked it into the portfolio. Based on Gideon's history, I can only begin to imagine what those contents might include.

31 January

We leave tomorrow. I move through the hours as if in a terrible waking dream. I never before realized that grief and fear feel so much alike.

[undated]

We set out at dusk and traveled for miles without speaking. We reached a place on the trail where one road went north, the other to Juan Noq.

"Here we part ways, my friend."

And I could not do it. I broke down and wept with the pure, raw grief of a child. He knelt beside me in the dust and took my hands in his.

"Verland, our hearts are one. Our souls and minds are one. You know this, so you also know that those things are greater than this body, greater than time, even. Those things can never die, can never cease to be. Feel that now. Feel me now, Verland!"

He gripped my hands tighter and his consciousness broke through my grief. "Verland, this is what will stay with you always; *this* is immortality."

Then we both stood, and I watched him walk down the path until he vanished from my sight. I turned and ran without looking back, I ran northward without pause for as far as I could go before exhaustion overtook me.

[undated]

He is going; he has just gone! I shake from head to foot as I write this, for he is gone!

[undated]

Gideon may have been wrong about one thing. For a long time now, I have not had even the slightest urge to write in these pages.

[undated]

For the first time since our parting, I opened the portfolio. I spent many hours studying the sketches of him, marveling at how the artist captured a particular expression or state of mind with only a few well-rendered strokes. On the inside of the front cover, I recognized his handwriting in the one word he had added to his master's collection: *Pentimento!*

[undated]

I have at last retrieved Gideon's chest. Using the map, I easily located the Calakmul ruins and the stele along the outermost ring. Despite its size and weight, I moved it without too much difficulty and dug a few feet beneath the place marked by the snake head glyph. I admit that I had half-expected some rotted contraption from Biblical times, but the chest was modern—metal, with a hinged lid and two latches that had rusted shut long ago.

Once I had it fully excavated, I realized that I had seriously misjudged how big it would be. It had been over twenty-four hours since my last feeding, and the exertion of the journey and moving the stone had depleted my energy. The beasts of the jungle were the only feeding source for miles around, and I cursed my foolishness at failing to consider transportation back out of the jungle.

In order to distract myself from my situation, I pried open the chest and examined the contents. How to describe the treasure trove of artifacts and objects carefully wrapped and stored inside that humble box? Gold and silver coins dating back thousands of years; exquisite pieces of jewelry and a dozen or more precious stones; canvases covered with paintings and sketches; scrolls filled with obscure writing from dozens of different languages; elaborate trinkets and artifacts from every far-reaching corner of Gideon's life. In that strange and ancient place, alone in the deepening shadows of dusk with the silent ruins as my only witness, I was overwhelmed by what lay before my eyes—not because of the value and splendor, but because the chest and its contents represented all that had been lost with Gideon, all of his wisdom and experience—so much he still had to tell! So much he still had to teach me! So much we still had to share.

I buried my head in my hands and wept with a sorrow deep and wide enough to swallow the earth and seas and still remain unfilled. I probably would have sat weeping among those stones until I turned to dust under the jungle sun, but instead I looked up and saw it: a sturdy gray burro less than six feet away, chewing on some dried brush and gazing at me with wise, placid eyes. I sat staring at it for some time, and it stared right back before finally throwing its head in the air and letting loose a tremendous braying noise, an absurd *hee-haw* that echoed through the ruins and across the empty jungle sky. And I realized that this donkey was *laughing* at me! It was unmistakable and fantastic, and I threw back my own head and roared at the sky along with it, roared long and loud enough to fill the emptiness, my laughter and my weeping mixing until I could no longer tell the difference between the two.

I lashed the chest to the donkey's back and rode it all the way to the nearest town before watching it go on its way, in search, no doubt, of that which comes next.

March 1971; Mexico City, Mexico

I have sold some of the pieces from Gideon's chest, and now have enough money to last for some time. It is strange to reenter society again after so many years of isolation. Many things have changed since I last lived among men, and I have much catching up to do. I am now once again headed to the United States, where I hope to resume some unfinished business from long ago. Gideon was of course correct all along; the next part of my story is ready to unfold.

Elle was about to restack the papers when she noticed something at the bottom of the last page—words written in such light pencil that she had to lean close to decipher them. *Dante's View, Griffith Park, noon tomorrow. N.*

Nyholm bustled in on cue, and she started to ask him if the time and place meant anything until the look on his face stopped her. His mouth was a twisted line of panic, his eyes bulging so strenuously that Elle expected them to pop out of his head and fly across the room at any minute. His forehead was damp, and it took a moment for her to realize he was sweating—Nyholm's skin was usually more akin to zombie flesh than the perspiring human variety.

"Did you finish the *whole thing*?"

This guy wasn't going to win any awards for subtlety. Elle almost glanced up at the corners of the room before she caught herself—Kingman's ever-present surveillance cameras.

"Yes, everything. When do I get to read the rest of it?"

"I'm not sure. When are you available?"

Elle thought about the best way to answer. Kingman and his gang of vampire hunters might be old hands at this espionage stuff, but Elle was a complete novice. She supposed that now would be the time to whip off a cryptic one-liner like the dicks in noir films, cigarette in one hand, highball in the other.

"Well, tomorrow afternoon I'm expected somewhere." Not exactly Cagney, but it would have to do.

"I am, too, actually. So that's agreed."

Elle was glad to see his eyeballs relax back into his head a little. He picked up the stack of papers and moved toward the door, a marvel of awkward jerks and spasms. If one of Kingman's goons actually was monitoring this conversation, he'd probably suspect Nyholm of quaffing one too many cups of coffee rather than passing secret messages. For any future cloak-and-dagger situations, Elle would have to remember that a profound lack of social skills could come in handy.

On the drive home, she wondered what Nyholm could possibly be up to with all of the subterfuge. If he was after Verland, Elle had no more idea of where he was hiding than Kingman did. But unlike Kingman, she didn't for one second think that a vampire was going to come swooping out of the shadows in order to discuss a book option for his life story. For some reason, though, Nyholm Quinn *was* going to swoop out of the shadows at noon tomorrow, and she could pretty much guarantee that there was only one book on *his* mind.

CHAPTER 16

By noon the next day, it was sweltering. In her pre-Kingman days, Elle wouldn't have even left the house in weather like this, let alone asphyxiate up a hillside to meet a vaguely repellent man she hardly even knew, and trusted even less. But then again, it seemed not much in her life *hadn't* changed since Kingman had entered it.

On the trail toward Dante's View, Elle thought about Gideon and Verland. Their conversations had swirled around her head for half the night, but either despite or because of this, she had woken up with a strange and unexpected feeling of peace. *The kind stitched together from the frayed remains of a great, unwoven sorrow...*

She reached the top just before noon, but Nyholm was nowhere in sight. Elle couldn't even imagine him in daylight let alone hiking up a mountain, and it crossed her mind that maybe this was some kind of a setup to test her loyalty or some crazy thing; or maybe she was becoming as paranoid as the rest of Kingman's team. She had decided to give it ten more minutes and then head back to the air-conditioning when Nyholm emerged from the picnic area behind the bench. He had either taken one of the back trails or been waiting there all along—making sure she was alone, no doubt.

Sure enough, before Elle even managed "Hello," he asked, "Were you followed?"

"No. I don't know. I'm not in the habit of looking for suspicious vehicles with tinted windows and shady looking men behind the wheel—which would include about half of L.A., actually."

When Nyholm failed to appreciate the joke, she added, "I'm pretty sure I wasn't followed up here, anyway."

It seemed extreme to plant spies along a hiking trail, even for Kingman; but then again, there *had* been that woman with the small white dog lingering around the bridge...did a dog *really* need to drink that much water? Elle could see where this spy stuff could get to a person really fast.

"That's all that matters, I guess," Nyholm said. "Come on, we have to go quick."

He lead her through some brush to a trail Elle hadn't known existed, even though she'd been hiking Griffith Park all her life, and within ten minutes, they emerged at the parking lot near Canyon Avenue.

"My friend is here to take us somewhere more secure."

They were on Los Feliz Boulevard and headed toward Silverlake before Elle had time to consider the wisdom of going to an unknown location with Nyholm and anyone strange enough to be Nyholm's friend. As soon as they'd gotten in the car, Nyholm had retrieved a large brown tote bag from the front seat, and he'd had it in a death grip ever since. Elle decided that it might be a good idea to establish her own death grip on her phone, just in case.

They stopped in front of a plain-faced little bungalow and filed inside; every blind was pulled down, giving the place a dismal, twilight feel even in the middle of the day. A stale smell lurked in the corners and along the walls, the buildup of many a fresh-air-free day. Nyholm motioned her into a small room at the end of a narrow hall. *This is where he knocks me over the head and I wake up in a secret dungeon that the neighbors will later swear they knew nothing about.* If she had been writing this scene for one of her books, she would have been screaming at herself to get out of the house right now without stopping to look back and stumble to her doom on a carpet edge. But everything about this story—Kingman's madman schemes, oddballs like Nyholm and Zor, and of course, the diary itself—all of it had pulled her in too deeply to turn back. The hawks, Verland's shadowy presence somewhere out there, always just out of reach... She followed Nyholm down the hall.

Every inch and surface of the room was filled with piled canisters of reel to reel film, old VHS tapes, and high-tech gadgets whose purpose Elle couldn't even guess. Dominating the mess was a huge contraption with enough reels, knobs, and buttons to qualify it as either an android or a piece of postmodern art.

"That's an RCA TD-sixty-six projector set to run twenty-four frames per second." Which Nyholm could see meant nothing to Elle, so he added, "It's used to transfer film into a DVD format. First, you run the film through there, then through a digital transfer camera, and it ends up on one of these."

He pulled a disc from his bag and held it up like a talisman, flicking it back and forth to refract the light.

"Before I got on Kingman's payroll, I used to help run this place. We mostly transferred old home movies, a few professional jobs thrown in here and there—audition tapes, promos. Small-time stuff like that. Still, it was pretty good money."

He slid the DVD into a computer along a side wall.

"But you don't care about that. You're wondering what any of this has to do with Kingman. Well, I'm about to show you. Pull up a chair; show's about to begin. It hasn't been adjusted for brightness or color, and the audio was completely unsalvageable no matter what I tried, but I think the visuals will more than make up for that."

What looked like a home video of the inside of someone's house was flickering to life on the screen, and she soon realized that it wasn't just anyone's house. The camera provided a stationary, wide-angle shot of one half of a room as crowded as this one, although meticulously arranged. A cabinet full of antique swords and daggers propped up an enormous replica of a space ship, a collection of military memorabilia shared cabinet space with a bewildering array of sci-fi figures, set props, and miniature scene replicas. Every inch of wall space was covered with film posters, modern art, and dozens of pictures of celebrities, businessmen, and politicians…and smiling into the camera right next to each of them was the architecture of it all—Eliot Kingman.

The footage continued without change for a full minute, and Elle started to wonder why Nyholm had gone through all of this trouble just to show her a film about the inside of a room. And then Kingman appeared on the screen. He was fussing around rearranging things, and then he moved to the cabinet. He removed one of the daggers with exaggerated, almost ritualistic care, and laid it on a side table. Elle felt her chest tighten; she gripped the edge of her chair.

Kingman remained alone for another half minute or so… something passed in front of the camera, obscuring the lens… and then he was there. Elle's blood was pulsing too hard against her temples. She desperately wanted to sit on the floor with her head between her legs, to stop the room from spinning…but the screen held her in its pixilated tractor beam. What had up to now been a half-believed fantasy made real only in the neatly typed pages of reassuringly acid-free, multipurpose paper had suddenly come to life right in front of her eyes.

He was dressed like any ordinary person: jeans, t-shirt, and a long coat worn loose and unbelted. But Elle knew that it was Verland. She had only ever pictured him in some elaborate nineteenth-century uniform or gentleman's attire, and yet here he was, as twenty-first century as the next guy. He stood at the far end of the room, almost out of range of the camera angle. He was just taller than Kingman's six-foot frame, but whereas Kingman was husky, Verland had the lean, muscular build of a swimmer or a runner. His hair wasn't blond, but it wasn't quite brown, either; more some odd shade between the two, almost an *absence* of color rather than a distinct color itself. It fell across his forehead and behind his ears—not the cropped military haircut she had been expecting. He had the exact kind of long, straight Roman nose that he had used as a template for figuring out Gideon's heritage, and sharp, high cheekbones. His attractiveness and physical stature alone would have set him apart in a crowd, but there was something else…something in his bearing, in the slow, deliberate way that he moved…

Kingman was doing most of the talking. He was putting on quite a performance, gesturing wildly and clutching his hands to his heart like an opera star. But Verland appeared unmoved. Occasionally he gave some short reply, and Elle cursed whatever audio gods had failed to capture their conversation. Kingman went on for a while longer and then pressed a button on a wall panel. A few seconds later both Kingman and Verland turned to look at a part of the room not captured by the camera. From the layout, Elle guessed it was the door.

And now a third person comes onscreen…David Klee, looking much younger than his twenty-eight years. He stands in front of Kingman, and they exchange a few words. Klee nods; Elle can see him form a word—"Yes." Kingman turns, picks up the dagger, and then, quicker than she would have expected, quicker and without any tense buildup of music, without any close-up shot at the moment of death, Kingman plunges the dagger into Klee's chest. There is surprisingly little blood. Kingman pulls the dagger out and looks at it as if it should know what's supposed to happen next. In his final moment of fidelity to the script, Klee clasps his hands to his chest and sinks to the floor, legs splayed out at an angle impossible in life. The scene becomes a still shot for the next few seconds…Kingman makes an awkward, forward-jerking motion, stops…Verland, motionless until now, goes to the body, kneels down…

Elle held her breath, waiting for his teeth against Klee's neck—she would have to leave the room if that happened, she could not watch that...but Verland picks up Klee's limp hands and holds them in his own, lowers his head in a moment of... what? Prayer? Grief? Then he stands up, turns to face Kingman, holds his gaze for an agonizingly slow four, five seconds, and then he's gone. Kingman looks at Klee for only a moment before gesturing and shouting to someone outside the frame, and then he, too, disappears. The camera turns its cold, impersonal gaze to the body now lying alone on the floor. It holds the shot for several minutes and then the scene goes black.

They both sat staring at it in silence for a while before Nyholm finally spoke. "There's actually hours more footage on the original tape, including the cops and forensics team showing up. But I only had time to transfer this part, which is all I really wanted anyway."

Elle's thoughts were spinning in spirographs of confusion, but she knew this would be her only chance to get some answers.

"So Kingman really did kill Klee." Not much of a start, but all she could manage for now.

"Of course he killed Klee. I thought everybody knew that. The real question was always why, though maybe now you've figured that out."

No, not really."

Nyholm seemed eager to talk. Elle guessed that too many secrets had been building up for too many years, and it looked as if Nyholm had chosen now to let them out.

"After Kingman's father died, he became obsessed with death; and for Kingman, an obsession always ends up as a film. That's where *By Night* came from. He hired three new research assistants to work on the film: Klee, Vita, and me. I was the oldest, the most sure of myself, I guess, so I became the de facto leader. 'Head' research assistant—that was one of the bigger crumbs Kingman threw my way. He already had a ton of assistants at his disposal, but this batch needed to be something different, something completely separate from any of his other work. He did his homework and found people who all had an interest in death and the afterlife, an interest that some would say crossed the line into obsession. It also helped that we were all a bunch of misfits who couldn't really make it in the mainstream. Drifters without any real direction or career prospects to worry about. In other words, just the sort of people ready to commit wholesale to Kingman's vision. And he was right—not one of us even hesitated to jump in just as hard and deep as he did."

"And this vision included more than making a film about vampires."

"Much more. Before his father died, Kingman had never lost anything in his life, and he decided that he wasn't going to let a little thing like death get the better of him. He set out to learn everything he could about the so-called black arts. Magic, blood rituals, communion with the dead. All of it. For Kingman, you learn everything you can about a subject, and then you conquer it."

"And that's where Zor came in."

"Right. Synchronicity, I guess. Zor and his stupid FBI program turns up a vampire right in the middle of making the film. Once he got the info from the program, Kingman tracked Verland down with the help of his goon squad. He studied Verland for a long time before he finally made contact, and his timing was perfect. *By Night* had just come out. You know from reading the diary that Verland has always been interested in the vampire legend and how they're represented, all the way back to Polidori and Stoker. He hadn't seen *By Night,* but it was all over the news, so of course he'd read about it, knew what it was about. Have you seen it?"

"Yeah, I've seen it."

It had been released in October with a lot of Halloween fanfare, and she and Gary had gone to see it on the opening weekend. There had been some good parts about the vampire trying to find his place in society, but the plot had mostly functioned as a setup for lots of body counts and flying blood. In other words, a typical Kingman number.

"Then you know that like anyone else who makes money in this town, Kingman can't tell a story with even an ounce of subtlety. But still, he at least showed the vampire as something other than the usual horror monster or teenage romance sort of thing, and if nothing else, the film got Kingman's name associated with vampires, which meant that he could use it to connect with Verland. I don't really know how much Verland ever told Kingman, whether or not he ever came out and said, 'Hey, yeah, I'm an immortal bloodsucker,' or whatever. But Kingman was obviously convinced, and he sold himself to Verland as the guy who would finally tell the real deal about being a vampire; or at least Verland's version of it, anyway."

"But Verland wasn't interested in Kingman being the one to tell it."

"I don't think a Kingman movie is quite Verland's style, do you?"

"No, I don't think so. Coppola, sure. Scorsese, maybe. But Kingman—not so much."

Nyholm laughed for the first time since she'd met him. "I don't completely know what all went on between them. I was never actually allowed any contact with Verland; nobody was except Kingman. He never wanted any one person to know too much. He made sure to toss each of us our own little scatter of crumbs, but no one ever got a complete piece of the pie. Only Kingman really knew what was going on. That's how he operates, how he keeps such complete control. But one thing everyone knew for sure—Kingman wanted immortality from the first second he found out about Verland. And he wanted it more than anything he'd ever wanted in his life—more than all of his success and money and talent combined. A thousand times more."

"But in the diary, Verland promises Gideon that he'll never transform anyone. And if you ask me, he doesn't seem like the kind of vampire to break a promise."

Nyholm gave one of his bitter smiles. "You don't know Kingman. He was born with that lucky combination of talent and superhuman ego, and Hollywood went and cemented the whole thing. He's spent the last thirty years in a town where men like him are considered gods. There's nothing, *nothing*, that Eliot Kingman believes he can't do."

Elle noticed his use of the present tense. "But he couldn't convince Verland."

"No. Somewhere along the line, even Kingman had to admit that Verland wasn't exactly signing up for the team. So he figures he needs some leverage. He sends his men to go find something he can use; they turn up the diary, and that's pretty much that. When Kingman thought he couldn't get Verland, he got the diary, which was the next best thing."

"Because he knew Verland would come for it."

"Exactly. And that's what you saw on the video. Verland coming for his diary, coming for what was his in the first place. Kingman set the whole thing up. That's why nobody else was around that night. Kingman didn't even want his security team directly involved; he wanted to run the whole show on his own. His big opening night, I guess."

"How does Klee come into it?"

"Kingman and Verland spent a lot of time talking about how vampires have to kill people in order to survive. Verland didn't think Kingman fully understood that part, the consequences of taking a life. So Kingman got it into his head that this was the one big thing standing in the way of his transformation."

"And killing Klee proves to Verland that he has what it takes."

"Exactly. He proves he can kill, but that's not all. Did Kingman ever tell you about his master plan—his vampire society fed by legions of the faithful willing to die for their survival? Well, Verland got to see the first convert."

"Klee knew what was going to happen all along?"

"Oh, yeah. That's why he started sending his family all of those 'I'm going to a better place' messages that Kingman's lawyers used to say he killed himself. It was suicide in a way, I guess. But not by his own hand."

"So Klee believed Verland was an actual vampire?"

"We all did, at least as much as anyone could without actually *knowing*, you know? At first we all kind of wanted to believe, if not in vampires per se then at least in Kingman. In his vision. Then, as things went along, we started to believe for real. The diary...that's what convinced us, I guess." Nyholm trailed off, trying to find the words. "You can believe something without actually *believing* it, you know what I mean?"

"Yes, I do." In fact, Nyholm had just more or less summed up her own feelings from the first time the word vampire had come into play, right up through the video she'd just seen.

"David—that's 'Klee's' name, you know—David's whole family, his parents and an older sister, were killed in a car crash when he was only three years old. He was with them in the car, the only survivor. His grandparents raised him and he had a completely normal life, hardly even remembered his family or anything about the crash. But who knows what stays with a person, you know? He never really got over how he was still around and they weren't. Never really shook the feeling that his family was out there somewhere just waiting for him to join them. I guess it's not surprising that he took such an interest in religion. He one hundred percent believed in God, in the afterlife.

"When Kingman stole the diary, I translated that thing night and day. I mean, I would sleep maybe four, five hours if I was lucky, eat whatever was put in front of me, and then sit with that diary and a stack of dictionaries and language books. Kingman didn't want anyone else to even know it existed, so I was on my own. The early parts were really difficult; sometimes I had to improvise in a few places where the pages were damaged or the writing was messed up, but once I got rolling, I managed to produce a working copy in a little over a month.

"With Kingman riding me every second of the day, I'm surprised it took that long, but at the end of the day, I'm still an academic. I wasn't going to cut any corners or make any mistakes. Sometimes I spent an entire afternoon with just one or two sentences, or hours on the possible meaning of one word. The longer the diary went on, though, the easier it got, and by the time I hit the Spanish, it was no problem at all. I've never really stopped working on it, though— reworking a passage or tweaking a word here or there. Perfecting it. That version you read is probably like my sixth or seventh one so far, and every time I finished a new one, I had to destroy the old one. Only one copy could ever exist at any time.

"Anyway, once the first version was finished, Kingman got us all together and we read it through from beginning to end. Then we sat for hours discussing it, and he watched us every step of the way—our reactions, our responses. He studied us like he studies everything. David was the one most moved by Gideon's death. He couldn't stop talking about it. It didn't take much for Kingman to push him into what you just saw happen."

"And Kingman thought it was a good idea to film himself committing murder?"

"Kingman's a filmmaker before all else. And David's death wasn't the point. That was just the prelude to what he thought would be his own transformation into the ranks of the immortal. Do you think Kingman could let that go by without capturing it for posterity? That room you see in the film is Kingman's 'memorabilia room.' It has a false wall built along one side big enough to fit a sixteen-millimeter camera. The lens is completely obscured among an incredibly expensive piece of modern art, and the false wall is so well constructed that no one's ever suspected it's even there. You'd be surprised at the things that camera has caught through the years."

Elle didn't think she'd be surprised at all, but she let it pass and waited for Nyholm to continue. When he did, his voice had dropped to a ragged whisper, and he had disappeared inside his own memories.

"I was there that night…not in the room—Kingman didn't want anyone else in the room. But I helped set up the camera, like I always did. I brought Verland into the house. You know, up to that moment, even with the diary, a part of me still believed it was all some fantasy, an idea we were working on, like some really cool grad school project, you know? But then he was *right there*, he was *real*, but also *not* real, you know? At a quick glance he could have been just anybody, but then you look closer and he's just…I don't know, *off*. His skin and the way he carries himself…his eyes. I don't know, his whole *self*… just *off*. I can't explain it."

Elle thought of Verland's strange presence, compelling even as an image on a flat screen. She didn't think Nyholm needed to explain.

"I never even spoke one word to him," Nyholm continued. "Just brought him back to the room. It was Kingman's final move in the game, and he never doubted for a minute he would win. He had two ace cards up his sleeve—David and the diary. Kingman tried to convince Verland to turn him without bringing David into it, he really did. I have to give him that. He played the game hard, and he played it well—the best role of his career! But it turned out Verland wasn't even in the game. After a while, I got the signal that meant I was supposed to bring David in. You know, after Verland went into the room, David came into the hall and just stood there, waiting. I was a nervous wreck, but he was so *calm*. He hadn't even *seen* Verland at that point. I'll never know whether he was so calm because he actually *did* believe in Kingman's plan and an afterlife and all that, or because he didn't believe *any* of it, didn't really think any of it would happen, you know?"

Nyholm paused for so long that Elle wondered if he had finished, but eventually he went on.

"We were all so caught up in Kingman's world, in his vision. He made it all sound so *important*... I know this is going to sound lame, but he made it sound so *exciting*, like one of his movies or something. None of us had ever done or been anything, had ever mattered even one bit in the world, and now we were finally doing something big, bigger than anything anyone had ever done before. And Verland was right, I guess. About the killing thing. I guess I just didn't believe that Kingman could ever kill someone. That David would really die. It sounds stupid, I know, like a child or an idiot, but..."

Nyholm closed his eyes and put his head into his hands. Removed from Kingman's haunted mansion, Elle finally saw him for what he really was—not some coldhearted ghoul or brainwashed pawn in Kingman's game, but a desperately confused young man amid the shattered ruins of everything he had once believed in.

"In the video, when Verland takes Kl—*David's*—hand like that. Why did he do that? Did they know each other?"

"No way did they know each other! They never even *met*. I can one hundred percent guarantee that. I have no idea why Verland did that. Maybe he couldn't believe Kingman had really killed him. That it was faked or something. I don't know."

"But he still wouldn't transform Kingman, even after he knew David was dead."

"No. In fact, he totally got out of there like two seconds later. Just *bang*! Out the door and gone before I even knew what happened. I looked into the room and that's when I saw David. Kingman told me to follow Verland, to not let him go no matter what I had to do. He was obviously half out of it from what had happened, killing David and all, because how could I follow a freakin' *vampire*, let alone stop him from going anywhere? I guess I had lost it, too, though, because I did follow him, out the back of the house and all the way up to the cliffs. I tried to keep up with him, even headed toward the staircase with the idea of following him down to the beach, but then I saw him go straight over the cliff and that was it. He was totally out of sight before I even knew it; there was nothing I could do."

He paused, lost in his own thoughts again.

"You know, at first, all of us—David, Vita, and me—we were just three people thrown together, feeling lucky to have gotten such a great gig. I mean, here we were in this unbelievable mansion, not just making movies with one of the biggest names in Hollywood but actually a part of his *inner circle*. We spent every day together, going deeper and deeper into this closed-off little world…we all got close—*really* close. By the time the movie came out, we were almost completely isolated from everyone else, even our own families. So standing out there in the dead of night with the Pacific roaring in my ears…one of my closest friends had just been stabbed through the heart by the person I admired most in the whole world, I was chasing a vampire who might just pop up any second and kill me, and I don't know… I just lost it."

Elle thought about what Gary had told her about the untraceable phone. Whether he had been aware of it or not, Nyholm's confidence in Kingman must have been on shaky ground even before Klee's death.

"You were the one who made the nine-one-one call."

He got up and began pacing back and forth. This wasn't easy with Gort parked in the middle of the room, and he eventually sat back down.

"I didn't go back to the house until way after Kingman had been arrested. The cops were still there, but the forensics team had finished and I was allowed back in the house. They never turned up the false wall. No one did. I didn't think I had a lot of time, even though it turns out that Kingman didn't even request a lawyer right off. He was still so sure of himself, still so caught up in his fantasies. I think he actually wanted to keep the game going, like, see how much smarter I am than all of you, worried about some stupid murder? Don't you wish you knew what *I* know? That attitude came back to haunt him in the end, but it bought me time. I waited until the room was cleared, and then I snuck in and got the film reel. I brought it here and transferred only what I needed in order to get it back as soon as possible. By the time Kingman wised up to at least some version of reality and got his lawyers to arrange bail, everything was back in place as if it had never been gone. Kingman never knew. At least, I don't think he knew; but I'm not so sure of anything anymore."

"But why show it to me now?"

Whatever had compelled Nyholm to betray Kingman on the night of Klee's murder, he had still kept playing on the team as far as Elle could tell. For all she knew, this whole thing was part of some elaborate setup. After all, Nyholm himself said that Kingman was always master of the game, always the one who made the rules and set up every play.

"In order to understand that, you'd have to understand something about me, and I seriously doubt you care one way or the other."

"Actually, I do care, Nyholm."

Elle realized that this was the first time she'd called him by his name. She leaned over and took his hands in hers; only much later did it occur to her that she had reenacted Kazamira's gesture to Verland on the night they had met, the same one he had given back to her when they parted. Then Verland had given it to Gideon on the floor of their volcano hut, and Gideon brought it full circle on the pathway to Juan

Noq. It was the same gesture Verland had enacted with David Klee—simple yet powerful in its immediacy, its intimacy—*I'm here*. Nyholm flinched, but he didn't pull away.

"Do you have any brothers or sisters?"

"A brother. Half, anyway, but I didn't grow up with him. I'm way older. More like an aunt or something."

"I have a brother, six years older than me. Just old enough to always be out ahead, always bigger and stronger and cooler, but close enough to still be buddies. He was like one of those guys you see in a teen movie or something—good-looking, a natural at just about any sport, smart, but not too smart. Friendly with everybody, but always the leader. One of those guys with every-thing going for him who somehow manages to not be a total dick about it, you know?"

Elle did know. She had just gotten a proposal from one of those guys.

"I know what you're thinking," Nyholm said. "But no, I wasn't adopted. Just the way the gene pool coagulated, I guess. Anyway, I completely idolized him. And I got lucky. He let me tag along sometimes with him and his friends. Taught me about sports and girls and all those other things I was so hopeless about. How to play all the cool songs on guitar—that kind of thing. He was a good brother, even to a loser like me who wouldn't even be allowed to sit *near* his lunch table in whatever parallel universe is out there where we aren't related. We stayed pretty close even when he went to college. When he got married, I was the best man, even though he had a social network prob-ably bigger than some small towns. But all that changed about six years ago. I was twenty-seven, just out of grad school; head filled with all kinds of lofty ideas, ready to reinvent academia. My brother was thirty-three. He and his wife had just had their first kid. She wasn't even a year old yet when he started having problems. It first showed up in his hands, losing dexterity and strength. He was tired all the time, which was totally unlike him. Do you know anything about amyotrophic lateral sclerosis, or what most people call Lou Gehrig's disease?"

"I've heard of it, but I don't really know anything about it."

"Most people don't. It's a progressive disease that affects nerve cells in the brain and the spinal cord. When the motor neurons die, the brain can't control muscle movement. That eventually leads to complete paralysis, then death. There's no treatment and there's no cure. Half the people diagnosed die within three years, ninety percent within six."

Nyholm took his hands from hers and began clenching and unclenching them in his lap. Elle knew that every time he told this story, he fought the same struggle against the old wounds that actually don't heal with time. At least not enough to prevent them from being ripped open again with even the dullest knife edge of memory.

"Another thing about ALS is that it works fast. Within three months, he couldn't do any of his hobbies, couldn't play sports, couldn't take his boat out. A couple more months, he had to give up his job. Restructuring computer systems or something like that. He went from making bucket loads of money and owning this big house to disability and a modest one-story with wheelchair accessibility. Within six months, it went from his hands to his diaphragm. His breathing started to go, and he couldn't swallow. He got a feeding tube, and in another year, he needed a full tracheotomy and ventilator to breathe for him. I would go to see him, and that thing would be trailing him like some evil little robot that had taken over his body, *pssssh-ke, pssssh-ke,* day and night, keeping him alive. He's now in a power wheelchair with almost no mobility left. He can only talk a little bit, and when he does, you can't really understand him. Without his speaking program, he'd be totally unable to communicate. And the thing with ALS—it doesn't affect the mind at all, so you know everything that's happening the whole way through."

"And your brother, him getting this disease, that's partly what attracted you to Kingman's plan?" Considering his brother's condition, Elle could only imagine the maddening temptation of Verland's powers.

"I just couldn't believe this was happening to him, you know? How do you go from being an athletic guy in the prime of your life, no major health problems whatsoever, to being immobilized in a wheelchair in less than two years? What kind of world have we been handed where something like that could happen? It's like all of the philosophy and history and big ideas I'd studied in school got thrown right out the window; like none of it meant anything, wasn't worth one tiny thing, in the face of what was happening to my brother. Diseases like that, they just level *everything.*"

He smoothed his hands across his legs. The worst part was over.

"When I met Kingman, I was just drifting around. I just couldn't care about anything anymore, didn't really want to do anything. Kingman changed all of that. All of a sudden, here was this thing, bigger than ALS, bigger than death, even. A way out, an option. It didn't matter if I thought vampires were real. It was the *idea* that mattered. The idea was real; Kingman's vision was real. And that's what mattered."

"But David's death changed all of that?"

"It definitely started there. From the second I saw his body there, I stopped making any conscious decisions, stopped thinking anything through. I actually did everything possible *not* to think, to just go through the motions, to keep going. Then the trial started and everything got really crazy. When Kingman was found guilty, no one ever thought that would happen, even though he practically convicted himself with his stupid behavior. Then all of a sudden he was gone, David was gone. I didn't want to just leave Vita. I didn't know what to do, where to go. Technically, I was an accessory to David's death. I guess it was just easier to stay there in the mansion, to hide from the world."

"So what changed all of a sudden?"

"It wasn't all of a sudden. No matter how much I pretended that nothing existed outside of the mansion, after David's death, a part of me wanted to get away from everything and everybody even associated with Kingman, with that place. A few months after Kingman went to prison, I went to visit my brother. I hadn't seen him for a couple of years. They're on the East Coast, in Massachusetts; I was across the country in L.A.… and to be honest, it was just easier to not visit, to not have to face what was happening to him. I know how selfish and shitty that is, but that's how it was for me then. After the trial, I was a total wreck. Going to see him was probably the worst thing to do given my state of mind, but I still wasn't sure what might happen, if I would eventually be charged with something or I don't even know what. I guess I wanted to make sure I saw him at least one more time before he died."

He rummaged around in his bag and pulled out a dog-eared photograph. "That's him. My brother, Joel."

Elle studied the picture of a handsome man in a wheelchair with a woman standing next to him. They were outside, and even though the sun was shining and the woman was in a summer outfit, Joel was under a heavy blanket. She could see the trach tube taped to his neck. They were both smiling.

"That's his wife, Christine. She's stayed with him through the whole thing."

"They must love each other very much."

"They do. That's the thing—I went to Massachusetts with some big dramatic deathbed scenario in my head. But when I got there, I found out that Joel wasn't in any way just sitting there waiting to die; in fact, he was totally engaged with being alive. You know, I never expected him and Christine to be so…*happy*, I guess. Don't get me wrong, I'm not sugarcoating things. Joel requires around-the-clock care now, and they've had to hire a part-time caregiver. They both have their bad days. Sometimes *real* bad days. But Joel showed me the computer site he built to help other people learn about and deal with the disease. In a section called 'Afraid of dying?' he talks about death and the fear that goes with a terminal illness, about his faith in God and how to carry on with your life. He volunteers on an online support forum, has all these friends he talks to from all over the world. His daughter is starting school this year. He's lived to see that when his doctors told him he might not make her third birthday. He knows the reality, the statistics. But he also knows that all any of us ever get is just a chance, and it's up to us to take that chance as far as we can go.

"When I left for L.A., the last thing he said to me was something like 'Life continues to be good and worth living.' That's it—nothing profound or earth-shattering, but I don't know, it just stopped me right there in the airport. The whole way home, I kept thinking of my brother, a complete prisoner in his own body, a guy who had the kind of life everyone hopes for and lost it. And yet in every way that counts, he was more alive than I was. He was busy with things he cared about, he was surrounded by people who loved him. He was doing things that mattered, helping people.

"And then there was Kingman, another guy who had lost the kind of life most people only dream about. Only he didn't lose it to some disease beyond his control—he *threw it away* for a chance at some dark and brutal version of immortality, to be trapped in his body forever in a way that even my brother couldn't begin to imagine. For the first time I really saw how crazy it all was. When I got back home, I reread the whole diary, and even though I'd spent so much time poring over every word and sentence, for the first time I really got it. What Gideon was trying to tell Verland, how all of it had hit home among those ruins in Mexico, with the donkey… I made the decision right then to get away from Kingman and leave the whole mess behind. The only problem was convincing Vita to come with me."

Elle was beginning to suspect that the "really close" relationship that had developed among the three of them had gone much farther than friendship; which couldn't have made things easier when Kingman decided to claim Vita for himself.

"But Vita remained loyal to Kingman. I mean, she went so far as to marry him before the trial."

"Yeah." The bitterness in Nyholm's voice all but confirmed Elle's theory.

"That was meant to help Kingman out with the press and for legal purposes in a worst-case scenario. They had been involved before that, but I don't know...after David's death, Vita got even more obsessed than before. With the vampire thing, with immortality, with Kingman—all of it. I knew I had to be very careful with what I said, because unlike me, she was totally loyal to him. I was still trying to sort out what to do when you showed up. That's when I realized once and for all that prison hadn't changed anything for Kingman. He was just as determined as ever, maybe even more so. I knew then that somehow, someday, he would find a way to overturn his conviction and get out of prison. And once he did that, he would come after Verland all over again. He would never stop until he got the ultimate prize, the only one that matters to him anymore."

"And what about Vita?"

"I kept trying with her, I swear I did. But the harder I pushed, the more she withdrew. I'm pretty sure she's already told Kingman that I want to leave, which is the reason for all the paranoia. It's like I've finally woken up from some nightmare, and to tell you the truth, I'm scared to death. I don't put anything past Kingman at this point, I really don't. I've seen firsthand what he's capable of, how far he's willing to go. That's what this is." He ejected the disc from the computer and put it back into his bag. "Insurance."

"What do you mean?"

"All I want at this point is out. I don't want any money, nothing. I want to go back to Massachusetts, get to know my brother again. Spend some time with my family, maybe go back to academics. Only now I think I'd be happy to just work in it rather than reinvent it. I want to rejoin the living, you know? I figure this disc is my get-out-of-jail-free card. I left a copy at the mansion before I left. Vita will tell Kingman about it. He'll know where it came from, but he won't know how many more of these there might be out there, or who knows about them. What's on this disc would keep Kingman in prison for the rest of his life, not to mention bring Verland to the world's attention, which he actually cares more about than his own situation. But all of it stays safe as long as I stay safe, and that's where it ends as far as I'm concerned."

Elle doubted if that's where it would end as far as Kingman was concerned, and she wondered if Nyholm had been watching too many noir films himself lately. "Why was Vita chosen?"

"What?"

"Vita. You said that Kingman chose each of you for a reason. What was Vita's?"

He hesitated. His loyalty to Kingman may have been long gone, but he was still reluctant to betray Vita.

"Unlike me or David, Vita's obsession with death was firsthand. She started having periods of depression and going through mood swings when she was a teenager. Probably even before then, but that's when it got bad enough for her parents to notice. They got her some counseling and things got better, but when she went to college, she just lost it. Couldn't handle the pressure of making new friends, being on her own. She tried to kill herself with some pills and booze during her freshman year. Said she just woke up one morning and tried to think of a reason to get out of bed, and couldn't come up with even one. The second time was at the end of her junior year, and she'd done her homework this time. Cut her arms, vertical and deep right along the arteries. She would have died if her roommate's professor hadn't overslept or had a date with his mistress or whatever else had caused him to cancel class at the last minute. Vita spent some time in a hospital for that one, but her parents had money, so it never went on record. The school had no problem with that; they sure as hell didn't want that kind of thing coming up at parents' weekend."

"But Kingman knew about it."

"Of course. It's like I told you—Kingman knew all about us, knew all about everything. At least, *almost* everything."

Nyholm reached into his bag and retrieved a book, an old one with a green leather cover that seemed to shift and change as Elle looked at it—the diary. Nyholm started laughing, clutching it to his chest like a little boy delighted with his own cleverness.

"Shocking, huh? You know how Kingman stole it from Verland? Well, *I* stole it from Kingman! Now that's justice for you!"

"Another get-out-of-jail-free card?"

"What? Oh, no way. Kingman knows that Verland will eventually come for this diary. If he knew I had it, he'd hunt me down for sure, video or no video. As much as this book has meant to me in the past few years, I have no intention of keeping it."

He released the diary from his chest and looked at it one last time before holding it out to her.

"I'm giving it to you."

Elle stared at it, equal parts sinister and compelling. She didn't want the diary, didn't even want to touch it. "What am I supposed to do with it?"

"Well, you can finally finish reading it, for one. The rest of it is in English. It goes all the way up to Verland meeting Kingman, actually."

"Why take the risk of stealing it if you don't want it?"

"Because Kingman doesn't deserve to have it. He never did. And when he gets out of prison—and he will get out, I don't know how and I don't know when, but he will—he's going to do whatever it takes to find Verland again. I decided he didn't need one more weapon to help him do it."

"I take it you no longer want Kingman to succeed with his plans."

"Like I said, a lot has changed for me since David's death. I sure as hell don't want someone like Kingman to become a vampire. But it's more than that. I used to think it would be the greatest thing in the world to have that kind of power, to live forever. But not anymore. I think Gideon was right; that's it's more like a curse to never die. To never find out what comes next. I think someday, Verland will come to the same place Gideon did, but that should be his choice. No way should he be taken out just so a bastard like Kingman can play god over some vampire kingdom."

Elle wasn't surprised that even now Nyholm didn't want to help destroy the creature whose story he had brought to life from the pages of that book, one painstaking word at a time.

"But won't Kingman know you stole the diary? I mean, you're gone, it's gone…"

"No one's even going to know it's missing, at least not until I'm on the other side of the country. I told you that Kingman keeps the diary in a top-of-the-line security vault. It has, like, five safeguards and a ton of elaborate codes. He was so paranoid about keeping Verland a secret that no one but him knew the codes all the way up through the trial. After he was convicted, though, he needed someone to handle the diary. Well, that someone was me. I'm the only person on earth other than Kingman who knows the codes. They're not even written down anywhere; they're all in here." He tapped his fingers against his head and smiled as if he'd covered all of the bases.

"But he'll tell someone else the codes once you're gone. Vita, maybe."

"He doesn't trust Vita. He knows how unstable she is, which is why he didn't want her anywhere near the mansion the night Verland showed up. The night of David's death. He'll eventually recruit someone else—who knows, maybe he has you in mind for the job. Now *that* would be some irony! But like I said, I'll be long gone by then."

"I don't know, Nyholm. Why should I step right in the middle of something that you yourself just made a pretty good case for wanting out of?"

"Because you're not ready to walk away from it just yet. Because Verland *will* come for the diary someday, and maybe you need to see him for yourself, like I did. The diary could give you that power, you know. Even more, if you want it. As soon as you walk out of here, you could give the diary back to Kingman, or even just throw it in the nearest Dumpster and forget you ever saw it. Or you could keep it—it's up to you. Here, take it."

She reached out and touched its surface, rough and cracked in places, worn smooth in others. She half expected it to ripple beneath her fingers like some ancient serpent stirred to life, but it just felt like a very old book. She watched Nyholm's fingers loosen their hold, watched hers tighten, and then it was in her hands.

He pulled out a notebook and handed that over, as well.

"This is the latest, greatest translation of the German and Spanish parts. Who knows, you may need it someday."

Elle sat there trying to think of something to say, but Nyholm suddenly shot out of the room.

"Wait here," he called over his shoulder, and she heard him rummaging in a closet in the hallway. When he returned, he was carrying a bag that looked as if it had been abandoned in a bowling alley somewhere around 1973.

"I realize it's not going to win any fashion awards, but you need something to carry it in."

Nyholm was right—if she exposed the diary to the Los Feliz hipsters breezing by, lattes in one hand, cell phones in the other, it just might burst into flames right there on the sidewalk. Not to mention that one of Kingman's men could be lurking around any corner.

"My friend will take you back to Griffith Park. You'll understand if I don't come along to see you off, but I've got a plane to catch."

Elle always wanted to say something meaningful at moments like this, even though she rarely managed it.

"I'm glad you decided to trust me, Nyholm. Not just with the video and the diary, but with David, your brother...all of it. I hope you find everything you're looking for in Massachusetts."

"Thanks. But I think I've already found what I'm looking for, maybe for the first time in my life. I hope you do, too, Elle—find whatever you were looking for that drew you into this thing in the first place."

She gripped the heavy outline of the diary all the way back to Hollywood, trying to figure out exactly what that might be.

CHAPTER 17

*I*n her apartment, Elle pulled all of the blinds and laid the diary on her kitchen table. She circled around it for a while, waiting for it to spring to life and lunge for her neck. Among the rooster-print wallpaper and orange teapot, it looked like a prop from some spooky movie that had ended up on the wrong set. Only this was no prop. For some reason she was reluctant to pick it up, as if handling it for any length of time would only add to its already potent draw. It certainly had consumed Nyholm, and Elle knew how difficult it must have been for him to just hand it over without even knowing what she would do with it.

She thought about the first time she had seen it, how the images on the cover had seemed to shift and blend the longer she had looked at it. She bent closer; there was the circular tree with the interwoven animals and leaves…and there were the faces again… She pulled away and wiped her palms on her shorts as if she had touched something disagreeable. But the diary drew her back like a gravitational force. She opened the front cover, turning pages of German and Spanish script until the words jumped into comprehension. Just as Nyholm had promised—good old English and an ordinary ball point pen. The place was also familiar this time, and she sat down to finally find out where Verland's story had ended.

August 1971; Los Angeles, California

I have a great deal of catching up to do with the modern world. Society keeps much better track of its members these days, and it is not quite as easy to simply disappear without a trace and reemerge as someone else. However, one thing has not changed: almost anything can still be acquired if one has means enough to get it. In fact, the modern method of assigning a man a name and a number has in some ways made it easier than ever to maintain a number of perfectly legitimate identities at the same time.

Living conditions are also quite easy to arrange. I now live in an apartment just like thousands of others all across the city. I have discovered a fascinating array of modern locking systems, and with blackout shades on the windows and the door bolted, I can achieve a level of isolation and security unimaginable in the lodging houses of nineteenth-century Berlin. In this fast-paced city of millions, it seems that no one complains or asks questions as long as the bills are paid on time.

November

I have discovered that in addition to live musical performances, which I still prefer, I can own an unlimited selection of recordings and play them at any time in my own home. I have been listening to Chopin's Nocturnes for several weeks now without pause.

Films are another newly discovered pleasure. Movie-making was only just beginning to gain popularity when I left Germany, and those early versions bear very little resemblance to the marvels of technology now found on every cinema screen.

19 February, 1972

In this new age without disease and starvation, without great swaths of the poor and forsaken left to their fates, I had thought feeding would prove more difficult than before. But I simply needed to look with different eyes—as always, mankind still pushes aside those who miss a step, those who stumble and fall too far behind in the ceaseless race forward.

April

Over the last few years, I have noticed a sharpening of my abilities, and for the first time I feel myself approaching some of Gideon's power. For instance, although it still takes tremendous effort to control a human's actions to even the smallest degree, my ability to connect with their thoughts has significantly improved. The experience is not akin to actually reading their minds like words in a book, but is rather more of a general impression, I suppose, of their emotions or thoughts at a particular point in time.

This ability comes in quite handy when feeding. Yes, we must kill in order to survive; but while walking the city streets or watching a crowd from the shadows, it is most helpful to be able to identify those whose departure from this earth will cause the least amount of sorrow—or even, in more cases than one might think, a great deal of relief.

Winter

I have opened an account identifiable by a code known only to myself and a restricted number of bank employees. The name of the account holder is completely protected, and this system will ensure that my finances are secure and free from scrutiny for many years to come.

March 1973

For some months now, I have been trying to locate Kazamira. I tracked down the steamship *Waldersee,* which set sail from Hamburg on August 12, 1914, only to learn that the journey was an ill-fated one: according to news reports, the ship was just offshore in the early hours of August 26 when a shipment of wool in the cargo area caught fire. The flames swept through the ship, trapping the passengers in their cabins. Most managed to escape by jumping overboard or making it into the lifeboats, but 212 people died and 15 were never found. The name on the identity papers I had acquired for Kazamira was among those fifteen.

I realized that there were only two possibilities regarding her fate. The first is that she perished in the blaze, which would explain why no remains were found. The second is that she abandoned the ship and swam to shore; unlike the other passengers, she would have had no need or desire to make her survival known. I decided to believe in the second possibility.

I wonder how long her promise had lasted to keep the same identity until we were reunited? Perhaps until the end of the war, at least—although knowing Kazamira, she may have changed it immediately, perhaps even been forced to do so through some reckless act or stroke of bad luck. By now she could be anyone, could be anywhere in the world. And despite my desire to believe in her survival, she could also, of course, be long dead. This possibility haunts me all the more because I cannot help but think that if she were still alive, I would be able to sense at least something of her presence; though perhaps I am crediting myself with greater powers than I yet possess.

January 1975

The city celebrates another new year. The diversions of the modern world have already begun to lose their charm. Occasionally, I take a human lover, but these encounters seem more and more meaningless with each passing year. The loneliness and malaise once again spread through me like a slow and deadly infection. Those precious years with Gideon caused me to forget the torments of solitude, the despair of finding oneself hour after hour, day after day, year after endless year, completely, utterly alone.

20 June, 1976

Some time ago, I contacted a scholar of ancient religions and arranged to sell some of Gideon's scrolls to a "completely top-secret" buyer. Many of the scrolls are already half disintegrated, and as I can neither decipher nor preserve them, they will be better off with those who can make use of their value. As I could provide no documentation about how I acquired these "artifacts," it took a great deal of elaborate testing before their experts were convinced of their authenticity—although I could have convinced them immediately had they wished it.

The scrolls date back to the time of Gideon's transformation, so who knows what secrets they may contain. The scholar has assured me that the contents will be made known to the public, and this may indeed prove so; but the cynic in me would not be surprised if I failed to hear of their existence for many more years to come.

I have also decided to part with the paintings, which surely weren't intended to molder away in the corner of a dank apartment with only my own poor self for an admirer. I could not imagine putting a price upon such treasures, so I simply boxed them up and sent them to a museum in New York City without explanation; I do not suppose they will have too much trouble authenticating them, as well.

September 1979

I have taken to traveling up and down the coastline in order to relieve the tedium. Occasionally, I consider moving to some new place, perhaps even an entirely new country. But why move about when all places end up being the same as any other? No, it is much easier to remain in Los Angeles, a city in which the present exists only in the brief moment between past glories and future dreams.

12 January, 1980

At a bar last night, I saw a man who resembled Gideon—something about the curve of the nose, the set of the mouth, the way he gestured when he spoke... I watched him from my dark corner of the room, and I felt something stir to life that I had not felt in a very long time. I was on my feet and advancing toward him, his name on my lips, before I realized what I was doing and retreated to the shadows. But my vigil continued.

He was with a large group of friends, and I waited until he was alone before drawing near. I entered his thoughts, but could discover no special bond or connection to tie him to Gideon. However, I was not deterred, and when he took leave of the place, I followed him.

Imagine my surprise when his path led to the apartment building right next to my own! It cannot be a coincidence that he resides so close to me, and I must find out who this man is and what role he is to play in my life. The most secret part of me cannot help but ask, cannot help but hope—is this Gideon, somehow returned to me?

14 February

His apartment is located opposite my own; from my living room, I can see two of his windows in the upper-right-hand corner of his building. Occasionally, his lights burn long into the night, and I often wonder what he is doing during such lonely hours, when most of his kind have long since given themselves over to their dreams.

13 March

I have finally spoken to him. Yesterday, I followed him to a café, and fate again intervened. He produced a book from his bag, a popular new novel about a subject most interesting to me—*vampires*. This was the chance I had been waiting for, and as we struck up a conversation about the book, I could not help but wonder if this author, like Bram Stoker, had come across an actual vampire and used what she had learned to create her story. Needless to say, I quite impressed him with my own knowledge of the vampire "myth."

Although I find this man intelligent and engaging, I have not yet had any real sense of recognition in regard to Gideon. Perhaps this will be revealed to me in time; or perhaps—should I permit myself to think it?—perhaps Gideon must become what he once was in order to truly return to me.

20 March

As our friendship progresses, I can no longer deny that I am heading down a dangerous path toward one most treacherous destination—breaking my oath to Gideon. How can I even think to go back on a promise made to him who means more to me than all others?

And yet if this man contains something of Gideon's essence, something of his soul that somehow returned to this earth, is that the same as some random transformation performed upon the ignorant or the unwilling? Isn't it rather a restoration of what was, of what is meant to be again? Only this time, Gideon's existence would be closer in length to my own; we could erase the long centuries that separated him from me, that caused him to leave me far too soon. That cannot truly be breaking the oath, but rather correcting a cruel and needless mistake of time!

3 April

I am meeting him at his apartment tonight. I have been pacing for hours, unable to sit or to read…even music fails to calm me now, and all that I can do is count each eternal second as it passes. I have not fed for two days in order to weaken my resistance and help me to overcome any lingering doubts, and both my hunger and my anticipation course through me now in raw, equal measure.

7 April

I have until now been unwilling to write about what took place. I entered his apartment in an almost hypnotic state of mind. My manner must have seemed even more peculiar than usual, for he was unusually nervous in my presence. And in that perfectly ordinary apartment with its record collection and stereo system and inexpensive Van Gogh reproductions on the walls, I began to grow just as uneasy as he was. I had not been inside a human dwelling in over six decades, and I became disoriented among the startling clutter—the knickknacks and ashtrays and potted plants and box of tissues—all the debris of daily human life, long since useless and forgotten to me.

I had planned to say some words in order to set the correct tone for the occasion, but my frayed nerves in combination with my hunger eroded all self-control. Before I even knew what I was doing, I rushed across the room and knocked him to the ground. I believe he was quite senseless when I bent to his neck, and my entire being seized in anticipation as I felt his skin against my lips, smelled the blood pulsing through his veins. But more intoxicating still was the knowledge that this blood would soon be mixed with my own, that soon I would create a magnificent new creature out of this frail and finite flesh!

My teeth had just begun to pierce his skin when I saw a pair of shiny black eyes peering at me from a bookshelf. They belonged to a plastic figurine, about six inches tall, with a pudgy face and large ears. It looked like the trolls I remembered from the Grimm brothers' fairy tales of my childhood; only this troll had a shock of bright orange hair standing straight up, and was holding a sign that said, "Can Ya Dig It?" In my time, such creatures were used to terrify children into behaving properly, and yet here was the updated American version, with neon hair, impish smile, and a slang vocabulary.

The longer I looked at it, the more it seemed to be considering me with its twinkling little bead eyes. The absurdity of the situation triggered in me a fit of laughter that overtook even the hunger. When it had passed, I looked at the owner of this odd little figurine, and I made myself say the words that my heart had known all along: this man was not Gideon, had no essence of Gideon, was an ordinary man like thousands of others in thousands of apartments just like this one.

I know I should have killed him then, but I had made the most fatal mistake that our kind can make—Gideon or not, I had come to care for him. I released him from my arms and fled the apartment in disgust at both my self-deception and my weakness. On my way out, I walked past the troll, and some impulse drove me to grab it by the hair and take it with me.

I went straight to the tunnel on Dix Street. It felt like hours before a group of three people came through, and I fed with an abandon I had not permitted myself for many years, with no thought or feeling at all as to who they were or what their lives meant.

Since then I have been sealed inside my apartment trying to avoid the fact that I must now leave this place. Though I doubt he wishes to make a police report about a strange man assaulting him for the apparent purpose of stealing a plastic troll, after the incident in the tunnel I can afford no risks. If nothing else, I have no desire to bump into him in a bar or a café, a feeling which I'm sure is quite mutual.

And so I must find a new place to live, but for now, it's easier to hide here a little while longer with the troll, who sits in the corner of my apartment grinning mischievously, the ancient keeper of yet one more secret.

10 April

I have decided to live by the sea. Venice Beach, with its narrow alleyways and footpaths that lead to nowhere, seems well suited to my present state of mind. The boardwalk is always crowded with street performers, sidewalk poets, fortune-tellers, surfers, bodybuilders, roller skaters—the whole human carnival converged in one place, wearing very little clothing. And things get even stranger once the sun goes down.

November 1982

This evening I studied my appearance for the first time in many years, and was shocked to discover that I have changed. Not in any fundamental or significant way; our kind does not seem capable of that. But the difference is there, at least to my own eyes—an oddly translucent quality to the skin; the features more even than before, as if smoothed over by a sculptor reworking his first attempt; and something about the eyes that I cannot quite figure out...something missing, and yet something added, as well, like a blindingly bright fixture installed to illuminate an otherwise empty room.

Gideon once told me that for many years after the transformation, we retain much of the mortal beings that we once were. Our appearance, our predilections, our habits and preferences—all of the things that once defined us are like imprints upon the soul, sharp and vivid at first, then growing more vague, more faded, with time. I look back through these pages and picture myself in the salons of Parisian society or the battlefields of World War I, and such things seem unimaginable to me now. Mixing so intimately with mortals, enacting the endless charades so necessary to take part in their world... I have passed beyond that now. In some ways, this is a great freedom; and yet I wonder if this pathway has only one way forward, leading to only one place—Juan Noq.

Summer 1986

I have noticed a curious group among the many drawn to Venice Beach like lost children seeking out the circus clown whose painted smile obscures the leer. This particular group is made up of young people dressed in elaborate black ensembles of anachronistic accessories like capes, top hats, and corsets mixed with modern fetish gear, fishnet stockings, and studded leather belts. I have learned that these young people are called "Goths," and their white faces, red lipstick, and blackened eyes are meant to simulate the undead. They congregate at the northern end of the boardwalk very late at night, drinking red wine from blue and green bottles and waving their arms about in what I can only assume is meant to be the dance style of the undead. I walk right past them every evening without drawing so much as a second glance.

November

I was passing the hours in a café when a mist rolled in from the sea and covered the windows in condensation. Some impulse compelled me to press my hand against the glass, and when I removed it, the imprint was there, but something didn't look quite right. It took me a moment to realize that I had not left any fingerprints. I examined the palm of my hand, and sure enough, the skin showed no trace of the usual lines and ridges and whorls. I later replicated the experiment with some paper and ink, and even this more precise method failed to produce even the faintest of prints.

April 1987

I have been brooding on my brush with transforming another. As hard as I've tried, I cannot forget what it aroused in me, the intoxication that almost overtook me at the moment of consummation. I will not break my vow to Gideon—but must I then live out this endless existence so wretchedly alone?

January 1990

Another decade. Living among men makes my own isolation worse, so I have left Venice Beach and rented a cabin deep within the San Gabriel mountains. Perhaps returning to the peace and solitude of nature will help to restore my frame of mind.

March

I spend the greater part of my time in that deathlike sleep so unique to our kind. I can no longer recall what it is to dream.

I have lost track of time. I sleep all day and well into the night, and when I awake, I feed. That is all.

20 February, 1993

I had a visitor yesterday who entered the cabin and shook me from sleep. I spent several minutes in that helpless stupor that our kind suffers upon waking, and when I regained my senses, I was so startled by this man's presence that I immediately lunged for his neck. I had him pinned to the floor and was seconds from opening his veins when I recognized him as the owner of the cabin. I released him and attempted to formulate some kind of an apology or explanation, but I found it difficult to think of the correct words, the correct mode of behavior.

His human presence was so alien to me that even the tone and timbre of his voice was strange and unsettling. He was quite shaken, and I could see that the shock of my attack had caused him to urinate in his pants. In the inevitable way of human males, his fear and embarrassment quickly turned to anger, and he began to shout about unpaid rent, unanswered eviction notices…on and on with such tiresome things until I quite seriously considered finishing what I had originally started.

When I couldn't bear the sound of his voice any longer, I threw a bundle of money at him and told him to get out, that if it wasn't enough he was free to come back for the rest. I saw him then look around for the first time, taking in the absence of furniture or any other item of human comfort—the dark, empty dankness of a lifeless place. He looked at me oddly and began slowly backing toward the door, threatening to come back with the police if I was not gone within the next two days.

He no doubt thinks that I am a drug addict or a degenerate or some such thing, and so once again, I must move on. Perhaps this time, I won't even bother to rent an apartment at all; I'll just live among the dust and the yucca bushes and wait for unsuspecting coyotes and landlords to pass by.

21 February

Today I was gathering my belongings when I came across Gideon's portfolio. I sat on the floor of the cabin and studied his pictures, and then went back and reread all of my entries from our time together. When I had finished, I put my head into my hands and shook from head to foot with confusion and shame. What have I become during these last few years, living like a beast without thought or purpose, without art or music or books, or anything that makes life worthwhile? Have I become so lost to human society that I can no longer understand anything of their world?

I once judged Gideon for wanting to end his existence, and yet in a *fraction* of the time that he lived I have become this monster, this *thing*—I cannot bear to imagine what he would think of me in this state...and yet if only he were here to help me, to guide me! I feel that I am losing my very essence, that I am being reduced to no more than the desire to feed, to survive. And mere survival is not living, not even for our kind! I must find my way back to something better than this existence, or else I see no reason to continue it...

3 October

For the past several months I have attended concerts and plays, watched countless movies, and read all of the latest books. I spend many hours walking the streets and shopping malls in order to be among humans and relearn the things that occupy and amuse them. I have not yet taken any into my acquaintance, and I'm not certain whether I'm even still adept enough at the deceptions required to make that possible. But I feel myself steadily regaining some sense of my identity; I must be very careful in the future to avoid such extreme solitude.

June 1994

I sold some pieces from Gideon's chest and bought a small house; it is situated on a quiet cul-de-sac near Griffith Park, and so affords an acceptable level of privacy without being overly isolated. I have electricity, and have filled the rooms with art and other decorative items. I have also purchased a magnificent piano and have begun to play again for the first time in many years.

Overall, I am quite delighted with my house, and spend many happy hours roaming about the rooms rearranging my possessions. It is very comforting to be able to touch and look at so many of Gideon's treasures each day.

Even so, I know that I must never become so attached that I cannot walk away without a moment's hesitation should the need or the desire ever arise.

October 1995

I have decided to travel to New York City and make another attempt to locate Kazamira. Perhaps by walking the streets that she once walked and seeing the places that her eyes saw, I can find something of her presence—that is, if there is anything left to find.

28 October

New York City: a crowded, dazzling monument to the human condition in all of its strange variety, a modern day Atlantis rising straight out of the Atlantic. I can easily imagine Kazamira on these streets, among these people that never pause, never stop rushing ahead in their maze of neon and steel. As for myself, I find it all rather claustrophobic, and more than a bit exhausting.

04 November

Today I visited the Metropolitan Museum of Art, and there in the European collection I found Gideon's paintings. I spent most of the afternoon gazing at them, imagining him there during their creation, perhaps suggesting a stroke of color here or a bit of shading there. It was quite moving to see them, after so many years in darkness, finally basking in such full and radiant light.

February 1996

I have been in New York City for almost five months and can find nothing of Kazamira. How foolish to think that in this teeming city of millions, I would somehow find her waiting for me as if we had just parted yesterday! I am quite weary and heavy-hearted and wish to return to my home without further delay.

11 December, 1997

For several weeks now, a young woman has been following me. She watches me in the shops and cafés, and once I even saw her lurking around my home, attempting to peer inside the windows. I have no idea who this girl is or want she could possibly want from me.

14 December

She has taken to standing across the street from my house, waiting. Although this did not bother me at first, I am now growing a bit disconcerted by her constant presence.

17 December

She comes almost every day just as dusk approaches; I believe that her goal is to follow me whenever I leave the house for the night. Considering that I can come and go as I please without her even realizing it, the foolish girl will have a very long wait.

18 December

I am studying her from my upper floor window. She is young, probably in her early twenties. Her skin is pale, and from what I can tell she wears very little makeup. Her hair is cut in long, blunt angles that frame her face like the wings of a crow. This evening she is dressed in a long black dress, big black boots, and purple opera gloves.

She has been standing across the street for over an hour now, staring intently at my house with alert, intelligent eyes so dark in color that the brown is almost indistinguishable from the blackness of her pupils.

20 December

Last night my mischievousness got the better of me. She had just appeared for her nightly vigil, but this time I strode out the front door, went straight to where she stood, and invited her inside. The poor child turned even more pale than usual, and for a moment I was certain that she would either faint or run away in terror. But she did neither, and instead followed me into the house without a word. How trusting these human souls!

My décor proved effective in calming her nerves, and she began looking about, chatting about my piano, my books, my artifacts… When I was able to get a word in, I offered her some tea. I had prepared for just such an occasion by placing a large potted ficus plant next to my chair in the sitting room, the willing recipient of the contents of my own cup. The ficus never let on, and I was delighted to have a somewhat normal social interaction with a mortal for the first time in many years.

She calls herself Tempest, and she is twenty-eight—older than I first thought, but I find that I am increasingly inept at judging human age; they all seem hopelessly young to me. She plays keyboards and sings backup vocals in a band called Violent Silence. She showed me their CD, the cover of which depicted four young people whose expressions suggested a recent discharge from the suicide ward of a psychiatric clinic. She next went to the piano and proceeded to play a few classical pieces with quite an impressive amount of skill and nuance.

After she had gone, the house seemed devoid of life in a way that it previously had not. However, I took comfort in the certainty that she would return, for I confess that I had entered her consciousness in order to discover the reason for her vigil: after watching me for some time, Tempest came to believe that I might be a vampire, and now she is even more determined than ever to find out.

13 January, 1998

She visits regularly, and knowing her rather forward way with my things, I have begun to hide certain items that might prove difficult to explain. I also had to purchase things like toilet paper for the bathroom and food items for the refrigerator, though I'm sure that I have overlooked a hundred other little necessities that any human household would include.

We spend many happy evening playing piano or having long discussions over a pot of tea, which the ficus has developed quite a liking for. She also asks a great deal of questions about me: my background, my heritage, how I earn a living. When we take our tea, I have noticed that she watches me very closely, but I am much too quick for her to catch on to my deception.

20 January

Tempest has been bringing over a steady supply of books and movies about vampires. I am quite astounded by the variety of these stories, and by the fascination that humans have with our kind. I know that she is struggling to come up with a way to ask me if I am a vampire, a thought which both amuses and alarms me.

When I asked her why she is so interested in vampires, she said, "There's just something cool about the idea of immortality, about a creature that doesn't have to play by the rules. I mean, ninety percent of the population does the usual plotline from start to finish: marriage, kids, career, retirement, grandkids, death. Hit button, repeat with next generation. Most people are completely happy with that—and that's cool, it really is. That's what makes the world go 'round. But there's the other ten percent who don't want that life, who don't fit the pattern; and if you're going to be an outsider anyway, why not be the kind that lives forever and never grows old and can pretty much do whatever it wants?"

Later on, I thought about this pop-culture phenomenon, and concluded that mankind has come full circle in regard to the gods and monsters that frighten and fascinate them in such equal measure: first, men believed in them without question; then came the doubt and denial of enlightenment; now, if men have not returned to *actual* belief, they seem to have developed a strange and perhaps even more powerful need—the *desire* to believe.

My relations with humans have often caused me to fear discovery of what I am; but I have never before faced a situation in which a human initiates a relationship with me *for the very purpose* of discovering what I am! I once again find myself asking the age old question: can our kind ever coexist with humans who both know and accept our ways? And yet the reality of our survival always leads to the same answer, and I very much doubt that Tempest would find me quite so cool if, after tea one fine evening, I ripped open her throat and drained her dying body of blood.

11 February

Several nights ago, I went to see Violent Silence perform in a local club. Afterward, the band and several of their friends came over to my house. Although I found their company quite engaging, I was unsettled to be around so many people, by the noise and activity, particularly within my own home. Fortunately, Tempest was astute enough to sense my discomfort and has not invited anyone else over since then.

30 March

Tonight after drinking an entire bottle of red wine, Tempest finally asked me if I am a vampire. I knew how long she had been planning the moment, and how important the question was to her, but her earnestness nearly caused me to burst out laughing at the absurdity of the situation. When I had control of myself, I told her that although I have an interest in ancient legends and superstitions, I am definitely not a member of the undead. I could feel the conflict battling within her: the rational side glad to have done with such foolishness, the other side terribly unwilling to let it go.

At any rate, the long buildup of tension had been released, and that, in combination with the wine, allowed her to move forward with the amorous intentions that she had been working toward all evening (only later did it occur to me that she had fully intended to be intimate with me even if I were a vampire; in fact, that possibility was probably the more favored outcome).

I reached out and touched her skin—always so warm and alive! But something was different this time; it felt almost perverse, this imbalance of power. How much I could take from her, so easily, so utterly, even if I spared her life! And yet also how easily, how utterly, the slave can become the master.

I withdrew my hand from her warmth. She was quite drunk, so I took her to one of my spare rooms, where I now sit writing this and watching her sleep. The flickering eyelids and gentle sighs of the dreamer; the innocent, childlike expression that steals in to soften the harsh wakefulness of day…so beautiful, human sleep.

9 April

Today Tempest stopped by to tell me that Violent Silence has been offered the opening slot on the national tour of a well-known band. Upon saying good-bye, we embraced, and she quite unexpectedly leaned forward and pressed her lips against mine. I returned her kiss, and she drew back in surprise. I held her fast in my embrace, and we stared at each other in silence as the emotions came to her in quick succession: confusion, realization, doubt, and then, finally, belief.

She pulled away from me and put her hands over her mouth, her eyes wide circles of shock. As I turned to take my leave, I couldn't help but smile. "Best of success on your tour, Tempest," I told her, "and remember that even though the dream may be an illusion, the dreaming is always real."

31 December, 1999

On the eve of a new millennium, people all across the world are in a state of frenzy at the arrival of the twenty-first century. I can remember when the dawn of the twentieth seemed like a monumental step forward. Including the thirty-three years of my human life, I have now been in existence for one hundred and sixty-four years.

November 2002

I am becoming increasingly aware of others of my kind, as if we are connected by some strange collective consciousness limited by neither time nor space… It is hard to understand or explain, but I must continue to develop it…for it may mean that someday I am able to find another.

December

I was in a state of deep and prolonged meditation when it happened—I believe that tonight, for the first time, I have finally felt the one who made me.

April 2003

I have been meditating every day for many months now, but I have not been able to go any further in my connections with others of my kind. I know that I must be patient; and yet I also know what is out there, just beyond my reach, and that is an agony almost impossible to withstand.

November 2005

I have made the acquaintance of a rather well-known film-maker. In the café that I frequent, we struck up a conversation about his most recent film. I had, of course, seen the advertisements all over town: a handsome, unusually pale young man, blood dripping from the tips of his sharpened fangs; the inevitable ravished, beautiful young woman draped over a gloomy tombstone. He began telling me about the research he had done in preparation for the film, and the café was closing its doors before we had finished our discussion. I found it fascinating to finally talk with one of those who create the many stories about my kind, and we have agreed to meet again.

16 February, 2006

My relationship with the filmmaker has taken an unexpected turn. I have come to believe that like Tempest, he, too, suspects that I am a vampire. Unlike Tempest, however, I find it quite difficult to connect with his thoughts, and therefore have no idea how or why he arrived at this conclusion. I am feeling somewhat paranoid about the fact that two people have now had reason to suspect my true nature. If I have grown careless, I must take more precautions to prevent any threat of discovery; I will admit, however, that I have no wish to return to lonely, wretched exile.

27 March

My conversations with the filmmaker have awakened in me a desire to share all that has been written in these pages. He wishes to make another film about vampires; however, like many others, he sees only the power of the vampire, and nothing else. And yet the idea of revealing my story—which also belongs to Gideon and Kazamira, to Aslan and Sally and all of the many recorded here—this idea has taken powerful hold of me. And if this man is not the one to help me tell my story, then I will keep searching until I find the one who can.

CHAPTER 18

There were blank pages left in the diary, but that was the last entry. And so that's where Verland's story had ended—with Kingman. Elle closed the book and ran her hands along the worn-out spine. She did the same with the tree design, as if mastering the book's externals could somehow unravel the mysteries inside.

One of those mysteries was a vampire's house somewhere near Griffith Park, probably within walking distance from Gary's place. She ran through all of the streets in the area and could only come up with one cul-de-sac. She'd driven past it countless times, and now it turns out that a vampire had been living there all along; talk about not knowing your neighbors. And yet some part of her still could not accept this as reality. What had Verland said? Not actual belief, but the *desire* to believe. Is that what had taken hold of her since first reading the diary? A desire to believe? And in what, exactly—vampires? Immortality? Some kind of an afterlife? Nyholm's words suddenly came back to her—*I hope you find whatever you were looking for...*

Things *had* been different since she'd started reading the diary, but that wasn't hard to understand; who wouldn't be compelled by the prospect of an actual vampire, not to mention Kingman thrown into the mix? But it was something else that Nyholm had said that she couldn't as easily explain away: *Maybe you need to see him for yourself, just like I did. The diary could give you that power, you know. Even more, if you want it.*

Kingman had purposely sought out people attuned to those low notes that vibrate outward from the darkest corners of the soul—the ones most people don't even acknowledge, let alone listen to. For Elle, those notes had jangled to the surface twenty years ago with the ring of a telephone, the siren song of death whose call we cannot bear to hear, yet also cannot fail to answer; and now Verland could silence that song forever.

She should walk away right now, should give the diary back to Vita and tell Sadie to give the Kingman story to someone else. She could take Gary up on his offer, get married like everyone else did, start working on her own stories for a change. Forget she'd ever known about a creature who had once been known and loved as Verland.

And yet her mind was already picturing the houses on that cul-de-sac. She knew that after everything that had happened, Verland would be long gone by now; but the need to see where he had once lived was overwhelming. For years, he had been less than three miles from her apartment—a ten-minute drive without traffic. If she drove up and down the street, she was certain she would know the right house.

She took the diary and buried it at the back of her closet beneath a pile of shoe boxes and sweaters. Her keys were already in her hand when her phone rang. It was Sam, and she considered not taking the call. Right now she was having trouble connecting with anyone and anything not connected with Verland, as if everything else were just vague details from someone else's life. Just like Nyholm and the rest of them, then— nothing matters except Kingman and his fantasy world... *Verland's* world. She answered the phone.

"Hey, Elle. What are you doing? Working on the book, I hope."

"Sort of. Listen, Sam..."

"Well, I don't want to interrupt money, I mean art, in progress, but the contracts have been finalized and I want to get them back to Greene Line ASAP. So whenever you get the chance, come by and give them one last look through before we sign everything."

Elle looked around her apartment. She thought about Nyholm and the video, the book hidden in her bedroom closet; the fact that she was about to drive off looking for the house of a vampire she didn't entirely believe in... And suddenly she was thoroughly sick of all of it—of Kingman, of the immortal undead who fed off of innocent people who just happened to walk through a tunnel at the wrong time, the same one that she herself had walked through a few times! Suddenly, Sam and his parrot seemed like a welcome change of direction from the one she had been heading in.

"I can come over now, actually, if that's good for you."

"Oh, perfect! I'll make some mojitos and we can catch up. Anything big going on with the story?"

"A few things."

And how did she intend to explain those "few things," anyway? She would have to deal with that later; but right now, she just wanted an evening free from death and vampires and Kingman. She was beginning to understand the strange complications of living in Verland's shadow world; it was like being caught in a rip current pulling her farther and farther out to sea, and all that she could do was try not to drown. For tonight, at least, she needed some solid ground.

On her way out, something in the hallway caught her eye—Nyholm's bowling ball bag. She'd pitched it there as soon as she'd gotten through the door, and for some reason, the sight of it crumpled in the corner like a puppy needing to go out made her laugh. Elle wondered what Maxine would have to say about such a hideous accessory. She picked up the bag, slung it over her shoulder, and stepped out into the sun.

"What happened to Maxine's hat?"

"She ate it. She's turning into such a glutton. But the nine-one-one thing is coming along nicely, even though yesterday she called my hairdresser. He'll never believe it was an accident, but, oh, well. I've been a fool for lesser things. Agh! What is *that*?" Sam took the bag and held it up between two fingers like a piece of road kill.

"I picked up this little gem from…a friend. I knew you'd love it. Think what a hit it will be on Seventies night at Club Blue."

Sam put the bag over his shoulder and orchestrated some moves definitely not intended for a bowling lane. "I love it! It'll go perfect with my brown-and-orange leisure suit."

Elle figured this was as good a time as any to break the news. "Well, consider it a peace offering, then."

"Ummm, for what?"

"Sam, I can't sign the contract."

The disco diva vanished and the agent appeared. "Elle, you have to sign the contract. I've been haggling out the details for over a week now like Churchill at Yalta."

She knew how much Sam wanted this, what it meant for both of them: success, and everything that comes with it. For the first time, they could stop worrying about money, could enter the kingdoms of status and wealth always right in front of their eyes—but just out of reach without that one big break. Kingman was that big break.

"Sam, I…"

As usual, she couldn't think of one thing to say; not for the first time, she considered the irony that so many of those who make a living with the written word have so little mastery of the spoken version. And then the tears were there before she even knew they were coming. She brushed her eyes and tried to turn away, but Sam stopped her and took hold of her hands…that gesture again…

"Elle, listen. I know that things have been going on with you lately, okay? I don't know what, and you don't have to tell me if you don't want to. But I want you to know that I trust you—completely. And I believe in you as a writer, Elle. More than you do in yourself, actually."

He let go of her hands and searched for the next words. "I don't know, maybe we're both at a place in our lives where things are changing. Maybe this Kingman story came along for a reason—like fate or something. And if you're not ready to sign the contract, then don't sign it. Now don't get me wrong here; I'm only saying that as your friend. As your agent, I still have to deal with Sadie, which could be the end of you and me both. But to hell with it! Right now, let's dance. I think the Bee Gees and Marvin Gaye are just the ticket, and believe me, Maxine knows all the best moves."

Elle let the combination of rum and the greatest hits of the Seventies work its magic, and by the time she stepped out into the early evening air, she felt better than she had in days. The heat of the day was just starting to burn off, and she didn't feel like going back to her apartment just yet. She drove up Highland and turned onto Hollywood Boulevard, which was packed with the usual slow-moving clumps of summer tourists whose sole function seemed to be disrupting traffic patterns. But Elle was in no hurry tonight. She turned onto Ivar Avenue, passed the Knickerbocker and the Alto Nido, and by the time she turned onto Franklin, toward Griffith Park, she didn't even try telling herself she was going to see Gary. Somewhere, on a quiet cul-de-sac in an otherwise perfectly ordinary neighborhood, a vampire had once lived.

She was almost there when her phone rang, but this time, Elle decided to ignore it. It kept right on vibrating for acknowledgment, so she finally pulled over and took the call. A woman with a croaky voice and a limited vocabulary was on the other end.

"Nine-one-one! Nine-one-one! Nine-one-one!"

Maxine. Elle was risking a ticket for being parked in a bus lane in order to take a call from a parrot.

"Maxine, much as I'd like to talk—" The call broke off and Elle sat staring at the screen. She hit redial and was immediately bounced to Sam's voice mail.

"Stupid bird. Sam never should have taught you that trick."

What if there really had been an emergency and she wrote it off as a parrot with a dialing problem? Couldn't a person be fined for placing a false 911 call? She closed her phone and sat watching the light change: red, yellow, green…red, yellow, green…

Elle did a U-turn at the light, drove as fast as she could back to Highland, and double-parked in front of Sam's building. The door to his apartment was unlocked, and when she stepped inside, it was dark and quiet—too quiet, and way too still. She was standing in the hallway trying to decide what to do when something burst from the living room and clipped the side of her head. She staggered back and cried out in panic—but it was only Maxine, circling around the bungalow screeching, "Nine-one-one! Nine-one-one!" over and over again.

"Maxine, be quiet, please. *Maxine!*" She held out her arm and tried coaxing her like Sam did, but the bird was beyond reasoning.

"Sam? *Sam!*"

Elle's stomach contracted into a tight little ball, and she put her hand against the wall to steady herself. She advanced into the living room and flipped on the light.

Sam was lying at an odd angle in a corner of the room. He wasn't moving.

"*Sam!* Oh, no, Sam, *no!*"

Her vision started to fade, and for a minute, she was sure she was going to faint. But Maxine *stuka*-bombed her again, and she made her legs move forward. She bent down and turned Sam over. His chest was covered in blood.

She called 911 and checked for vital signs the way she had seen it done dozens of times on television. Only this wasn't television, and it was impossible to distinguish Sam's pulse from the pounding in her own head, to measure his breathing against her own hyperventilating. His breath was coming in rapid, wheezing gasps…she tried to remember some of the first aid Gary had taught her, something about covering a chest wound with plastic… Or was she supposed to leave one side open for an air valve? *Get it together, Elle, get it together…* Forget about the air valve and apply direct pressure to the wound in order to slow the bleeding… She got a towel from the bathroom, and when she pressed it against Sam's chest, he stirred and let out an awful, watery sound.

"*Sam*…it's Elle… I'm here. The ambulance is on the way right now. Please hold on, Sam…"

She noticed something in the middle of the floor. The bowling ball bag, turned inside out.

"Sam, who did this to you? Sam, can you talk to me? *Who did this?*"

But Sam was gone again, on his way to some other place.

She checked to make sure that he was still breathing, and suddenly the EMTs were there, someone had her by the arm, was steering her toward the kitchen. She heard the sound of voices filling the room, the stretcher clanking open…and then somehow Gary was there, she was being placed in his car, and there was his partner, Dave. What was Dave doing here?

"Maxine…someone needs to take care of Maxine… Did she get out? When the ambulance came? Because if she got out and flew away we'll never find her…"

"Elle, Maxine didn't get out." Gary stroked her hair. He was talking very softly. "I'll make sure someone comes by and looks after her."

"Gary, someone shot Sam."

"I know. We're going to follow the ambulance and go see him. He'll be fine, thanks to you. You got there in time to save him, and he's going to be fine."

Later, Elle could remember nothing of the ER, nothing of the endless wait as they worked to stabilize Sam, nothing of the flurry of doctors and nurses and sterile corridors and paperwork and police questions. The first thing she did remember was the Intensive Care Unit, Sam's strangely motionless form made even more alien by the jumble of tubes and machines. She was vaguely aware of Gary coming in and out, of being lead into a hallway.

"Elle, the doctors say Sam is in the clear. It's almost midnight, and you need to get some rest. I'll take you back to your apartment and stay there with you, and I promise we can come back first thing in the morning."

"I need to be here when he wakes up, Gary."

"Well, that's definitely not going to be tonight. He needs his rest, Elle, and so do you. Let me take you home."

When she didn't answer, he said, "At least get out this room for a little while. Go walk around; get a cup of coffee. Things will look better then."

"Okay. A cup of coffee I can do."

"I'll come with. I could use a cup of bad coffee myself right about now."

"No, Gary—you have to stay here with Sam until you can get a police guard on him. Promise me you'll make sure that someone keeps watch on him all the time."

"OK, I'll stay with him. But I need a reason in order to request a guard, Elle. What's going on here that I don't know about? 'Cause if you or Sam are in trouble—"

"No, Gary, it's not like that… I'm not really sure what's going on… Just trust me on this one, okay? Please."

"OK, I will, but—"

"Gary, please. Just make sure that someone stays with him."

At this time of night the cafeteria was almost deserted. The food line had long since closed, and only one solitary worker remained to guard a forlorn row of coffee pots. A few equally dismal-looking vending machines offered chips and stale cookies to the desperate. Elle found the most isolated corner and slouched into a plastic chair designed to fit no human body that she'd ever seen. Her phone was beeping with its usual lack of respect. She considered ignoring it, but for once she actually welcomed the distraction. After what had happened to Sam, she knew that she had some serious reckoning to do about everything that had been going on. She had to get her head together, but right now, she couldn't even manage a lousy cup of coffee.

She flipped open her phone, and forgot all about the coffee: in the past six hours, Vita had called twenty-four times, every quarter hour on the dot. She hadn't left any messages. Elle hit redial, and Vita picked up on the first ring.

"*Where have you been?* I've been trying to call you for *hours*. You have to come here *right now*—to the mansion. I think I'm in serious danger."

Elle's head whirled. Whoever had shot Sam had been after the diary, and that meant Kingman. But why would Kingman send his own people after Vita?

"Look, you have to call nine-one-one right away. I'll even do it for you. In fact—"

"No! No police! You *cannot* call the police! I need you to come here *now!*"

"Vita, I can't come anywhere right now, it's twelve o'clock at night and—"

"*He's here.*"

"What?" Elle had heard her clearly enough, but it was the meaning behind the words that she needed to confirm.

"He's here—*Verland*. He's come for the diary. He's on the grounds *right now*. I'm watching him on the security cameras as we speak, but I don't know how long he'll even *be here*, he could leave *any time! You have to come now!*"

Elle hesitated only a moment before hearing herself say, "I'll be there as soon as I can."

She didn't go back and tell Gary. She didn't wait for Sam to wake up, and she knew that she would have to live with that decision for a very long time. But right now, she had been given the kind of chance that might not ever come again—the chance to finally find out, to *know*. She walked out of the hospital and got into her car.

Unless Sam's shooting had been an extremely random coincidence, Nyholm's paranoia hadn't been misplaced—Kingman's men had been tracking them. They must have known about Elle's meeting with Nyholm, must have seen her leave with the bowling ball bag, which could only contain one thing. They'd watched her take the bag to Sam's house—and then come out *without* it; Sam had almost gotten killed over an empty bowling ball bag.

She hesitated, gripping the steering wheel. Once Kingman's men had realized that Sam didn't have the diary, they'd probably gone back and ransacked Elle's apartment top to bottom; the diary was probably long gone by now. And if the diary was gone, that meant that she could walk away right now, could turn around and go back to Sam and Gary and forget Kingman and his vampire diary even existed. But Nyholm had been right; she did need to see Verland. From the moment the hawk had appeared at the library window—the moment she had begun to believe—she had needed to see him, needed to know that he was real. She turned her phone off, pulled onto the freeway, and headed toward Malibu.

The gate to the mansion was wide open. Elle drove slowly down the winding driveway, searching for him around every turn, in every shadow. But only Vita was there to greet her.

"*Where is the diary?*"

"First of all, where is Verland?"

Vita circled the room, rubbing her hands together and muttering to herself.

"Vita, please calm down and tell me what's going on. Is Verland here?"

Vita turned on her with burning eyes: the eyes of fanaticism, of dangerous obsession. The realization of how careless she had been surrounded Elle like cold, bracing water. She reached into her pocket for her cell phone, and it starting vibrating the instant she turned it back on—Gary.

"Where is the diary? Give it to me *now!*"

"I don't have it."

"I know you do! Nyholm told me! He told me he gave it to you in that stupid bag!"

"Nyholm? When did you talk to Nyholm?"

Elle's phone vibrated again. Vita picked something up from a corner table and suddenly there was a pistol pointed straight at Elle's chest.

"*Turn it off, or I swear to God I'll kill you right now!*"

"Vita, it's my boyfriend. I called him right before I got out of the car." *Think. Think of something fast...* "His dog, Bosie— that's his dog's name—got really sick just before I came out here, and I told him to call me right away if he got any worse. If I don't pick up, he'll get really worried. He's a cop, Vita; you must know that. He'll think something's wrong if I don't pick up."

Elle saw her hesitate. Unlike Kingman, Vita was no chess master, just a very confused young woman right at the edge of the abyss. Elle wasn't exactly a chess master herself, but she wasn't completely out of her mind, either. Not yet, anyway. Vita gripped the pistol tighter.

"Get rid of him *right now*! If you say anything suspicious, *one word* that doesn't even *sound* right, I'll shoot you! Believe me, I have nothing to lose, *nothing*!"

Elle didn't doubt her for a minute. Gary's voice came over the line like the world's last refuge of sanity.

"Elle, where the hell are you? A call just came in from headquarters. One of Kingman's assistants—a Nathan Quinn, or something like that—his body was found in an abandoned building near Downey. He was shot twice in the chest. Elle, I need to know—how is this connected to Sam?"

Elle paused, her eyes on Vita. She would have just one chance. "So you think Bosie should go to the vet?"

It took Gary only a second. "You're in trouble…"

Elle put both hands around the phone to keep it from shaking.

"Yes."

Vita advanced a few steps toward her.

"Elle, keep your phone with you, and we'll track you. Can you do that?"

"I don't know. No."

"Are Kingman's people responsible?"

"Yes, that's the best place to take him, that's where I would go—"

Elle felt a shockwave of pain as Vita swung the pistol hard, knocking the phone out of her hands. It skidded across the floor and came to a stop against the wall, and then the entire room exploded into shrapnel pieces of flying metal and plastic. Blood was streaming into Vita's right eye from a deep gash across her forehead, but she didn't seem to notice. She had fired three times, and Elle tried to work out how many bullets she had left. Didn't the bad guys always run out of bullets after six shots? Or was that only in westerns?

She forced herself back to reality; Gary would call the Malibu police. It would take them ten, maybe fifteen minutes to get here. All she had to do was keep Vita distracted until then—which was easier said than done with Vita aiming the gun back at Elle and demanding the diary again.

"Vita, I have the diary in my apartment. I'll give it to you, I swear, we can go and get it right now…"

Elle had to change the subject; if the goal was to keep Vita calm, talking about the diary was guaranteed to achieve the exact opposite. "Vita, how did you know that Nyholm had the diary?"

"Because Eliot *told* me. He *knew* Nyholm would steal it! He *knew* he would betray us! I couldn't let him betray us."

"But why kill him, Vita? You knew that he had given me the diary. That's why you called me, right? He told you I had it, even told you what kind of bag it was in."

Elle tried to think through the timeline of events, but things weren't adding up. If Kingman's men knew that Nyholm had stolen the diary, why not just grab him off the trail in Griffith Park and take it back? Why let him give it to Elle in the first place? And how had Vita come into the picture?

"Nyholm had to be *stopped*. Eliot said Nyholm could make sure he *never* got out of prison, and he was *right*. I *saw* the video he made! Nyholm was going to *destroy* us, destroy *everything* we'd worked for!"

"So Eliot told you to get the diary back and take care of Nyholm?"

Once again, things didn't make sense. Why would Kingman send Vita for a job like that when he had a top-notch security team just ready and waiting to go? The truth came to Elle like a hard punch to the gut, and she gasped and took a step backward.

"*Stop moving!*"

Vita thrust the gun forward, and Elle put her hands in the air; just like a noir film—only she was definitely on the wrong end of the smoking gun. "OK, OK... I'm not moving. But I need to know something, Vita. Why didn't Kingman have his security team get the diary back? Why didn't they take care of Nyholm?"

"What?"

"Kingman's security team. I know all about it—ex-CIA, military guys. They're experts in this stuff, so why not send them to do it?"

"Because the security team is *nothing*!"

Elle was beginning to realize which three people were nothing in Kingman's scheme, but Vita had other ideas.

"You just don't *get it*, do you? Eliot only trusts *me*—I'm the *only one* that knows the whole truth! And *no one* is going to get in the way of our plans. *No one!*" She leveled the gun at Elle.

"Vita, listen to me."

Her finger was on the trigger, and Elle was out of time.

"Eliot set you up. Don't you see it? He tells you to go after the only person who can prove that he killed David. Vita, all that Kingman wants right now is to get out of prison, and now you've given him—"

"*No!*"

"You've already shot *two* people, Vita, and one of them is dead! If you put the gun down and tell the truth about everything, there's still a chance that you can—"

A beeping noise came from the hallway. The front door security system.

"Vita, the police are already here and—"

Elle turned toward the door, and the room exploded again. She felt a strange cold sensation spread across her left side… blood…why was there so much blood? And then the pain burst open like a mushroom cloud. Vita wavered before her eyes, and she felt her legs giving way.

"Get up! *Get up!*"

Vita grabbed her arm and they stumbled down a hall and out the back door of the house, the gun never leaving the side of Elle's head. The Pacific roared to life in her ears; if she was going to die, at least she couldn't ask for a better location. Vita let go of her arm and Elle fell to her knees. They were less than twenty feet from the edge of the cliff. Vita started toward the access stairs, swung back to Elle, advanced a few steps, and stopped.

"Vita, there's no place to go. You know that. Please…"

Vita drew back her arm and threw the gun as far as she could over the cliff. She closed her eyes and turned her face toward the sky. For the first time since Elle had met her, she seemed completely in control.

"There's always someplace to go," she said. "Always."

She advanced to the edge. With the wind whipping her skirt around her legs and her head thrown back, she looked like some tragic Greek poet, a modern-day Sappho ready to dash herself against the rocks for a pain no illusions could repair.

"Vita, *no!*"

Vita looked back at the house one last time, and then she was gone. Elle heard sirens and shouting as if from some faraway place. Her field of vision narrowed to a pinpoint and then faded to black until nothing was left but the ebb and flow of the tide.

CHAPTER 19

*eep...beep...beep...*Where was that beeping coming from? Elle had been floating at the bottom of a deep, still pool for what seemed like a very long time, and she had no desire to surface just yet. But every time she tried to drift back down, something beeped its way into her brain like techno water torture. *Beep... beep...beep...* It didn't seem to be going anywhere, so she decided that she might as well struggle upward toward the rather unwelcome light. Her eyes would not focus; the room was a painful blur of white until a familiar set of features emerged.

"Gary?"

"Hey, you're finally awake. I know you like to sleep late and all, but this is getting ridiculous."

"I feel terrible."

Elle attempted to sit up and discovered her tormentor—the same beeping, blinking array of machines that had stood guard around Sam's hospital bed. The fog in her head cleared and the jumbled fragments of memory began forcing themselves back together: Vita and the gun…the cliff…Sam crumpled in the corner of his apartment…

"Gary, where's Sam?"

"Sam's fine. He's recovering in the hospital, and so are you; which is all you should be worrying about right now."

"Where am I?"

"You're at the Urgent Care Center in Malibu. But now that you're up, we can work on getting you out of here. You were lucky—no major organs involved. You'll be wearing a bikini again in no time."

"I never wore a bikini in the first place, Gare, bullet hole or no. How long have I been here?"

"All last night and what's left of today. But don't worry—I sent Lupita to get the cats. They're ganging up on Bosie's tail as we speak. Maxine's there, too, and let me tell you—the cats are one thing, but Lupita is not at all happy about that bird."

Elle's head felt like Gary's drum kit after a particularly vigorous practice session, and she now understood that *splitting headache* was not a figurative term.

"What about Vita?"

Gary frowned. "We don't have to talk about that right now."

"I want to talk about it."

He threw his hands up in a gesture of surrender. Gary understood that for Elle, not knowing a thing was usually a worse torment than the thing itself.

"Vita's dead. She shot you and then did a swan dive over the cliff. Broke her neck and died instantly."

"And Nyholm? She killed him, too, right?"

"You mean the assistant guy?"

Elle nodded. Somewhere in his cop's brain, Gary had just filed away the fact that she'd used his first name.

"According to statements from a friend of his, Quinn was headed out of L.A. He was on his way to catch a plane when Vita intercepted him. Probably called him with an emergency or something like that."

Like a vampire stalking her, Elle could have added.

"She got him to that building in Downey and killed him. The gun was the same one used to shoot Sam. And you, for that matter."

Elle knew better than to ask if the police had found the disc in Nyholm's bags. After all, cleaning up loose ends had been Kingman's plan all along...*Kingman*—Elle jerked upright as the remaining pieces of the puzzle fell back into place.

"Elle, what?"

"Kingman's lawyers are going to appeal on the grounds that Vita killed David Klee. That Vita was the third person, and he was trying to protect her the whole time."

"Maybe." Gary frowned, looking at her closely; she was going to have to be very, very careful in the next few days. "And maybe that *is* what happened, for all we know. It's looking like she had a history of mental problems, plus she had more of a relationship with Klee than Kingman did. So it actually makes more sense if she did kill him. And it doesn't exactly paint a picture of innocence to shoot three people and then jump off a cliff."

Elle thought about those images on the computer screen: Klee opening his shirt, Kingman drawing the dagger. What had Nyholm said? His first willing sacrifice.

"You're probably right."

If Gary, with his cop's instinct and penchant for skepticism, had already pinned Vita as the actual murderer, then Kingman's conviction might as well be overturned right now, to save time; and no DA on earth would even consider a retrial. Nyholm had hinted about copies of the video stashed away for "insurance," and even at the time it had sounded more like a plot from some spy movie than an actual plan. Then again, maybe proof of Kingman's guilt would sit gathering dust in an unclaimed safe-deposit box somewhere for years to come.

"If Vita did kill Klee, that would also explain why she killed Quinn," Gary said, bringing Elle back to more immediate speculations. "After all, Quinn was heading out of town pretty fast. Maybe he didn't want to keep her and Kingman's secret anymore; maybe he was even considering a little blackmail—who knows. But either way, it looks like Vita wasn't taking any chances."

He paused, unhappy about what was coming next.

"Elle, you're going to have some questions to answer about all of this, and not just to me. A lot of people want to know what happened here."

Elle wondered what that police report would look like: "Hollywood filmmaker hunts for vampire in order to start elite society of immortals; three people dead so far." She knew that some kind of story would have to come out of this, but it wasn't going to be the truth—whatever the truth even was at this point.

"I know, Gary; but I don't even have everything straight in my own head yet."

"I know you don't. And right now I just want to make sure that you're safe. Remember that offer I made at Griffith Park? Well, it still stands."

"What, you're still interested in a girl with some lead in her belly?"

Gary laughed, and in that moment, it was the best sound in the entire world.

"Are you kidding? I've been waiting all my life for a woman like that."

She didn't have to think it over this time. "The white wedding part is going to have to wait. But if you're looking for a roommate, I'll take your offer and throw two cats into the bargain. No extra charge."

Gary jumped up and kissed her forehead. If Elle hadn't been tied down by the tubes and wires, he probably would have picked her up and spun her around the room like the lead character in some 1950s romantic comedy who finally gets the girl.

"Your cats are way ahead of you; I don't think they had any intention of leaving. But one thing we have to agree on right now if this is ever going to work—the minute Sam gets out of the hospital, that bird is a goner."

Elle spent the next few months doing nothing. She woke up late every day and sat on the porch drinking tea and watching the sun make its way across the sky. She took Bosie for long walks in Griffith Park and messed around in the backyard trimming the bougainvillea or thinning out the herb garden. One week, she did nothing but reread her favorite books with the cats piled on top of her and Bosie snoring at her feet. Sometimes she didn't leave the house for days at a time, with Gary and Lupita her only contact with the outside world. She let time drift by like an easy-flowing stream, steering clear of any currents that might take her too close to rocky shores.

Sam's injuries had been more serious than hers. As he liked to recount to Elle and anyone else who would listen, the bullet had ricocheted around in his chest "like a pinball," coming within centimeters of hitting a major blood vessel. He had spent almost a week in the hospital recovering from two fractured ribs and a punctured lung, and Elle knew that she would be hearing about chest tubes for a long time to come.

He remembered very little about what had happened, which hadn't stopped him from talking to the press, who were of course going crazy for the story. Maxine had been able to replicate the 911 call that had saved Sam's life, and they had become something of a media sensation, making the talk-show rounds and getting invited to all of the best parties. Even though Elle couldn't imagine how fame would add to Maxine's already considerable opinion of herself, she didn't begrudge either of them any of it—just as long as it didn't involve her.

One day she made a phone call to Joel and Christine Quinn in Somerville, Massachusetts. Nyholm's bags had been placed in police evidence, and she had asked Gary to let her know when they were ready to be released to the family. When that time came, she had a request to make.

"Hi, my name is Elle Bramasol, and I'm trying to reach Joel Quinn. I knew—I was a friend of his brother, Nyholm."

"This is his wife, Christine. Joel is mostly paralyzed and can't talk on the phone, but if you wait, I'll go get him and put you on speakerphone. Hold on just a sec."

Elle waited, wondering what in the world she had been thinking. She had spoken to Nyholm exactly four times, and only once that really counted; she could hardly make the claim that they were friends. She was trying to come up with some way to end the call when Christine came back on.

"Okay, Joel can hear you now."

With no quick exit in sight, Elle just started talking—about the things Nyholm had told her about them, about how much their example had meant to him. She told them that on the day he'd been killed, Nyholm had been on his way to catch a plane back to Massachusetts in order to be a part of their lives again; she told them that before he died, Nyholm had finally found peace. They talked for a long time, and eventually Elle was ready to ask.

"This is going to be an odd request, but Nyholm showed me a picture of you and Joel—the two of you in a yard. He had it with him when he died. Nyholm's things are being released from police custody, and I was wondering if you would con-sider letting me have the picture. I know it sounds strange, but the picture and what it meant to him... I know we've never even met, but...it's kind of like a reminder of the things he told me, the things he came to understand..."

Elle trailed off, unsure of what else to say. For one terri-ble moment she thought her request had offended them, but Christine's pause didn't last long.

"Of course you can have the picture. We've got them all on the computer, anyway, so we can make copies any time."

Elle put it in a simple wooden frame and wrote "Life continues to be good and worth living" around the frame. She put it in the top drawer of the desk Gary had cleared out for her to use, and she took it out whenever she needed to remember.

Kingman's lawyers had started the appeals process before the bodies were even in the ground, and it was just a matter of time before his conviction was overturned. Elle no longer wanted to share the same planet with Kingman let alone the same city, and she and Gary had been talking about moving north—San Francisco or Santa Cruz, maybe even leaving California altogether. They had looked at Oregon, with its misty forests and towns with names like Sweet Home and Wolf Creek. Neither of them could really imagine leaving behind Southern California and the way of life that went with it; but then again, that way of life had been changing even before Kingman had come along.

Gary had also returned to the idea of putting in his notice with the force, and Elle was on equally uncertain ground with Greene Line. If the Kingman story had been big before, now it was the hottest ticket in town. Even though Sadie had told her to take "all the time she needed," Elle knew that every day that went by without a book took at least a year off of Sadie's life. But Elle didn't even want to think about Kingman let alone write about him, and unfortunately for both Greene Line and her career, she couldn't see that changing.

The police questioning had been surprisingly easy. It hadn't hurt to have Gary on her side, and she found that as long as she eliminated any reference to the diary or to Verland, the story held together. Kingman had contacted Greene Line to write a book about his case. No, she didn't know why he had specifically asked for her; no, he hadn't revealed anything new about the murder. Yes, she had gone to the mansion several times to discuss the story. Yes, she had met with Nyholm on the day he was killed. He said there were problems between him and Vita, that he was leaving L.A. to be with his family in Massachusetts; no, he most definitely was *not* going to blackmail anyone. After leaving Nyholm, she had spent the evening at Sam's, gotten the call from Maxine, found Sam, called 911. Vita had called her at the hospital with an emergency and asked her to come to the mansion.

That part had been trickier. Why hadn't she called the police? Her friend has just been shot, Vita calls out of nowhere in the middle of the night—surely she hadn't thought it was a coincidence? The only thing that Elle could do was keep insisting that she hadn't been thinking at all, that at the time she'd had no reason to connect Vita with Sam's shooting. Not the most solid explanation, but in the absence of any other, it had been enough.

The detectives assigned to the case had eventually come to the same conclusions that Gary had: convinced that Nyholm was ready to expose her as David Klee's killer, Vita lures him to an isolated spot and confronts him. In an increasingly paranoid state of mind, she thinks Nyholm arranged a secret meeting with Elle in order to tell her the truth about the murder. Vita kills Nyholm and goes looking for Elle. Completely out of control by now, she ends up at Sam's house and shoots him, too. Not realizing that Sam survived, she lures Elle to the mansion, at which point all unanswered questions go over the cliff with her.

Case closed as far as the police were concerned—but Gary was a different story. Even though he hadn't yet asked her any questions she couldn't answer, Elle knew that someday those questions would come. Right now, though, she just wanted to retreat: from Gary, from Sadie, from everything.

In the hottest part of the afternoon on one of the last days of summer, Elle set out for Griffith Park determined to sweat her way to Dante's View. She hiked hard and fast, and by the time she reached the top, her mouth was parched and her eyes were stinging with sweat. She had left Bosie at home this time; for some reason, she had needed to do this one alone.

She looked out at the hazy L.A. landscape filled with cars and houses and people going about their lives, and she allowed herself to think about Verland for the first time since that night at the mansion. When Vita had told her that Verland was there, she had gone without hesitation—not for the story, not for Vita, not even for the diary. She had gone for him. And what if Verland had been there? Would she have grasped for that Holy Grail just like Kingman had? If she had been willing to go that far for a possibility, how far would she have gone for the real thing?

She hadn't been forced to answer those questions, though, because Verland *hadn't* been there—had never, in fact, been proven to even *exist*. The diary existed, that much she could accept, whoever had actually written it. And someone had been in that room with Kingman when he'd put a dagger through Klee's heart. But there was nothing to prove that this man was a vampire, nothing to prove that a vampire named Verland even existed, or had ever existed. Elle had almost gotten both herself and Sam killed, had lied to Gary and played deadly games with a sociopathic murderer and his delusional followers, for nothing more than an *illusion*, a fantasy—for nothing more than the desire to believe.

Elle stretched her legs and turned her face toward the sun. She needed to let her mind drift for a while, to not think about vampires, or Kingman, or young people dead before their lives had even begun. She was floating along with the patchy little tufts of clouds when she saw it: a golden hawk circling overhead, its wings creating a dark silhouette against the blue sky. If she waited, she was certain that it would come in to land. But it stayed high up, circling; Elle kept waiting, and then the hawk suddenly cried out three times and began coasting away. She jumped to her feet, shouted, "Wait! Come back!" into the empty air before realizing where it was headed—south, toward a past-its-prime apartment building at the wrong end of Sunset.

She raced back down the trail as fast as she could and stopped just long enough to reassure Bosie before going to meet the owner of a book that was long overdue for a return.

Her apartment had the stale, musty smell of neglect. The blinds were drawn and the place was gloomy and dank in contrast to the brightness outside. It was stifling hot, and she turned the air conditioner on low, unwilling to open the windows and break the tomblike atmosphere. She went to her closet, tossed aside the sweaters and boxes—and there was the diary, right where she'd left it.

She took it into the living room and sat down, but she didn't have long to wait. Before she even had time to register the door opening, he was in the room, standing right in front of her. He looked just as he had in the video: same lean, muscular body; same oddly uncolored hair falling in waves across his forehead and behind the ears. His features were as smooth and unlined as a statue, his skin so pale that in the gloom of the apartment, he seemed to give off a faint luminescence, like moonlight in a dark night sky.

She stared at him, and reality collapsed. She felt weightless, slowed down, like being underwater. She wanted to touch him, to make sure that he was real, but her body had lost its ability to move.

He broke the stasis by speaking first.

"Each year, from September to November, the hawks of North America fly southward—millions of them. In a place called Chichicaxtle, between the Sierra Madre and the Gulf of Mexico, a bottleneck forms, and all of the hawks must funnel through this one place. It's the greatest concentration of raptors in the world, yet very few people know of it."

His voice was deep and clear, flecked with the persistence of accent.

"The hawks travel by riding the thermal currents, and sometimes thousands of them soar within one column of air. They all turn in the same direction, riding the sky like a river, making visible what had, until that moment, been invisible. Many people weep when they see this."

He crossed the room and sat down beside her. He was so near to her now that she could see the smoothness of his skin, could see the crescent-shaped scar above his right eye, almost imperceptible now, but still visible this close-up. His eyes were a strange shade of blue—bright, almost *too* bright, but also... *translucent*, somehow, like a flame burning behind ice... She forced herself to look away. She laid the diary between them.

"You're here for this?" Her voice came out weak and shaky. She was surprised to hear herself form words at all.

"I am. But I'm not here to take it from you; I'm here to give it to you."

"Why?"

"Because you are the one to tell the story written in that book—the many stories written there."

"Why?" Elle cursed her monosyllabic repetition, but her mind was turning too slowly. His eyes, the strange vibrations coming from him...it was too hard to think...

"Because there are things in that book that mankind should know of. You see, for many years, I believed that humans fear my kind because we can harm them. But then I considered that most anything in this world can do the same, including humans themselves. And I realized that people fear us most of all because we know death—know it so intimately that we have become it. And so our very existence refuses your laws and your science, your religions and your philosophies. But this refusal is not a negation; it is not a destruction. Rather, it can be a way forward."

"You mean a way forward from death...like Gideon?"

"Yes. Like Gideon."

Elle thought of her mother. Even if everything Gideon had believed was true, her death would remain a raw, open wound. "But it doesn't make death any easier to bear. That's why people like Kingman are so obsessed with immortality—a way around death."

"Death is not an obstacle to be gotten around; it is a part of the pathway itself. Only those who have gone down that pathway can truly understand this. For those who remain, something breaks inside of the soul, and you will carry that something with you always. But that pain which has so broken you can also help to restore, for it means that you will never love any less."

Elle felt herself threatening to come undone. She wanted to reach out, to touch him...

"But death is not meant to be a lover, Elle." Her name sounded strange on his lips, as if he were addressing someone she hadn't yet met. "And too great a hunger for what has been or what is yet to be quickly becomes starvation."

She thought of Nyholm and Vita, of Gary. Had she been starving for the last twenty years without even realizing it?

"How do you want me to write it? Your story, I mean."

He smiled, wistful, with neither sadness nor joy. "That is for you to decide. You are the writer; you will tell the story the way that you choose—the way that you can."

She had to know. "Why me?"

"Because you have looked into the darkness and seen the flame that burns there, the light that is a part of darkness itself. A man like Kingman wants to master the flame—wants to set the darkness ablaze and drive it away forever! But the flame cannot be mastered; it is meant to illuminate the darkness, not destroy it."

"But…" She felt odd even saying it. "No one will believe that any of it is true."

"Some will believe; some always do. As for the rest—they don't have to believe in the story in order to believe in the idea, and the idea is what matters. That's the way it has always been—the history of mankind is the history of fictions made into truths, and truths made into fictions."

He reached out and picked up the diary. His movements were measured and slow, like a dancer or an actor in a silent film. He ran his hands across the cover and then held it out to her. She grasped the edge, but he did not yield his grip. It hung between them like a bridge across time and space, and she felt it—the bond between creator and created. Only this time, the transformation was not that of his kind, but of hers—his story, the pain and loneliness and death and love, yes, most of all the love that made it all bearable and worthwhile—his story transformed into her story, into *our* story—the one we need to believe in as strongly as we need to tell it. He let go, and she laid the diary between them again, creator and created inextricable, one.

He stood up and was almost at the door before Elle realized that he was leaving.

"Wait!"

She took a few steps toward him, stopped. She held out her hand, then dropped it to her side; she was shaking all over and could not make herself stop. Verland turned, considered her for a moment, and then he was right in front of her, his presence surrounding her, blotting out the world outside, the room around her…she reached up and put her hands against his chest, ran them across his shoulders. He was so solid, and yet so *still*. She looked up at him, ice blue eyes so close now. He took her hands, leaned down, and pressed his lips against hers…gently until she returned the kiss…his lips were as smooth and hard as polished marble, and just as cold. So very, very cold. She could feel her heat transferring to him, warming him, and she pressed closer against him, into him. She wanted to give him that warmth, to give him the very essence of her own life force running through her veins… She pulled away, took a step back. He smiled, fully this time, with a flash of teeth…the *teeth*…and then he reached out and touched the side of her face for just a moment before turning away.

"Where will you go?"

"I am going in search of that which comes next. Nothing more and nothing less."

And then he was gone. Elle ran to the front window and pulled up the blinds; the light flooded in, but there was no trace of him, only the blinding midday sun that casts no shadows.

CHAPTER 20

"What you're looking for is called a 'kettle.' That's when they form that whirlwind like you're talking about. Tomorrow, I'll take you to a place way out in the open territory, and we'll find one for sure."

Elle and Gary had been in Chichicaxtle for over a week now. On any given day, thousands of hawks could be seen gliding across the sky, but they had yet to see one of the swirling gyres that Verland had described. Their guide, an enthusiastic, energetic fellow named Rigo, had promised to find one for them, but it would have to be soon. In two more days, they had to return to L.A. and pick up the pieces they'd left behind.

When Elle had finally told Sadie that she wasn't going to write the Kingman book, it had gone a lot better than she'd expected.

"I'm not going to say I'm not disappointed, Elle. With the publicity around this story, having your name on the cover would have been the kind of thing that comes around once in a career. Having said that, I don't blame you one bit for not wanting to do it. To be honest, I wouldn't either if I were you. But I want you to be sure. You know I need to get that book out *yesterday,* and every writer I've ever said 'hello' to wants a chance at this story. Once you pass on it, that's it. So I want you to be sure."

Elle had been sure.

Gary's departure from the LAPD had been equally smooth, although he hadn't been as happy about that as Elle had been about Greene Line. His partner had tried for two weeks to talk him out of it, and his chief had been sorry to see him go, but by the time he'd cleared his desk and turned in his badge, he was just one more name in a file somewhere.

"Can you believe they had my replacement picked out before I'd even finished the resignation process? Just a tiny little cog in the big wheel that just keeps on turning, always some new cog to come along and take your place."

"Well, I'm glad that this particular cog has sprung its socket. My wheel doesn't take replacement parts quite so easily."

But Elle knew that it would be hard for Gary to adjust to being an ordinary civilian again, and with L.A. looming back into view, she also knew that Gary was trying to figure out what came next. They had both needed to just leave everything behind and take off for Mexico for a while, but sooner or later, you had to go back.

Gary put his hands behind his head and gazed up at the clear, endless sky, unbroken by buildings or billboards.

"You know, our first few nights here, it felt like something was wrong. I couldn't put my finger on it, and then it hit me— I'd forgotten what silence sounds like. In L.A., there's always some kind of noise going on; the drone of the freeways alone is like a soundtrack that never shuts off. You don't even notice it after a while; but this is true silence."

"Maybe we should move here." Elle didn't really see that happening, but she enjoyed trying out the idea.

"Hey, you're the one who said you weren't ready to leave L.A. yet—which is probably a good idea until I can figure out how we're going to make a living. My savings isn't going to last forever, and at least the house is paid for."

Despite Gary's concerns, Elle suspected that his "savings" would last for quite a while longer, and it definitely hadn't come from saving leftover pennies from his cop's salary.

"I'm not going to worry about money just yet. We'll make a living somehow. In fact, I've got an idea for a new book."

"For Greene Line?"

"No. Something…different this time." That was one way to put it. She hadn't even figured out *what* she was going to write about Verland, let alone how. The diary and its untold stories was just one more thing waiting for her back in L.A.

"Well, I don't mind being a kept man for a while, but don't get any ideas for the long run."

"I was thinking—maybe you should start playing drums again. You always said one of the things you missed being a cop was not having time to do music anymore."

"I can't say it hasn't crossed my mind through the years. It wouldn't have to be anything major. Definitely no touring or anything like that. But getting some people together to play around, do some shows here and there. That wouldn't be bad at all. As long as you don't mind the competition, that is. Musicians really pull in the chicks, you know."

"Shows what you know. Once my new book comes out, *I'll* be the one fending them off. Successful women really pull in the men, you know—especially the *young* ones."

"Let me show you the benefits of age, and those schoolboys won't stand a chance."

At eleven o'clock the next morning, they were barreling down a dusty road with the sun frying a hole through the roof of their tiny white rental car. Over an hour later, Elle was about to suggest calling it a day when Rigo swung the car hard to the right.

"There's one forming now, right there to the east of us!"

He drove straight at the kettle and jerked the car to a halt. Elle and Gary tumbled out, heads craned toward the sky, and sure enough, there it finally was: hundreds of hawks billowing upward in a silent, swift-rising column of wings and air. Standing directly underneath the spiral, Elle felt as if she could rise from the ground and join them, could feel nothing but the wind and the sky and the miracle of flight.

"*Hermossisimo,*" Rigo murmured. "So beautiful."

In less than a minute, the kettle began to dissolve, the hawks streaming off the bottom like a ribbon unfurling in the air. They gradually faded to dark specks against the brilliant sky, letting more and more light come through as they spread farther apart. Watching them go, Elle felt a loosening within herself, a lightening, as if all of the hardness and heaviness were dissolving, weightless as air. She knew that she no longer needed to search for the hawks. She finally understood that they had been there all along.

Back in L.A, Eliot Kingman was on every news screen. His conviction had been overturned and he'd been released from prison, as free and guiltless as anyone else. Gary refused to watch any of the news stories and advised Elle to do the same. She knew that he was right, but one weekend when he and Bosie were away on a kayaking trip, she couldn't fight it any longer. She flipped through the channels until she found a gossip show replaying footage from the press conference he'd given after his release. There he was, commanding a horde of reporters, fans, and gawkers who were hanging on his every word.

"I've learned a thing or two about how the justice system works. Or rather how it *doesn't* always work," he said, smiling affably.

The crowd guffawed its assent, amazed at his magnanimity. A few reporters shouted out questions about Vita, and Kingman bowed his head in a truly effective display of grief.

"Of course, I would have done anything for her—to try and protect her. But in the end, I couldn't protect her from herself."

So the press had decided to cast Kingman as the hero of this tale, the white knight willing to sacrifice his own freedom for the woman he loved.

"I'm just sorry more people had to get hurt. If I would have known it would turn out that way, I would have done things differently. But right now, the future's the important thing."

This set off a barrage of new questions: Would he go back to making movies? Had prison changed him? Was he going to make a film about what had happened?

"I will go back to making films. That's what I do. And yes, my next film will reflect what I've been through. But right now, as you can imagine, I'm anxious to just enjoy my freedom again…"

Elle turned off the television. She suddenly felt the need for some fresh air; maybe it would help to dispel the lingering stench of Kingman.

Synchronicity…or not. She had just crossed Franklin when the black Mercedes pulled alongside her. The passenger door swung open, and Kingman leaned over, smiling.

"We meet again. Please, get in."

She considered ducking into a store and calling 911—but what would she say? That Eliot Kingman had offered her a ride?

"Do you think right now I would risk so much as a parking ticket let alone harming someone? Please, get in. We have things to discuss."

Elle had known this meeting would have to take place sooner or later, so she figured today might as well be sooner.

They stopped in front of one of the luxury apartment buildings that had sprung up all over Hollywood in the past few years. In the elevator, Elle sized up the two bodyguards whose restless, wary eyes never stopped scanning for threats. At the top floor, Kingman showed her into a spacious penthouse apartment.

"This is home for now. I had to sell the mansion after everything that happened. Hated to do it—that place was special to me in so many ways. But sometimes you just can't go back."

He led her into a luxurious living room with a view of downtown.

"Anyway, it beats an eight-by-twelve-foot cell, so I can't complain. Sit down." He dismissed the bodyguards with a curt wave, and they were alone.

"Would you like some coffee? Tea, maybe?"

"No, thanks. I'd rather know what you want."

"First of all, I want to tell you that I'm very sorry about what happened to you and your friend. That was never my intention."

"And what was your intention, exactly? To kill off Nyholm and set Vita up as David Klee's killer? Which also conveniently gets you out of prison?"

Kingman smiled, but unlike his press conference, this one was cold, ruthless. "You give me far too much credit, Ms. Bramasol."

"Actually, I didn't give you *enough* credit. Apparently, neither did Nyholm and Vita. Why play games, Kingman? If I were going to tell the police the truth, I would have done it by now."

"Oh, I never thought that you would tell the police the truth. We have far too many secrets for that, don't we?"

That smile could put frost on the midday sun.

"Then what do you say we get them all out, starting with how you convinced Vita to go after Nyholm?"

"Very easily. I told her that he had the diary, and that she had to get it back at any cost."

Another piece of the puzzle fell into place; Elle was once again left breathless at the depth of Kingman's cunning. "You let Nyholm steal the diary."

"Of course I let him steal it! You see, everyone has a fatal flaw, Ms. Bramasol. Shakespeare understood that, and that's why his stories still speak to us all of these centuries later. Nyholm's fatal flaw was one of the most fundamental of them all—*ego*. After I was sent to prison, that fool actually thought that I had entrusted the diary's security to him alone." Kingman shook his head in amused contempt.

"But how did you know he would steal it?"

"I didn't know one hundred percent. Nothing is one hundred percent, obviously. But I knew that he had betrayed me on the night of Klee's death. Of course I knew! So I also knew that eventually, he would betray me again. One way or another, he would betray me again. Shakespeare, Ms. Bramasol; it's all there in Shakespeare."

"And then you could use that betrayal—by using Vita, as well."

"Ego again. He never even realized that Vita was reporting his every move to me all along, just waiting for him to cut and run."

And so the harder Nyholm had worked to convince Vita to leave Kingman, the easier it had been for Kingman to convince *her* that he was a threat. Kingman had played them off one another perfectly; the master chessman right up to the end.

"And when he did cut and run, you made sure that Vita went after him—with a loaded gun."

"Like I said, nothing is one hundred percent. For instance, I didn't know Nyholm would go to you or that your friend would get involved. Wrong time, wrong place."

"But you did know how unstable Vita was, that putting a gun in her hands and sending her on some desperate mission to save you and the plan—that couldn't end up too many different ways, could it?"

Elle replayed the sequence of events all the way up to the cliffs. "What if Vita hadn't killed herself? Or was that a part of the plan, too?"

Kingman shrugged. "It wouldn't have mattered either way. Think about it—here we have a mentally ill woman who had sexual relations with both Nyholm *and* David Klee—I can prove that, by the way—shooting Nyholm in cold blood. It would have been child's play for my lawyers to connect the dots back to Klee's murder. And if Vita had been looking at growing old in some psychiatric prison anyway, it probably wouldn't have taken much convincing to get her to confess to Klee all on her own."

"And you end up cleared of the murder with no one left to prove otherwise."

"Unless you count Verland, that is."

Verland—Elle had been wondering when he was going to come into it. "So is that why I'm really here? You want the diary back?"

"If I wanted the diary back, I'd have had it a long time ago. That's partly why I let Nyholm take it in the first place. With me stewing in prison, I thought Verland might finally turn up for it. When that didn't happen, I realized it was all but useless as long as I had it."

Elle held her breath before answering. She had to watch every word, every facial expression and gesture. She wasn't going to underestimate Kingman again. "And so you think he's going to come to me for it?"

"Maybe he will, maybe he won't. Understand one thing, Ms. Bramasol—I will never stop trying to find Verland—never. He was the first, the one who opened up the possibility of an entirely new existence. But he's not the only one out there. I've already set up teams in New York and Chicago, and I'm working on international targets next. I'll find another vampire if it takes every last penny I have. And I'm not going to lose him this time." He smiled, his eyes burning with the pure, hot flame of fanaticism. "Or her."

Elle paused, stalling for time. She had no idea if the gamble she was about to take would pay off, or cost her dearly. But she had to take the chance. "And what makes you think I even still have the diary? I could have burned it or tossed it in a Dumpster somewhere. For that matter, what makes you think Verland hasn't come for it already? Maybe he has it back and is long gone by now."

Kingman leaned back, completely at ease—completely confident. "That's an interesting theory, Ms. Bramasol. But I know he hasn't come for the diary. And I know that you still have it."

And now for the final move in the game. Elle leaned back, completely at ease—completely confident. "An interesting theory, Mr. Kingman. But maybe you don't know as much as you think you do."

"Don't take me for such a fool! Do you think I'd have let Nyholm just take the diary if I couldn't keep track of it?"

If Kingman was right about everyone having a fatal flaw, then he and Nyholm shared the exact same one.

"Then you'll know if I ever do get rid of it."

"You won't. I haven't been wrong about anything yet, have I?"

It was Elle's turn to smile. "No, I guess you haven't."

He stood up and within seconds his bodyguards reappeared. "One of my men will drive you wherever you need to go. Perhaps our similar interests will draw us back together some time, Ms. Bramasol."

"I doubt that very much, Mr. Kingman."

He lingered at the door, wanting to say something more. "I'm not evil, you know."

For the first time since she'd met him, he sounded unsure—vulnerable, even. He lowered his head and frowned, searching for the right words, and Elle got a glimpse of the ragged, broken edges beneath the seamless exterior.

"We all begin the same, Ms. Bramasol—half good, half bad. Everybody—*everybody*. And sometimes, depending on a thousand different things, the good wins out. And sometimes the bad does."

"And which is going to win this time, Mr. Kingman? The good or the bad?"

"Maybe both. Who knows? That part of the story hasn't been written yet."

Elle retrieved the diary as soon as she got home. After Verland had appeared out of nowhere that afternoon and then disappeared just as fast, she had taken the diary with her and then spent days trying to figure out what to do with it. Eventually, she had stuck both the diary and Nyholm's translation on the bottom shelf of a bookcase in the living room. She figured that if Gary ever found them, that would be the time to start answering some of those questions.

She felt along the inside cover of the diary, fingering every fold and crease, and then did the same with the spine. Along the bottom of the inside of the back cover, she found what she was looking for—something small and hard at the innermost corner, imperceptible unless you were looking for it. She got a knife from the kitchen and carefully cut away the paper, and there it was, pressed into a neatly gouged out recess about the size of a half-dollar—a tracking device. Elle had never seen one so small, and she guessed you couldn't buy one like it in any store that she knew about. Kingman had probably put it there during the trial, figuring that if things did go wrong, his men would need some way of keeping track of the diary. Or maybe he'd done it as soon as he'd stolen it from Verland—either way, one of his special-effects wizards would have no trouble restoring the back cover and re-creating the wear and tear of time as many times as necessary.

Elle put the tracking device in her pocket and drove out to Santa Monica. She walked out to the end of the pier, past the parents tugging small children and the gangs of teenagers, past the restaurants and the Ferris wheel, all the way to the outermost railing, where a few solitary fishermen sat waiting for the day's catch. When she was sure that no one was watching, she drew her arm back and hurled the tracking device as hard and as far as she could. It arced through the air and hit the water with a splash; on a computer screen somewhere, a small blip had just registered about two thousand feet too far from the Pacific shoreline. She thought of Kingman's men trolling around the ocean floor for the disintegrating remains of a book that wasn't even there, and she smiled.

"Checkmate, you bastard. Checkmate."

The afternoon had faded to dusk by the time she got back home. She sat on the porch watching the night come on, and then called Sam.

"Elle! When did you get back in town? You're such a stranger lately."

"Hey, that's not my fault. You're too in demand for me these days."

Sam sighed. "Well, to tell you the truth, Maxine and I have had enough of the fast lane. Our fifteen minutes were fun, but we're more than ready to return to the sofa with some Fritos and *Star Trek* reruns. Oh! But I almost forgot to tell you. Something good did come out of our small brush with fame. Go ahead, ask me what."

"Okay, Sam, what good came out of your small brush with fame?"

"I met someone! His name is Jay, and he's the one. Ask me how I know this."

"How do you know this?"

"Be*cause*...he's a professional bird trainer.

"A professional bird trainer?"

"It's a very lucrative field, believe it or not. Do you think all of those parrots in the pirate movies just know what to say on their own? And guess what else?"

"What?"

"Jay has a magnificent cockatiel named Gus, and Maxine just *loves* him. Is that fate or what?"

"That's fate all right, Sam. I'm really happy for you."

"And what about you? Did you call to tell me that you and Gary secretly got married in some romantic little village in Baja? That's what you were *really* doing in Mexico, wasn't it?"

"Oh, please. Actually, I called to tell you that I'm working on a new book."

"For Greene Line?"

Sam had been the first one Elle had told after she'd decided to let the Kingman story go. It had been the biggest break of his career, and he'd shredded the contract right then and there without a moment's hesitation.

"No. And that's what I want to talk about. This story is going to be…different."

"After what we've been through, different has taken on a whole new meaning in my life. Is it fiction or true life?"

"Well, it's *based* on a true story. But I guess it will end up being called fiction."

"We'll have to find a new publisher then."

Elle had been dreading this part. "Actually, Sam, I've decided to self-publish. I've got to do this story my way, with no interference or bottom line getting in the way. And trust me, no publisher is going to want to take this one on under those terms."

"Well, that actually makes things easier for me," he said, surprising her with the relief in his voice. "This Kingman business has really forced me to take a look at my life, Elle. Cliché, I know, but almost dying has that effect on a person. Anyway, I've been thinking that it might be time for me to move on from the agent thing. Try something new."

"Like what?"

"Well, maybe Jay could use a partner. I always said that Maxine was just born for show biz!"

When Elle hung up, she sat for a while watching the darkness creep in from the shadows. The night jasmine had opened up, delicately scenting the air, and she could hear the faint howl of a coyote from somewhere in Griffith Park. She went back into the house and sat holding the diary. She thought of Verland and Kazamira, of Gideon, and emerald lakes in Guatemala. She thought of smoke rising from the depths of ancient volcanoes, as eternal and inscrutable as time itself. She sat down at the keyboard and closed her eyes, traveling backward to an unusually overcast day in the middle of June, to the place where the story began. She opened her eyes and started to type, slowly at first and then faster, more sure.

It was a good day for talking with the dead...

Made in the USA
Lexington, KY
08 May 2012